A Manhattan-alignme

ISBN: 97988445

Thor

Thor

For S, K, J, J & J

Thor

Thor

Looting (Hindi lūṭ [he] steals)—referred to as sacking, plundering, despoliation, pillaging, is the indiscriminate taking of goods by force as part of a military or political victory, or during a catastrophe, such as war.

The Nazis plundered cultural property from every territory they occupied. This was conducted by organizations created to determine which public and private collections were most valuable to the Nazi Regime. Some of the objects were stolen for Hitler's intended Führermuseum and for other officials such as Hermann Göring, whilst other treasures were traded to fund Nazi activities. Approximately 20% of the art in Europe was looted by the Nazis.

Switzerland is said to have launched an investigation into whether Argentina deposited stolen Nazi loot into its banks after the war. In 1947, the then First Lady Eva Peron, on a brief trip to Switzerland, may have opened at least one secret Geneva account to stash funds and valuables she allegedly received from Nazis in exchange for Argentine passports and visas. The findings were never published and the country still remains uncooperative.

When Israel was admitted to the United Nations in 1949 they applied pressure to recover the systematically looted art by the Nazi regime and looked to the USA to use their navy to block the known routes to the South Americas. But Dark Forces will always try to be one step ahead...

Thor

Thor

Daughter of Thor

By
Joey Morino

A Manhattan-Alignment Publication

Thor

Part One
THOR goes to New York.

Thor

Thor

1

1955: Stella Elisabet Bergstrom hugged and kissed the two couples who came to say goodbye at the Winona railroad junction. The conductor raised the green departure-flag and blew his whistle. She quickly climbed on board and leaned from an open carriage window to wave her final goodbye as the Amtrak-train started its long journey to New York.

The group remained on the platform until the train became obscured by the collection of lumber mills and grain silos that over the past century had formed into a vast storage complex. This took advantage of Amtrak's daily service to New York, Maine and Canada. The train's distant siren echoed, and then faded to finalise her departure, so the two women walked arm in arm back to their cars. The two men remained staring along the empty track, but suddenly turned to follow the women.

Stella's mother broke the silence—

'I do worry about her being on her own, especially doing that work.'

Her companion squeezed her arm. 'She seems to be coping well. All we want is her happiness. We must give her time. It's only been two years.'

Thor

Stella made her way along the carriage to find the window seat her parents had reserved as part of her recent birthday treat. She hated family platform-gatherings and would rather have come on her own and let the hugs and kisses happen back at her parent's house; but it was what they wanted. She was in her mid twenties, of average height and her slate-green eyes, fair hair, and strong features suggested a Scandinavian background.

She stacked her case in the baggage rack, adjusted her light-green shift-dress and unbuttoned her jacket before sitting down. Out of habit, her hand reached under her jacket, but of course she was still on vacation, so there wouldn't be any gun until she became Thor again.

The train slowly passed the last of the BNSF humped marshalling yards, slowly picking up speed before entering onto the vast red-wheat plains. She leaned her head against the window, hypnotised by continuous miles of golden wheat rolling past; she ran a finger down the scar on one cheek. On the horizon, an orange-gray dust rose above a line of giant combines busy with industrial efficiency; the harvest now in full swing with the promise of a bumper crop. She started to count the telegraph poles as they flashed past with their mesmerising cables moving up and down: e*ighteen poles to the mile* Charlie once told her; her smile distant; *who was interested in strange statistics?* The memories came flooding back as she fingered her wedding ring. The past two years without Charlie had been difficult as she struggled to come to terms with Black Saturday, as she called it, and so she had thrown herself into her work with the FBI. This coincided with her annual assessment that all field agents have to go through. This included a chat with the psychologist and his report was not favorable to her attitude, especially so near to Charlie's death. The director had withdrawn her from field-work hoping this would give her time for recuperation. Stella was furious when she found herself transferred into administration. But the director insisted he had no choice as she needed more time to restore the belief in her own ability. She also had to regain the trust from her fellow officers; or leave the service.

Every few weeks she would report to the director for one of his friendly 'fireside chats' to see how she was getting on. On one of these occasions he asked her to read the final page of the psychologist's report. This confidential report was certainly not intended for her eyes.

Thor

It concluded: "... *because the patient's agent husband had been violently killed trying to stop a bank raid, even though not on duty, which in itself makes the patient even more vulnerable, there always remained the possibility, placed in a dangerous situation with others, she could, or would, experience a revenge reaction that could, or would, cloud her judgement and endanger her fellow officers."*

Stella had exploded at the word "patient". She threw the paper back in his face, swept her arm across his desk and tried to storm out! He blocked and forced her back into the chair. It was here that she finally broke down to sob uncontrollably for the first time since Black Saturday. This was the reaction he had hoped for. He was of the old school, having misgivings with this new "awareness" approach of using the psychologist's couch, and he knew that by even showing her just part of the confidential report could jeopardise his own career. His agents had become family and any emotions they felt were also his. It would be dangerous to send them into the field stressed out with personal problems, so they learnt to trust him enough to share their worries.

He guessed the word patient would get

some sort of reaction from her; good old fashioned shock treatment hoping to kick-start the recovery process. He gave her time to calm down and poured a glass of water for her. Then they both knelt on the floor to tidy the mess she had made.

She apologised and he asked her, 'OK Stella, so where do we go from here? How'd you want to play it?

'Carry on with that damn couch I suppose,' she agreed, 'and those upstairs can keep ticking their boxes so they can feel important.' They suddenly realised how ridiculous they must have looked having this conversation on the floor and they both burst out laughing.

The ensuing reports contained the psychologist's delight with, "*the patient's gradual improvement*".

When six months later, a request for a female operative on a temporary transfer to New York had landed on her desk, she felt that this was the opportunity to prove her confidence was back. At first the Director had overrode her application, still unsure if she was ready and guessing that if she failed New York, then that could mean her leaving the service; but Stella wouldn't let it go, so he reluctantly agreed.

After lunch in the restaurant car, she returned back to her seat and reflected on her recent vacation away from New York. It had been good, catching up with old friends and then the surprise visit to see her elderly music teacher. The two played a duet again in the front parlor with the same piano she was taught on all those years back. Her parents had also invited Charlie's parents for a few days and they made such a fuss over her. But now she was on her own, so the quicker she was back in New York and involved again with Lieutenant Carver and his unit, the better.

Two hours later, the Amtrak train stopped at a request-halt to allow an agricultural travelling salesman to climb on board. He entered her carriage, trying to steady himself on his elevated shoes as he slowly looked around. He took a swig from a hip flask as his eyes alighted on the empty seat facing the attractive young woman staring out the window. Ignoring the sign to use the provided baggage-rack, he dropped his sample-case on the floor by her feet. As the train suddenly lurched forward, he flopped down onto the seat and leaned forward to pull his case away with an apologetic mumble, relaxing back to stare at her with small beady eyes. She felt her tension rise as she caught his bourbon breath. He licked his moist lips as hooch sweat started to trickle down his forehead. Removing his porkpie hat, he pulled out a suspect handkerchief to wipe his fleshy face, then to dab the bald patch in the middle of his hair that some cheap barber had tried to dye ginger. He glanced at her wedding ring and finally his eyes settled on her legs.

She repositioned her hem-line, wishing for the ticket inspector's arrival and getting angry as he ignored the non-smoking sign.

At about the same time in Brooklyn, Frederic Vermeer Maliseet pulled on his denim jacket. He was in his thirties, tall and athletic looking, the dark complexion suggested a Native American Indian heritance in contrast to his unusual blue eyes; '*intelligent eyes*' she would later call them. He was well groomed and wore a blue, Boston button-down shirt and tailored jeans. His long, raven-dark hair was tied neatly behind his head.

As he opened the door that led onto the outside landing, he paused for a final, rueful look on leaving his bachelor apartment: the neat, well ordered lounge still with its lingering smell of coffee and tea; the dark-brown leather sofa and several easy-chairs taking up the main space; rugs casually scattered on the wide colonial planked floor. Sun streamed through the French patio-window to catch the vibrant colors of six framed Indian oils grouped alongside a glass cabinet. Inside this cabinet, he had arranged his grandfather's Maliseet tribal costume, together with a beaver hat and sealskin moccasins. Wall and standing floor-lights specially positioned for a balanced and soft, theatrical effect. At the far wall stood a large mahogany French-style cabinet, the shelves filled with dozens of classical LPs and singles. The latest hi-fi unit sat next to a matching mahogany cabinet, in which, discretely hidden by a sliding grill, was a television and radio provided by the broadcaster *ABC* for his work as a radio scriptwriter.

Before he closed the door, he made a simple gesture of facing the palm of his left hand towards the room and murmured, 'atewiktuati.' This meant he regretted his departure, although it was only a temporary assignment. Even as he locked the door, Freddie gave a sigh. He picked up a kid-leather case and his portable typewriter and rode the elevator-car down to the main entrance where his yellow taxicab waited. The driver turned out of 70th. Street into 20th. Avenue, to leave the area of Brooklyn before passing over the iconic bridge towards Greenwich.

One hundred miles from New York City, the Amtrak train's siren sounded as it started to slow and finally crawl into the main distribution marshalling yards. Its bogie wheels clattered metal on metal as they crossed junction rails towards the east-bound platform. It is here the Winona freight wagons will be disconnected, and then the passengers can continue the final leg of their journey directly into Grand Central.

The Jewish conductor started his long walk through the carriages, cantor calling, '*New York passengers stay on board*!' All part of an efficient rail service.

Stella quickly grabbed her case and struggled through the few passengers who were getting ready to disembark. She entered the rest-room and locked the door before quickly changing into torn jeans, running shoes and a loose fitting T shirt. Next she checked the chamber of the .38 gun before strapping on her covert-fit shoulder holster. She pulled on a loose fitting bomber jacket, zipped it up and tied a yellow bandana round her head. Carefully she removed her wedding ring and slipped it into a leather pouch which she placed in her luggage case; for a moment she fingered the pale ring-mark on her tanned hand and finally looked in the mirror: the face of Thor stared back, giving her that usual tingle of excitement. Shutting the case, she checked the room before making her exit, oblivious to the curious stares of the passengers as she joined those waiting to disembark. There was no sign of the beady-eyed travelling-salesman with his funny pork-pie hat and sample case. He must have jumped off at the first available stop. He certainly won't be ogling females again in a hurry; she couldn't help grinning to herself as the train finally juddered and screeched to a halt.

The New York bound passengers stared from the windows and watched inquisitively as the young woman in the yellow bandana alighted onto the platform, quickly refused the services of an over-eager, red-cap porter and hurried from the station. Outside she crossed the street into a covered parking-lot and paid the young attendant who tried to sum up her appearance. She strapped her case on the back of her Harley-Davidson and pulled the motorcycle off its stand, wiped the mirrors clean before kick-starting the engine. The young parking attendant quickly came from his office to stare at the bike with envy as she slowly drove past him into the street, turned east and twisted the throttle hard over. As the bike accelerated, she filled her lungs from the fresh wind cutting across her face; so exhilarating after the past few hours in that stuffy carriage, preferring to complete the final leg into New York on her beloved “Harvey”.

She was Thor again and loving it!

2

Freddie's story: He rolled yet another fresh sheet of paper into the typewriter and had one of those hopeful perceptions ... *maybe today would be different?* But then he thought that at the start of every new day. He tried to forget his trash bin with its screwed balls of paper and concentrated on the patterns forming within his cigarette smoke. Most writers have to start even with a simple line, so today he shrugged and typed ... "In the far reaches of the heavens, Mars and Venus start their alignment—"

He jumped as the phone shrilled.

'Hello Sam ...' He glanced at his single sentence. '... yeah it's coming on fine, lots of ideas ... how did I know it was you? It's always you ... nobody else knows this number, remember ... OK, tomorrow.' Sam Spiegel always rang every morning wanting to know how his new movie script was progressing. That's when he had his champagne breakfast in bed. That's when he started his daily routine of barking down the phone. He replaced the receiver with a sigh, *ever since Spiegel made that damn Waterfront movie he's gotten worse ... thinks he's God.* He growled, 'personally I think he has an open line to the governor upstairs.' He made a quick note on his pad: "*...open line to the governor upstairs*".

'I like that, could be useful.' Stubbing into the overflowing ash-can, he lit another Winston.

He rose from his chair, stretched and peered through the window, squinting against the early sun just breaking above the Mulberry roof-tops. He wiped the dusty glass and focussed his eyes to stare out to the new Manhattan day with its distant rumble of morning traffic; the odd banshee-wail of a cop car heading towards yet another incident? *That's what I could do with,* he pondered, *a good old fashioned homicide*!

He had worked as an assistant with his hero Budd Schulberg the year before, making last minute suggestions to the film script of Waterfront when location shooting around the New York docks. He knew his contribution had been small, but apparently Sam Spiegel had been impressed and one day he had a call from the man himself. As usual Sam didn't have to introduce himself as his timbre accent spoke volumes. 'Freddie I vanna do another mafia type movie ... I'm looking vor ideas ... I liked vot you did on Vaterfront and Budd speaks highly of you so come up viz a few ideas—'

Freddie had started to say, 'how about money Sam', but the phone went dead; he could almost smell the king-size Cuban cigar.

Before he agreed to Sam Spiegel's crazy, spontaneous idea, he had rung a fellow writer buddy who tried to reassure him. *'He'll pay you Freddie, you have to chase him ... but he'll have several others doing the same ... that's how he works. At this moment he needs you ... so don't forget when you chat next. He liked your contribution to Waterfront. He'll ring every day, same time, but get in with the money ... quick. He thinks we're all loaded like him ... remember ... in the movie world, it always comes down to money! That's the only language these people speak.'* The voice clicked dead. That was three weeks back.

The Italian lady in the next apartment started her violin scales; she could have been in the same room with those paper-thin walls.

The next morning a disgruntled Freddie gently lowered the gramophone arm down onto a worn LP of Chopin's 2nd piano concerto. He kept the volume low so not to disturb his immediate neighbors, taking for granted the appreciation of his violin-playing female in the adjoining apartment. The music played in the background as he brewed a fresh pot of Assam tea. Sitting back at his desk he waited for that phone call. His mind cast back to his days at ABC radio working with a team of writers on two popular comedy shows and also contracted to script three, one-hour plays per year. Money was good and he didn't have to chase it. Then one day at a luncheon, he sat next to Sam Spiegel, the Hollywood mogul. He had been restricted by his ABC's contract wording and didn't have the artistic freedom and creativity that he yearned for. Meeting Sam Spiegel was that opportunity when the movie mogul invited him to work on the Waterfront movie and learn the difference of writing visuals, as opposed to economy, manipulating the radio listener's own creativity.

The phone rang usual time but this time he got in first. 'I need money up front Sam. I've got bills to pay.'

'OK!' came his reply. 'Man of my vord.'

Later that afternoon, an asthmatic voice croaked over the tannoy: '*S.P. Eagle sent a package for you, gotta hand it over ... make sure you get it ... in person!*'

Freddie pressed the entrance button. The voice belonged to a short, wizened Irishman in dark shades dressed in the uniform of an Astor Hotel bell-hop; his chocolate-box cap perched at a rakish angle on the bald head. Before handing over a sealed package he sniffed and demanded with his strong Irish lilt, 'gotta sign 'ere.' As Freddie signed Spiegel's spider-scrawled note, the man took in the room, shaking his head, wheezing '...an' I thought my place was a dump.'

Freddie looked around the room from the acid remark. Yes the little Irish bell-hop was right: the only light coming from the ill-fitting window overlooking the busy Mulberry Street humming below. Once upon a time, each floor of the block contained a spacious apartment. But with the influx of refugees arriving from war torn Europe into their area, the residents had moved further out into the suburbs. Now the whole street had been converted into small apartments and his block into three cramped units per floor. Fortunately his still retained the original telephone party-line, so Sam pulled strings and it was quickly reconnected as a single-line....*money always talks*! The angle of the sun pouring through at that hour didn't help as it illuminated the sparsely furnished room at its worst: the dark woodwork desperately in need of fresh varnish; the peeling floral wallpaper; the creaking floorboards sculptured concave by decades of unforgiving feet. A threadbare carpet stretched central to the room with just a couple of neglected easy-chairs. His precious typewriter sat on the only table, now acting as his desk with a collection of pencils, a stack of typing and carbon paper, and a black office-style telephone. Next to the table was an old, patched, but comfortable office swivel-chair he managed to scrounge from the second-hand furniture outlet opposite, together with a couple of creaking dining chairs; one chair had a stack of recent newspapers. Freddie would scour the dailies, always at first through the crime section trying to pick just one headline that might trigger an idea. On the wall next to the window, he had hung his baize progress-board with two sheets of paper, one headed: "*plot-line*", the other: "*character-appearance tree*"; both sheets blank as a constant reminder of his lack of progress. In one corner of the room stood a large wooden crate he had disguised by covering with an old curtain. He referred to it as his corner of escapism with its collection of LPs and singles together with an electric player. A short hall had just one room leading off as his bedroom, and opposite was a large walk-in cupboard the landlord had converted into a kitchen. It had a small glazed sink with a very noisy, gas water-geyser, an old electric cooker, that was more than useless, and one wall-hung grocery cupboard with its door missing. On a small worktop, stood his sacrosanct coffee machine and kettle that he had brought with him for his beloved morning mug of tea.

He shared a bathroom along the outside corridor with his Italian musician neighbor, but he had the luxury of grabbing a taxi and escaping back to his apartment in Brooklyn for a welcome shower. He understood from his other neighbor, a noisy French family living opposite, that six Belarusian immigrants had been the tenants in his apartment before he came: how could they have possibly lived in such cramped conditions? Maybe they had given up and headed west for a better life?

He was intrigued that they left behind two items: a large colorful poster with Old-Russian script had been taped on the far wall. It had a picture of Jesus with intense blue eyes that followed you around the room. One torn corner hung down as if waiting for someone to either repair or tear off. Directly above the poster, was a heavily-carved wooden clock: the Russian maker just legible on its dusty face; the key still in place, and a curious Freddie had gingerly tried winding it. He was delighted that it worked and kept excellent time; although its constant tick, a reminder that his allocated days were passing and adding pressure; the poster and the clock remained abandoned and he would often wonder why? Maybe the immigrants were just grateful to have arrived, Jesus and time of no importance in this new land. He was lucky to get the apartment, or Sam was, but only by using his connections and, although Ellis Island had closed down the year before, immigrants were still pouring in from war-torn Europe, many illegal hopefuls trickling over the Canadian border.

"C*heek to jowl with human despair"* was how Freddie had described the immigrants in a letter to his father, Joey.

'*Live in the place an' get a veel of the characters, Freddie,*' proclaimed an agitated Sam with his thick mid-European drawl, as usual on the phone from his luxury suite at the Astor. Freddie couldn't help feeling guilty by taking an apartment maybe needed by a desperate family?

Jostling amongst the immigrants, Freddie's thoughts would occasionally drift back to his ancestors living by the Penobscot River on the west coast of Maine, as they must have watched their new immigrant arrivals from a time past:

Thor

"...in the land called people of the dawnland ... long before the arrival of pale men with beards who come on large white clouds", was how it had been written.

He suddenly realised the sniffing Irishman was waiting with a look that bell-hops have across the world. So he dropped a quarter into the expectant hand and the little man winked and touched his box-cap with his finger. 'May the angels protect *yer honor*!' He flicked the coin up in the air to catch it before scuttling down the stairs two steps at a time, whistling the latest Tin Pan Alley hit. Freddie closed the door and sat down at the typewriter to tear open the package. He found himself whistling the same tune as he flipped through a wad of notes. 'Must be a thousand bucks? ... better get moving.'

That was one week ago and Loretta Ponte eyed with dismay the floor covered in balls of crumpled paper, the empty Jack Daniels bottle on the table, the overflowing ash-can, the bleary-eyed Freddie staring out of the window, reflecting ... *damn Sam's great idea of so called living with the people, it ain't working ... interesting characters don't necessary create interesting plots.* He glanced at his pin-board with its blank "*Plot Line*". He thought of his comfortable apartment in Brooklyn ... *hell I must get my life back again ... back in control. Maybe working for Sam wasn't such a good idea.* He had agreed to a timetable, dictated of course by Sam, and there was only one more week remaining. Sam didn't bother with people that couldn't deliver, so unless he could come up with an idea in the next few days that would blow Sam's imagination, then bye-bye any future thoughts of writing for Hollywood.

He felt his unshaven chin as his Italian cleaning lady waved her arms in despair. 'Signor Freddie, what are you up to ... trying to kill yourself ... this drinking, she no good for you'. Her voice droned on as she collected the empty bottle, emptying butts and ash into her trash bag, but his mind was suddenly drawn to the roof garden opposite. Since he moved into his rented apartment he had become aware that the roof appeared to be a meeting place for dubious, zoot-suited grifters.

Loretta pushed him to one side, heaving up the dusty window, letting stale nicotine out and noisy Manhattan in. She continued her weekly clean as he leaned against the window cill to watch the two men who had appeared on the roof and now sat at a bar-table surreptitiously removed from Deno's bar directly below him in Mulberry Street. They started the morning ritual of dealing cards.

On the other side of the roof, a black-haired, Italian teenage girl emerged to hang fresh laundry on the support wires attached to the framework of a large flashing Cola sign; this was her morning ritual, seven days a week. The two men remained unseen behind one of the huge air-extractor shafts and unaware of her presence. She removed the previous day's washing before disappearing back through the roof door; for her, the normal daily drudge.

By now the two men had started arguing, gesturing with their hands. They stopped the card game and one man removed papers from an attaché case lying on the table. Freddie went into the bedroom and returned with his binoculars. One of the men sported an obvious ginger toupee. He was tall and gaunt, towering above the other man who was of slight build with a toothbrush moustache, walked with a stiff leg and clutched a cane; his appearance reminding Freddie of Charlie Chaplin.

Suddenly three Italian ginzo monkeys came on the roof. They stood as if waiting for someone and kept checking the time. Two of them looked like twins; both men were tall with matching pencil-moustaches, and no doubt hoping they would appear dressed by an expensive tailor with their matching charcoal-gray suits, slim cigarette-leg pants, oyster-white silk shirts and plain narrow-ties; their pale olive skin and black sleeked hair framed by matching gold-tinted shades. Even with his elevated black-and-white Daddy-shoes, the third ginzo couldn't have been more than fifty inches tall. He swaggered around as if the leader, twitching his shoulders, mouthing. He wore a fedora hat arrogantly angled down his forehead gangster-style; the black and silver-striped hat with white trim-ribbon, matched his silver-striped shirt with its matching white narrow-tie; he could have stepped straight from a Sears's catalogue *... must take hours to get dressed.* To complete his fancy-dress, he wore an expensive looking steel chronograph watch that glittered on his tiny wrist. Even at that distance he looked like a stand-in for Peter Lorre *... all we need now is Sydney Greenstreet.* The twins stood either side of the dwarf, as if anticipating his instructions.

The two men, hidden from the newcomers behind the ventilation shaft, looked startled and jumped to their feet. They quickly gathered the papers together.

Thor

Freddie had the feeling he was now watching a silent movie: The man with the ginger wig scurried away with the papers leaving the attaché case on the table. He hid behind another vent shaft as Charlie Chaplin limped into view and greeted the three visitors. They stood in line and faced Chaplin as if he was about to perform with his cane. For what seemed ages the group remained fixed with the dwarf Peter Lorre look-a-like, mouthing and gesturing until he spotted the attaché case and peered inside? He threw it down and grabbed Chaplin. Then he began to shout and slap the clown. Only yards away, the tall ginger man remained crouched and watched with horror from behind the shaft. Suddenly Chaplin seemed to step back and Freddie caught an orange flash; it seemed ages for the sound, as if from a backfiring car, to cross Mulberry but by then Chaplin had fallen.

Freddie gasped. 'What the hell!'

One twin knelt down to rummage through the clown's pockets. The dwarf turned and raised himself up on his toes to start punching the other twin holding the gun.

Freddie couldn't believe what was happening. 'You weren't meant to do that smart arse.'

The dwarf stopped his punching,

adjusted his fedora and tie before looking in the case, quickly glancing around the roof as if looking for the papers.

Freddie re adjusted the binoculars and felt his adrenalin starting to race ... *wonder what's so important about those papers?*

The trio started to argue with each other, but realised they were on view and hurried to the roof door. Both twins had to duck as they made to exit through the door. The dwarf looked back at the body of Charlie Chaplin still gripping his cane. He paused, twitched his shoulders, and suddenly glanced in the direction of Freddie's window. Freddie instantly drew back as the little man made his exit, short enough without having to duck or alter the angle of his fedora.

Manhattan sounds melted away from Freddie's thoughts. He grabbed the phone and started to dial ... *must get an ambulance ... call the police!* But then bizarrely, Charlie started to move, trying to pull himself up, half turning and then collapsing down onto his back, the cane pointing directly at Freddie's window.

Freddie cut the call as the tall ginger man emerged from his hiding place behind the shaft. He ran to his companion to stare into the silent features and appeared to panic. He quickly put the papers back into the attaché case and hurried back to the vent shaft where he lifted up the cowling to put it into some sort of void. Freddie stared intently through the binoculars ... 'third shaft from the door.' The imaginary reel ran out as the man hurriedly took his exit - *stage left – cut.* The movie now over!

Freddie's adrenaline continued to race. He hesitated, thinking fast, guilt making him pick up the telephone again ... s*hould call the police of course ... but the man is dead. Surely Ginger would call them, it's his friend. I wanted a good murder for a plot and I witnessed one ... nobody saw me ... maybe they did?*

He was lost in thought and feeling unsure with his new status as a witness; torn between his story and Charlie the victim; but there was nothing he could do to help the little clown. He replaced the receiver to stare back at the surreal scene.

'Freddie, are you OK ... Freddie?'

He became aware of Loretta shaking his shoulder. 'You drink too much mister Freddie, I am going now. Look, I have taken my money and I make coffee ...' She pointed. 'There on the table next to your typewriter.' He sensed the sudden aroma of coffee in his nostrils.

He stared at her for moment, trying to get his thoughts back. 'Yes ... yes thank you Loretta ... I appreciate it.'

Before closing the door she glanced back at the man staring intently out the window. She called across, 'drink your coffee and I see you in maybe three days, OK? ... Ciao Freddie.'

Freddie turned and smiled at her. He gestured with his hand. 'Yeah. Sure. Ciao Loretta.'

Loretta stared at him for a moment and frowned before she closed the door.

He turned his thoughts back to the roof ... *can't believe I actually witnessed a murder*, trying to excuse himself ... *but then I wanted a good murder.* He sat back at the Remington and suddenly for the first time in ages his fingers were busy and the keys were clicking; the adrenaline had now been replaced with an excitement. He started to relax with a feeling that the roof opposite had given him the seeds of a good story. The coffee tasted good and he lit a Winston. He rose and closed the window, studying the crime scene. His eyes narrowed thoughtfully and he started talking to himself. 'It's all being enacted for me. All I have to do is type as it happens. Others are thinking up the ideas.' He pondered over the morning events. 'Yes Mr. Sam Spiegel, or S.P. Eagle, or whatever you want to call yourself, I do have a plot forming, but now you'll just have to be patient.'

The rest of the day he kept an eye on the roof, but apart from a seagull hopping around looking for crumbs, nobody came to see the sprawled Charlie Chaplin look-a-like. Freddie felt uneasy with the cane pointing at his window. He kept returning to the typewriter, adding notes to his pin-board as dusk descended to swallow his imaginary movie-set just across Mulberry Street, and now only lit by the flashing red Cola sign.

That evening he had a drink in Deno's bar directly below his apartment. He sat at one of the outside tables directly opposite the entrance to the apartment block with its grim secret still undisturbed on its roof; no hint that a homicide had been committed. A Plymouth two-door prowl-car pulled up and one of the cops went into the bar to leave his driver to inspect and run his hand along a fresh dent in the rear fender. The first cop came back out with two coffees and fresh bagels and used the cab roof as his table, ignoring his companion's excuses for the dent. As he chewed and sipped his coffee, he stared absently into the night sky, intentionally turning a deaf ear to his chattering radio-traffic.

Freddie reflected over the day's

events as he watched the cops ... *you'll be here tomorrow, but not to eat fresh bagels*. He couldn't help feeling uneasy he hadn't made that telephone call.

Had he been seen at the window, watching Hooker?

Thor

3

The appearance of Hooker: Freddy rose earlier than usual with a feeling of apprehension, but also a sense of excitement as would a birthday kid for his special day ahead. He quickly surveyed his pretend movie-set. The lonely seagull was now perched frivolously on Charlie's head and busy cleaning itself; the cane still intimidating Freddie by pointing straight to his window. He looked at his watch, another hour and she'll be on the roof to hang out her laundry. He felt for the young laundry ragazza, after all he was letting her find Charlie and had a silly urge to warn the girl after all her hard work as she was bound to drop the laundry ... *if she doesn't appear then I'd have to call the cops and say I've just noticed the body ... his friend with the ginger hair, why didn't he report it? He should have made one of those anonymous calls. The cops would want to know what Charlie and Ginger were doing on the roof. There must be a good reason Ginger had scarpered. I bet there's a story waiting on that roof in those papers? Love to get my hands on* *them before the cops.*

He pulled the table over to the window so he could type and watch the next reel of his movie. For the umpteenth time he looked at his watch and up again to the Russian clock ticking the time away, so he went into the kitchen to brew a pot of tea and calm his nerves.

The small hand on his watch pointed to ten as the action started to roll. The roof door opened exactly on time with the girl carrying her laundry. He adjusted his binoculars as she moved over to the Cola support wire to start her daily routine with Charlie laying not twenty feet away.

He whispered to her through the window, 'come on girl ... surely you must have seen him?' She finished removing the previous day's washing and started pegging out her fresh laundry. He now moaned louder, 'come on for Christ's sake girl ... look he's there ... are you blind—' He jumped as the phone started to ring and looked at his watch. 'Go away Sam ... trust you to ring early ... this is your story ... go away.'

The girl inspected the new laundry before picking up her basket. She made for the exit, opened the door and stepped through.

Freddie now shouted at the window, 'what's wrong with your eyes girly?'

Then it all happened, frame by frame, as she started to close the door. She paused, at last something had registered in her young, innocent mind.

Freddie watched the following movie reel as in slow motion, later typing the action: "*...the girl slowly turns to stare at the body, the basket jerks and floats sideways to the floor. The laundry tumbles out, her face screws up in horror, her hands clutch her head, and her mouth opens to scream...*"

In a movie of course, her sudden scream would drift down and stop the Manhattan traffic. But of course it didn't and the road noises continued.

As he rolled in a blank sheet of paper, he explained to his typewriter, 'now this is where the story really begins my friend. This is where you start to earn your money!' He lit a Winston and balanced it on the ash tray when the phone suddenly rang. 'Hello Sam. Yeah, sure I've got the money as promised, thanks ... I'm working on it as we speak ... you're gonna love it ... that's my promise!'

With Sam now off his back for the rest of the day, he started typing, keeping one eye on the roof. Only twenty minutes passed from the scream to the approaching police siren. He looked down into the street as the car screeched to a halt. Two cops jumped out and disappeared into the building. They cautiously reappeared on the roof with drawn guns. He recognised them as the coffee and bagel cops with the bent car-fender. Eventually more sirens and more excited cops appeared on the roof.

He typed: "*...excited cops now treading the evidence around, just a gangland killing.*"

Forensic arrived, and then came the flashes from their cameras. An excited press horde was allowed in with their flashing bulbs. They all eventually calmed down to form a half circle, staring down at the Chaplin look-a-like and making notes. Then they looked bored hoping maybe for Chaplin's funny walk? The seagull had perched itself on the vent shaft in which Ginger had hidden the papers with its head turned sideways as if trying to hide a grin. He typed: "*...seagull watches from V-shaft containing mystery papers*".

A stretcher eventually appeared and poor Charlie was carried away. No more laughs so the press suddenly disappeared, hoping to catch the midday editions. Forensic decided to pack up and follow them. Two detectives remained taking a statement from the distraught laundry girl. Through his binoculars he recognised Lieutenant Sherman Hooker with his sidekick, the overweight Sergeant "Toby" Jugg, still wearing his beloved gold-frame shades. Freddie had come across them before and assumed, perhaps unfairly, he only made the rank of Sergeant because he married Hooker's sister. Jugg remained the quiet cop, preferring to be Hooker's shadow but always dependable in a tight corner. The redoubtable Hooker was different: he liked to dress smart and had a sharp and intelligent mind, always one step ahead. He could turn his gray eyes into ice on a whim, and he enjoyed being the local bogey-man!

He recalled meeting the two on the Waterfront set as a "PR" gesture by the mayor. The two cops had been loaned during filming to give helpful advice. Hooker was furious, protesting at being dragged away from his real job, having no say in the decision made right from the top. After a few days kicking his heels around the set, he not only upset the director with his deliberate interference, but the actor's union was drawn in and threatened to blacken the film unless he went. Hooker had made his point and immediately recalled to his day job of catching real criminals.

Freddie knew he would have to tread careful with Hooker, *he's certainly no fool. However he might come in useful.* He paused typing as another thought came into his head ... *as I'm committed, perhaps I should get a look at those papers before Ginger comes back to recover them, be one step ahead of the Lieutenant.* He contemplated that as perhaps a foolish thought. Tampering with evidence might return to haunt him. All good ideas usually have a final sting in their tail, especially with Hooker on the case!

The young girl finally left the roof with the Sergeant, but the Lieutenant remained and knelt down where Charlie had lain. He held the cane in his hand and pointed it in the direction of Freddie's window, exactly as Charlie had done. He stood up, brushed his trousers, had a final look round and made his exit from the roof.

Freddie looked at the Russian clock and said to it, 'I'll give him one hour.'

Exactly one hour and five minutes later came a rat-tat-tat at his door: not the expected Tannoy buzz, but then Lieutenant Hooker wouldn't do the expected on principle, not his style! Freddie noted the time and pulled the table away from the window. He rolled a blank sheet into the typewriter before he opened the door.

Hooker's eyes immediately made him uncomfortable, as if compounding his guilt. Hovering and peering over the

Lieutenant's shoulder was Sergeant Jugg. He too stared at Freddie, his heavy jaws moving side to side, shifting gum with an irritating click.

Hooker flashed his shield. 'Lieutenant Hooker, homicide and this is—'

'Sergeant Jugg,' growled his shadow.

Hooker pushed past Freddie uninvited into the room. Dressed in his belted trench coat, the fedora hat at a slight angle and with Chaplin's cane under his arm, he walked in like an army officer on an inspection. His eyes swept the room as if looking for dust before settling on the typewriter. He pushed his dark-blue Fedora to the back of his head and leaned over the desk to scan the crossword with its one remaining unfinished line: six letters? He tapped the puzzle with the cane and muttered under his breath before placing it slowly and deliberately on the newspaper. He glanced with curiosity at the pin-board before moving to the window to stare across at the crime roof.

He asked over his shoulder in a casual voice, 'did you see anything?'

'I saw all the commotion this morning with you guys tramping over the evidence.' Freddie enjoyed his own quick response, but instantly regretted it.

Hooker kept his back to Freddie. 'Wise guy, eh?' he drawled slowly.

'Say Lieutenant, I thought the cops only said that in movies?'

'Say what exactly ... *Sir*?'

'Wise Guy!'

Still keeping his back to Freddie, he shrugged his shoulders. 'Maybe I've seen too many cop movies. You've got a good view from here.' He glanced at the binoculars on the table. 'Must have seen something?'

'I was aware of all the camera flashes, and of course the cop sirens. What happened? ... I saw a body being taken away.'

The Lieutenant shrugged his shoulders again. 'Gangland slaying I would call it. Small time hood called Alberto Broccento ... one of life's losers. Wanna wrap this up fast. All I need is a witness.' He turned round to stare at Freddie, putting his hands into his trench coat to stand and arch one eyebrow. 'So ... how about you, what sort of witness would you make ... *Sir*?'

Freddie had also kept one eye on the Sergeant who shuffled flat-footed around the apartment, clicking his gum, prodding, as if looking for clues? His dark-brown trilby was clutched in one hand, and his crumpled dark-brown suit and red tie had possible signs of breakfast. Freddie couldn't help comparing him with

Hooker's neat appearance: even his dark-blue trousers had a crease you could shave with, as if to compliment the highly-polished black shoes. Freddie spotted the tiny Intelligence-Corp Association silver-flash on the matching blue silk tie.

Hooker removed his Fedora and ran his fingers through his thinning hair. He picked up the cane and looked at it as if studying an

antique. 'Strange how his cane was pointing straight at your window, maybe he was trying to say something.' He looked at Freddie and his face suddenly showed recognition ... 'Hey don't I know you? Now where could that have been?'

'Try the set of Waterfront. I was involved with the script.'

The Sergeant came to the table and flicked the blank paper in the Remington. 'Yeah, of course, I remember you. What's this ... another movie?'

Hooker growled. 'That's right ...Waterfront. Huh, what a farce that was. Now where were you at this time yesterday morning? Forensic suggests he died about twenty four hours ago. There was a shot, you must have heard something?'

Freddie raised his shoulders. 'I leave the window shut to keep the traffic noise out. It's difficult to concentrate over that traffic.'

Hooker glanced at the blank paper. 'Not doing very well are we?' he suggested.

Freddie tried to ignore the remark. 'Look, I didn't see anything until this morning with all that commotion going on.'

The Lieutenant murmured to himself and spied Freddie's record player playing quietly in the corner. He walked across and picked up a record sleeve. 'Chopin? I would have said you were a jazz man like me.'

'Sure, I like jazz, Lieutenant.'

He studied a theatre ticket. 'See you're off to a piano recital on Thursday. Carnegie Hall eh! Artur Rubinstein. Can't say I know him. Still, I envy you. I should take my wife there sometime.' He looked across at the Sergeant who was now staring at the poster of Jesus. 'Toby's an Elvis man, aren't you Toby?'

The Sergeant ignored the question, as if mesmerised by the intense blue eyes. He lifted the torn corner and pressed it back into position and then scratched his head before grunting with a nod.

The Lieutenant picked up a roll of Scotch tape. 'If it bothers you Toby, then repair it.' He swiftly threw it at the Sergeant.

Freddie couldn't believe the fast

reaction of the Sergeant who grabbed it without turning. He tore off a strip and repaired the torn corner.

Hooker grinned at an impressed Freddie. ‘Best catcher in the police team ... should have turned pro ... ain’t that right Toby?’

The Sergeant grunted and threw the tape back at Freddie who fumbled and dropped it.

The Lieutenant moved back to the window and looked through Freddie's binoculars to the roof. ‘How about before yesterday, see anybody?’

‘Sure, when I'm lost for ideas I often look out the window. There's usually the odd balls there ... dealing cards ... arguing ... and every morning that girl pegs out her laundry.’

‘What kind of odd balls would you say?’

‘They all look like hoods ... gangsters ... well the sort of hoods I’m trying to write about and if you want descriptions don't ask, they all look the same to me ... always Italian suits, hats and wearing shades.’

Sergeant Jugg adjusted his shades, aware they were both staring at him. Hooker picked up the cane. ‘OK. By the way, remind me of your name.’

‘Freddie Vermeer.’

‘Yeah, I remember ... Freddie Vermeer.

Make a note Toby.' He unfolded his billfold and took out a card. 'My direct number is on there, if you remember anything, call me ... OK?'

He suddenly moved to the door, grabbed its handle and yanked it open. The startled building supervisor stood there with his mouth hanging. He clutched a broom in one hand and looked guilty as hell. His droopy eyes flicked nervously side to side, trying to look as if about to sweep the corridor.

Hooker growled, 'hello Speedy, I was wondering where you were hiding. Don't go away as I'll be having a word with you later.'

Speedy backed from Hooker's icy stare, tripped over his broom and scampered down the wooden stairs. The three listened, mesmerised by the sound of his feet thumping down the two floors. Hooker grinned at Freddie and adjusted his hat before a quick glance across to the unfinished crossword on the table.

He said, 'Humphrey ... White house. Not the Washington White House, but Casablanca ... the movie. Six letters ... Bogart's your answer. Surely you remember him saying, "Wise Guy". Surprised you didn't get that Freddie, in your business.' He handed the cane over to the Sergeant and then nodded at the poster. 'What do you reckon that message across the top is telling us, Freddie?'

'Maybe I'll meet someone who reads Russian before I leave Mulberry, Lieutenant.'

Freddie tried to close the door but Hooker continued, 'you're sure you didn't see anything? Um ... it's strange about Broccento's cane.'

Freddie shook his head. 'No!'

He watched the lieutenant as he walked next door to the violin-playing neighbor and tapped on her door. Sergeant Jugg followed, using the cane as if trying to practice a limp.

Freddie tutted as he peeled gum off the frame before shutting the door, and after the Lieutenant's dig about the crossword he went to check it. 'He's right of course ... Bogart ... damn him!' Grabbing a pen he completed the puzzle. He realised there was no turning back after Hooker's visit. Wonder if those papers were really worth a man's life.

He filled the kettle to brew a pot of Assam tea.

4

Lieutenant Hooker's World: Early the next morning, Freddie opened the roof door that opened onto the crime scene. He slowly and cautiously looked around to check the roof was empty. It seemed smaller than seen from his window and certainly had an unwelcome feel to it. There was Charlie's chalked outline still marking his demise and his apartment window stared back with glass reflecting the gray morning sky ... Hooker's eyes.

He hurried past the laundry waiting to be collected by the young girl, and on to the third ventilation shaft where he lifted the cowling and pulled out the case. He quickly made his exit back through the roof door, his heart pounded as he hurried down the stairwell into Mulberry Street. He had that feeling the whole world was watching his every move, and the attaché case handle seemed to burn in his hand. He side-stepped a street cleaner and crossed to Deno's where he ordered a much needed coffee. What had he done?

Freddie acknowledged Speedy-Super sitting at the far end of the bar chatting to Deno's good lady as she mopped the floor. Speedy-Super nodded back but quickly averted his droopy eyes, pink creeping up his neck having been caught snooping outside Freddie's door. Deno Spiro, the generously overweight Greek bar owner, grinned good morning and slid last evening's paper to Freddie as he heated the milk. He raised his voice over the hissing steam, 'hey Freddie, we're big news ... got our own murder. Whispers say Broccento double crossed someone. Even his buddy Snuffy Ginger hasn't been seen, inseparable those two. Wonder what's happened to him?' His expression became furrowed and morbid as he leaned over the bar to whisper, 'seems like a bad omen to me. I can't believe Broccento was sitting on your stool only two days ago.'

Freddie looked down and felt uneasy sitting on Broccento's stool, so he unfolded the morning paper and studied the headline with the mug shot of the deceased splashed across the front page ... *Jesus, he did look like Charlie Chaplin.*

He waited until the machine had stopped hissing and asked, 'what's the latest Deno ... have they got anybody for it?'

Deno grinned. 'No my friend, Chinese proverb ... Confucius say, "*Never double-cross big shot - sky fall on you*".' He then laughed at his own humor. 'They'll never get anyone. The police will lose interest soon. Say, you live above here ... did you see anything?'

Freddie shook his head. As he sipped his

coffee he studied the colorful poster behind the bar advertising a special run of Guys & Dolls.

Deno nodded. ‘Thinking of seeing that show, Freddie? You need look no further as those characters hang around my bar every day.’

Just then the bar suddenly fell silent and a shadow crossed the newspaper. They both looked up at Hooker framed in the doorway with Sergeant Jugg floating behind. A ‘somebody’ coughed and another ‘somebody’ whispered. A third ‘somebody’ laughed out loud. Freddie aware of the sudden strained atmosphere with Hooker’s appearance; he made a mental note.

The Lieutenant smiled. ‘Ah it's my friend Freddie, the writer. It’s funny how your name comes easy to mind ... Freddie Vermeer.’ He paused, ‘I was waiting for your call, but sadly it didn't come.’ He moved over to lean against the bar, pushed his Fedora to the back of his head and cast his eyes round, enjoying the silent attention. Speedy-Super had already turned his back to look the other way as Hooker’s eyes now concentrated on individuals: the shadow-men; the table-crouchers with their eyes down all suddenly dealing cards; Damon Runyon characters anxiously checking the morning's racing papers with an obvious silence; the local radio station back-droning with the usual inane chatter about forthcoming weather affecting that evening's charity baseball game; the aroma of strong Greek coffee mixing with smoke drifting from brown cigarettes with foreign names ... *exactly as Sam would demand,* went through Freddie's thoughts ... *a heady, sepia-atmosphere.* In the far corner sat an attractive Italian woman with jet-black hair, in her thirties and busy studying a sheet of music. She adjusted the violin case on her table and looked up to smile across at Freddie.

Hooker's eyes dropped down to Freddie's feet. 'Been shopping so early Freddie, I thought you writers were night birds?'

Freddie's heart sank; he'd forgotten the attaché case. He swallowed, changing the subject. 'Lieutenant, it occurs to me that as I'm looking for ideas, and this murder of yours has the type of material that could be of interest to me, from a movie point of view you understand, I wonder if I could be involved in your inquiries? I was going to mention it to Sam Spiegel later on today. See if he could use his influence.'

Sergeant Jugg's eyes lit up. 'Yeah, Sam Spiegel ... good idea.'

Hooker didn't respond at first as he

studied the picture of Charlie Chaplin spread across the paper. 'Sam Spiegel. .Huh! Well, we'll have to think about that Freddie after that last run in with your mister Sam Spiegel. I'd like you to come down to the Precinct and look at mug shots ... see if there's any face you recognise from those hoods you keep seeing on the roof.'

'Sure, I'll be down later, what time?'

'Like now? No time like the present ... you did say you wanted to get closer to the action.'

Just then the Italian woman dropped the sheet music into her bag, picked up her violin case and came to the bar. She looked warmly at Freddie as she paid for her coffee. 'Bongi'orno Freddie ... come sta? I hope my practice no disturb you?' Her accent was strong and appealingly cultivated.

He stood and smiled. 'Bongi'orno Signorina. Not at all. I guessed after hearing your playing next door that you're professional.'

She nodded and grinned at the three. 'Yes, and I must go, I have to catch the Cruiser coach. We have big concert out of town tonight. I hear much typing now. I say to myself, our Freddie must have lots of inspiration. He now work very hard. Good luck with the story.'

'And good luck with your concert, Signorina.'

She glanced at Hooker who tipped his hat. 'Arrivederla Signorina.'

They watched her leave the bar and Hooker turned to Freddie.

'Now she's the type of dame you could do with. I had a chat with her yesterday after I left you. Nice type. She'd keep you on the straight and narrow.'

Freddie shook his head. 'I've got Spiegel on my back, can't deal with any more problems.'

Hooker stared at him. 'Interesting? Wonder what she meant by sudden inspiration, Freddie?'

Freddie gulped down his coffee, threw a quarter on the bar and bent to grab the case but Hooker reached down to it first. He handed it over to the Sergeant. 'You can take this Toby ... do something useful for a change.' Jugg pouted and headed for the car parked outside.

Hooker picked up the newspaper and refolded to the leisure page before studying the crossword. 'Mind if I take this paper Deno?' Deno shook his head and so they left with the bar voices noticeably picking up.

Speedy-Super waited till they had gone before darting over to Deno's diner-payphone. He lifted the receiver and his finger shook as he dialled ... the dime clicked down ... a voice answered, but suddenly a hand appeared over Speedy's shoulder and a finger pressed the cradle down. He turned his head sharply to find Hooker's ice-gray eyes inches from his!

'That's quick Speedy? Who you reporting in to, eh?

The face drained and his eyes flickered left and right. 'Er no one ... er my mother ... yeah my mother. Wanna see how she is!'

'Funny, I thought your mother passed away two years ago?'

'That's right Lieutenant, fancy you remembering.'

'So you're ringing her!'

'Um ... no, I meant someone who knew her.'

'And who might that be then Speedy?'

'Um ... my brother ... yeah my brother.'

'So your brother knew his own mother ... a close family ... I like that!'

Hooker grabbed his lapels and shoved him against the wall. 'Listen Speedy, when we chatted yesterday you said you'd get in touch with me if you heard anything about that killing opposite.' He pressed him harder. '24 hours have passed. Not a word. You're disappointing me Speedy!'

Speedy squealed and shook his head, his eyes continued to flick. 'Honest lieutenant, ah ain't heard a thing.'

Hooker let go and straightened the twisted lapels, straightened the tie and brushed dandruff off the weary shoulders. 'OK Speedy. Just remember, I'm keeping a close eye on you ... don't forget.' Hooker patted one of the man's cheeks and turned to leave, suddenly putting his hand into his pocket to pull out some change. He took a dime and pressed it into Speedy's hand. 'Here, sorry I lost your dime, most rude of me.'

As he left, the bar voices picked up again and a shaky Speedy- Super watched Hooker's car pull away before he tried re-dialling; this time, with one droopy eye on the doorway; you never trust Hooker!

As they weaved through the morning traffic, Hooker sat in the front with one hand firmly gripping the attaché case, staring at the morning crossword, the occasional mirror glance at Freddie who was trying to avert his eyes away from the case.

Freddie broke the awkward silence. 'Deno reckons this was all caused by some big boy getting double crossed.'

Hooker grunted but remained silent.

Sergeant Jugg drove into a yard at the rear of the Precinct. Any interviewee should be taken through the front of the ten-story granite building, but as the rear structure gave a clandestine appearance of doom, Hooker's modus operandi was to convince any suspect that he was already guilty and sentenced before he stepped inside. There were a few police cars parked, and in the far corner two familiar looking cops were standing next to a mechanic in a blue coverall, who was busy making notes and measuring the dent in the prowl-car fender.

Freddie followed Hooker up the worn stone steps with the Sergeant close behind. They entered into a spacious lobby through swing-doors marked: Police Staff only.

The lobby's embossed ceiling was decorated with green olive-leaves. The tile-covered floor had a tessellated picture of the scantily dressed Greek Goddess Themis. To the uninitiated, she was sitting blindfolded on a Manhattan bar-stool. The assumed intention of the Greek-born interior designer was to remind all those cops who entered this edifies, their duty to the principles of justice; however some had other ideas about the way the young lady had perched herself. On the far left was the public street-entrance where Sergeant Ponte leaned on his reception-desk and held his head in his hands as if covering his ears from the group of excited Japanese shouting at each other like a passing gaggle of wild geese. The Desk Sergeant looked across to Hooker as if appealing for help and shook his head. The Lieutenant laughed. The mosaic tiles and geese-like noise suddenly ended as they pushed through another pair of swing-doors into a cream-painted corridor, their footsteps echoing from floor tiles now changing into soothing olive leaves. Freddie was certainly feeling the pressure of an accused man with the lieutenant clutching that goddamned attaché case. The Sergeant followed behind, making his forefinger squeak as he ran it along the wall.

Hooker suddenly turned left to take a short cut through a door marked: No Admittance. They entered into the noisy communications department, busy with female civilians operating the precinct's PBX system. Further on, they entered into the patrol vehicle's communication section manned only by uniform; non-stop chatter from prowl-cars reporting in from across their region.

Leo Grant, the balding supervisor, looked up from his desk with a hang-dog expression, giving the Lieutenant his usual excited greeting with a slight twitch of his fluffy black eyebrows that was accompanied with a sigh, and that was about as much enthusiasm the Lieutenant ever received from the man; but he knew his job and reliable. Leo had mysteriously diverted Hooker's phone so all the Lieutenant's calls, in and out, always came via Leo's own personal PBX where he could act as the Lieutenant's filter; an arrangement suiting Hooker to keep him away from routine calls. The only pain involved by the occasional square bottle of whiskey appearing in Leo's deep desk-drawer. They passed into yet another corridor, still continuing with the olive-leaves. Hooker suddenly paused to greet a thick-set man who came from an open doorway. He had a friendly face and his sandy hair had speckles of premature gray. His pince-nez glasses perched on a wide nose and the deep blue eyes twinkled at the Lieutenant like a mischievous kid. His light-blue trousers were held up with gaudy red strap-braces, a dark-blue shirt sported a large red bow-tie.

A young, gum-chewing female followed, closed the door and waited, staring down at the tiles as if bored, hands pushed into her oversized leather bomber-jacket, jeans torn at the knees and scruffy sneakers on her feet. Freddie noticed a tease of blonde hair showing under the yellow bandana round her head. Her body language suggested an arrogant street girl and the scarred cheek gave the message: *don't mess with me*! But despite her apparent unfriendliness, Freddie felt strangely drawn. As he squeezed past to follow the Sergeant, she suddenly glanced up and looked into his eyes as if wanting answers.

Freddie walked on still sensing those eyes; he also noticed the blush on her scar; was it prejudice?

Hooker remained talking to the man and the girl called Thor continued to watch the tall stranger as he followed the sergeant. His long, raven-black hair tied back, his dark complexion ... an American Indian exoticism ... *but blue eyes*?

The Sergeant continued along the corridor before eventually opening a door marked: Interview Room 13. Freddie betting that was Hooker's lucky number. The Sergeant paused to change, Vacant to Engaged, before nodding at Freddie to follow him into the room. A slight, middle-aged, Italian scrubwoman was busy mopping the floor. She looked up at the intruders and made to pick up the bucket and her box of cleaning materials, but the Sergeant shook his head, growling, 'leave it, we won't be long.'

She seemed to do a slight curtsy before scurrying from the room still clutching her mop. He grinned at Freddie. 'She thinks we'll pinch it and not often a woman does what I ask.'

Freddie took in the cheerless room. A squeaking hum came from a shaded part of the high ceiling as a struggling ventilator tried dealing with the tart-odor from a freshly disinfected floor. There was also a suggestion of stale sweat, probably from past Hooker interrogations. The grilled window positioned high with just a glimpse of gray sky; no chance of a desperate villain jumping out, and he certainly would get lost in the precinct's maze of corridors. Four hard chairs grouped around a wooden table covered in cigarette burns. A single canopy-light had its coned-beam just wide enough to illuminate the well thumbed identity-albums Hooker had ready for Freddie. Next to the albums lay Charlie's cane: *this would be Hooker's technique of course, never miss a trick.* On the table, a battered, Remington-Rand typewriter waited with paper and carbon sheets. A chipped *Red-Sox* mug contained chewed pencils. This table had already been set up for Freddie's confession: *one couldn't design a better movie set.*

In the far corner stood an empty coat-tree, so the Sergeant threw his hat, but it bounced off the peg and fell to the damp floor. He swore and sat down with a thump, put his feet up on another chair and motioned Freddie to sit at the other side of the table.

Footsteps echoed outside on the corridor's tiled floor. Hooker entered and made a point of carefully placing the attaché case on the table between himself and Freddie. He whacked the Sergeant's feet off the chair with his newspaper before removing his hat. He aimed and threw it onto the peg where it stayed. He undid his trench coat and carefully hung it on the tree hanger, picked up the Sergeant's hat from the floor, tutted as he brushed it with his hand and hung it back on the peg. He then smoothed his hair, straightened his tie and sat down. Freddie viewed their double act with a lack of certainty; maybe Hooker's version of good cop – bad cop? The Sergeant groaned, stood up and leaned against the wall, his jaws continued to chew and despite the gloomy room, he still wore his shades.

'Toby get some coffees ... do something useful,' snapped the Lieutenant. The Sergeant muttered quietly before leaving the room. Freddie offered Hooker a cigarette and they both lit up. Their smoke curled and hung in the coned light-beam.

As Freddie opened the first album he

asked, ‘who was the female with the yellow bandana, lieutenant?’

The Lieutenant shrugged, uncommitted. ‘Oh somebody ... just somebody Freddie.’

Freddie slowly flipped the album pages over with a sense of unease, looking at staring faces that couldn't, or wouldn't, fit into a normal society. Mug shots lit with harsh light against a hatched height-measuring background made even the most innocent faces threatening. They flipped over and over until suddenly a face startled him: there was no mistaking the worried face of a very young Deno Spiro, Greek owner of the Mulberry Street bar.

Hooker leaned forward to look at the face. ‘You never know who you're rubbing shoulders with.’

He opened the second album: the very first page had a photo of a bald, gaunt-faced man with sticky-out ears and scared eyes. Freddie frowned and tapped the photo.

Hooker leaned across again to cover the baldness with his hand. ‘Recognise him?’

‘Of course,’ exclaimed Freddie, ‘but he's got a ginger wig now. I've seen him on the roof.’

Hooker made a note, nodding. ‘Yeah, I thought you would recognise him ... carry on.’

The Sergeant returned with two mugs of coffee, handing one to the Lieutenant. He started to lean against the wall when Hooker grabbed the other mug and gave it to Freddie. 'You're not thinking of our guest, Toby.' The Sergeant growled and helped himself to one of Freddie's cigarettes before stamping from the room.

Freddie identified two more faces he had seen at times on the roof. No sign of the Peter Laurie look-a-like, or the tall twins. Hooker scrutinised him as he closed the last album, studying his face with those unsettling cold eyes. Freddie painfully aware of the attaché case sitting between them with the Lieutenant playing his cat and mouse game of chess.

After a while the Lieutenant stood and stretched. 'We've only just started and yet it seems to have been a long day already.' He started his measured pace around the room that he had worked on over the years. 'This is how I see it ... that morning of the shooting you're looking out the window doing your thinking, as you like to call it, when others come on the roof. Forensic found different sets of footprints, obviously meaning there were several shade-wearing goons there. Forensic pointed out to me that the shoe prints were of the Italian winkle-picker style ... pointed toes.... no wonder Italians walk strange.' He continued his measured prowling and growling. 'The evening before, we had heavy rain, any old prints would have been washed away and so the ones we found had to be from that morning. Now, why would theses goons be there? Intuition tells me there was an arranged meeting of sorts.'

His voice lowered, becoming scornful. 'I can read these hoodlums like a book. I know how they operate, and usually they only meet in a group when money or something illegal is being handed over. Broccento wouldn't go on his own ... he wouldn't be that stupid. He wasn't that steady on his feet and only walked like a penguin, so there would be at least one companion with him.'

The lieutenant was now behind Freddie who suddenly felt his shoulder being gripped. The Lieutenant leaned over and breathed in his ear. 'The man with the ginger hair ... his name is Leonardo Vente; known to his cronies as Snuffy Ginger would you believe. He was Broccento's shadow. They were like Siamese twins, mates and buddies. Those two are what are called grifters, looking for the small swindle, the small time con-artists. They suddenly found a chance to make real money ... in other words, they got greedy, but someone else always pulls the strings. So where was Snuffy Ginger whilst this big-time meeting was going on? Did they take him with them? Was he a witness to his friend being shot? He's disappeared from the face of this earth. And why was Broccento shot? Because someone got over-excited and the gun went off accidently; I've seen it so many times ... trigger happy. They've watched too many of your movies Freddie. They're too dumb to be a Gary Cooper.'

Freddie began to understand why Hooker was known as radar. He had to admit a sneaking admiration for the prowling man with his uncanny instinct of analysing your mind.

Freddie waited as Hooker considered his next move: *the leopard moving in to trap and snare his victim*; he made a mental note to remember that line, except this time, he was the victim!

Hooker took his hand away and blew a smoke ring before walking round to face Freddie. He narrowed his eyes. 'I reckon Snuffy Ginger, mister Vente I mean, was there, hidden ... his job to see how things were going ... he had the money, or whatever they were after, and only appear to hand over, *if,* things go to plan.' Hooker's face became animated and his gray eyes opened wide and warmed, shining with a boyish excitement. 'But they didn't because some Sicilian bonehead pulled the trigger. That wasn't in the script, so they panicked and scarpered ... run like these sewer rats always run. The newsboy recalled three men making a hurried exit from the building...' he held up three fingers to Freddie, 'just three ... no forth Ginger man.'

He sat down and swallowed his coffee as the Sergeant entered. Hooker took Jugg's coffee. 'I could do with that Toby ... go and get another.' The door slammed shut behind the Sergeant. For one brief moment the corners of Hooker's mouth imparted a ghostly smile and his eyes seem to twinkle at Freddie across the table.

Freddie began to feel an unexpected surge of affection for the man.

Hooker continued. 'You say that you watched Broccento on the roof many times, and having been there myself I guess he must have been aware of you keeping an eye on them every day.' He gazed at Freddie over the attaché case as if trying to draw him out. 'Is that a fair assumption?'

Freddie reluctantly nodded.

'So when he fell, he guessed you must have seen the shooting. So in that split second, he must have realised he was about to leave us,' he picked up Charlie's cane and pointed it across the table at Freddie, 'so he pointed his cane towards your window, just like I'm doing. Was he leaving a message for *me*, his old buddy, Hooker the cop? ... I can hear his croaky voice ... "*he saw it Lieutenant ... up there in that window ... he knows who shot me ... the man with the binoculars*."' Hooker put the cane down on the table and looked at his hands now pressed together. He slowly moved his head, side to side, his voice becoming almost reverent. 'His last words were probably for me Freddie, how moving.' He looked up and grinned. 'Freddie, come on, such loyalty.'

Freddie tried not to smile, gathering his thoughts with the Lieutenant making another chess move; this time with humor. He lit another Winston and tossed one to Hooker.

'Lieutenant, what an imagination you have. I could use you ... fancy being my partner—'

'The point is Freddie, your cleaning lady, Loretta, is married to the Desk-Sergeant here, and she was telling him she was worried about your drinking and claimed you were inebriated that morning. *Inebriated* ... my, that's a big word for an Italian Desk-Sergeant. This was about the time we reckon the killing took place, so I thought ... no ... in that state Freddie wouldn't have noticed anything. So I nearly crossed you off my list. But my motto Freddie reads as, "*the three Cs*" ... Check ... Check ... and Check again. But then I recalled you from Waterfront, and you didn't strike me as somebody that would get inebriated. Ok the odd tipple, but an upstanding citizen like you? So I had a quiet word with Loretta. She said you were standing at your window with your binoculars, completely gone. She had to shake you to say goodbye. So I said to myself, was he drunk? No ... maybe in shock ... possible! But why did he have his binoculars? Never come across a drunk with binoculars before. Maybe you were deep in your *thinking* and could see a good story out there for Mister Spiegel.'

They heard footsteps in the corridor and the Sergeant entered with yet another coffee. Hooker threw him Freddie's Winston pack. 'Toby, go outside, drink your coffee, then enjoy a smoke with Freddie's cigarettes and at the same time get some fresh air ... don't like the way you're looking this morning. I can't have my sister ending up as a widow ... just yet!'

The door slammed with heavy footsteps walking away.

Hooker stood up and put one foot on the chair to study his highly polished black shoe. He leaned over and pulled a yellow duster from the cleaning lady's box. He then folded it into a square and carefully wiped some dust from the toe. He repeated the action with his other foot.

Freddie viewed this intriguing game the Lieutenant was playing as he returned the folded duster to the box, and then continued prowling.

'Now Freddie, what would your friend Snuffy Ginger do in this situation? He would still have the money ... or whatever they were after, and he wouldn't want to be caught leaving the building with it in case the mob was watching. I know what I would do Freddie ... I would hide it. Come back later when the coast was clear. But supposing somebody else saw him hide it and gets to it before he returns; you know ... curious like. Get my drift?'

Freddie tried to resist glancing at the attaché case.

'Now, if our witness has got his hands on the prize that someone has died for, and as Broccento was aware of you, why not Snuffy Ginger? Maybe he'll think badly of the man with binoculars that keeps an eye on them every day. Ginger's in danger if he can't hand it over, and if he's not careful, he'll end up with Broccento in that, holy take-a-way in the sky, where all good Italians want to go.'

He held his hands together as if in prayer and looked up to the struggling vent grill ... 'Where the guv'nor, with a long white beard, serves pizzas behind a gold and marble counter.' He paused, maybe wanting Freddie to appreciate his strange humor ... No? So he continued. 'That's why he's hiding. My guess he'll be back one dark night to recover his missing "*whatever*", that his friend died over. Maybe he's already told someone about the man with the binoculars—'

He suddenly leaned over and whispered, 'I'll let you into a secret Freddie; in fact even the Sergeant doesn't know this. I like to put myself in another person's shoes to see how they fit.' He leaned back and his voice rose, 'but your shoes pinched, which told me your story doesn't add up, particularly with the cane.' He deliberately pushed the attaché case nearer to Freddie. 'So my advice Freddie is this: lock your door at night and look behind you when you walk down the street. Maybe we should give you protection? How would you like Toby to be your companion? Problem is he snores. I'm sure my sister wouldn't object to you borrowing him.'

Freddie felt his wits being stretched. Maybe this was the sting-in-the-tail of his good idea. *He's got me, no doubt about that ... problem is, what is in that attaché case?* He cleared his throat. 'If your prognosis is true Lieutenant, you have placed your witness in an impossible position. If he agrees, then it means he's guilty of withholding evidence and that makes him an accessory, *after* the crime.'

Hooker flopped down in his chair to stare over the intrusive attaché case. 'Oh Freddie ... I'm not interested in you. You're out of your depth here. I'm after mister big and all the other scum out there. I'd like to think that I have an idea who's behind all this, but I don't ... and I don't care if they wipe each other out.' His face darkened. 'The more the merrier. Normally I would toss this in with all the other unsolved homicides, but I have a feeling this has a bigger picture. This isn't a planned gang killing ... it's a hand-over that went wrong. Snuffy Ginger and you witnessed it, so Ginger knows who they are and I don't want him frightened off. Once we find him I'll get one of my team to pull him in with several of the crowd he hangs around with. Just to ask routine questions as he was a close friend of Broccento, put pressure on him, frighten him and then let him go. Maybe he'll lead us to the boss?' He shrugged his shoulders. 'You're after a story, that's fine. I'd do the same in your shoes, but they're maniacs.' His eyes glared and showed his anger. His voice rose and he thumped the table, making the pencils in the mug jump. 'They shouldn't be in this country. In fact they're abhorrent living within a decent society with their so called "*Omertà of Silence*". That's what the war was supposed to be about. A lot of my friends died whilst they sat back here with their grubby hands in the till, waiting for others to sort the war out—' He fell silent, distant, then his voice lowered as he continued, 'you'll discover that I don't stick to so called rules. I'd never nail bastards with hands tied behind my back. So Rule One: I never break or bend the law Freddie ... but just occasionally I might put a slight curve in it. I'm quite happy to file it unresolved ... but there's more to this ... that's what I'm after ... and I need your help, and you need your story.'

He raised his eyebrows and looked over the attaché case at Freddie. 'So we both know where we stand. OK?'

Freddie nodded and Hooker continued, 'I'll get a feather in my cap and you'll come out of this smelling of Spiegel's favorite roses.' He drummed his fingers on the leather. 'What we have inside this attaché case will be an open book: the beginning, the middle and the end, amen.

I'd stake my pension on it, but I don't want to have to look inside unless you ask me. You have done me a favor by finding it and handing it as a concerned citizen ... right?'

Freddie nodded. Hooker stood up and offered his hand. They shook and Hooker beamed. 'Christ Freddie, you're hard work, thought Toby took some beating.'

He sat down and picked up four sheets of the yellow copy paper from the pile and slipped carbon between. He rolled them into the typewriter and stared hard at Freddie. 'Another Rule One Freddie: never dance with a goofball, they can't keep time and eventually it's you who'll trip and fall. Lucky for you, this time I'm here to catch you. Before we open that attaché case, let's get a statement, so start at the beginning when you were chewing your pencil and looking out the window ... thinking.'

He typed with two fingers as Freddie related that morning, getting irritated having to thump "t" occasionally as it kept jamming. He nodded at the description of the trio and laughed. 'Yeah, that's the three who were seen sneaking from the building, they're the Angelica brothers. I heard rumors they were born in the jungle and escaped from a three-ring circus when in town. The dwarf is known as Dandy-

Dandy. He's a loaner and odd one out. The two other brothers are identical twins. We've never been able to pin anything on them. Even when they've been pulled up for a minor traffic violation, the traffic cop gets confused when they both get out the car and claim, "I wasn't driving officer", so he lets them off with a warning. You should be a witness at an identification line up; better than going to the vaudeville if you felt like a laugh. Dandy-Dandy's also clever but when he's up to no good, which is most of the time, he gets his big twin brothers to look out for him, so it must have been important to take them to the roof.

They both stared hard at the leather case on the table.

Suddenly the irritated Hooker pulled the statement from the typewriter, screwed it up into a ball and tossed it into the trash-can.

'I think we'll worry about your statement later, see how things work out! Next time I'll use the machine in my office and you can type. The point is Freddie I'm sticking my neck out on this. A clever defence lawyer could make mincemeat of this case, and a cantankerous judge could give you a stretch for removing important material evidence from a crime scene. But first we need to know what's in there that someone died for.'

Again they both stared hard at the case sitting on the table.

'You need to put it back exactly how you found it, that's important because Snuffy might twig someone's been there and ruin what I have in mind. Until then, I'll keep a cop presence on-going outside the building entrance to keep Snuffy away.'

Freddie looked worried. 'But it'll be on my statement about removing the case and putting it back.'

Hooker rolled his eyes and leaned forward. 'Freddie, politicians pass unworkable laws to keep the public happy; the press change useless facts to suit ridiculous stories that keep their readers happy; I work to my own rules that make the criminals unhappy; so in the end, we're all happy, and that's my version of democracy! I'll dictate your statement *after* we work out the facts that suit this investigation. Just keep your mouth tight. I have a use for you in all this and in return I'm getting you off the hook. I didn't fancy using the good cop, bad cop routine on you. Actually that's only used in movies.' He laughed. 'I prefer the blackjack across the neck, saves hours. Why do you think I kept the

Sergeant away from our chat?'

Just then the door swung open and the man in question looked in to lean against the door frame. The two men stared at the Sergeant who asked, 'am I supposed to be in, or out, Lieutenant?'

'Get in here Toby ... what's the matter? You can't keep still. Come over here and sit down. Do us the honors Freddie.'

Freddie unlocked the catch with a loud click making him jump; he noticed his unsteady hand. Hooker peered inside and took out two folded blueprint sheets. He shoved the typewriter to one side of the table. 'Have you been typing your life story on this machine here Toby? The "t" keeps sticking.'

The Sergeant grinned at Freddie and replied by pitching a wad of gum into the trash can with a tinny thump.

Lieutenant Hooker unrolled the first sheet and they huddled together, studying a working elevation drawing of a proposed stone building with the title: Manhattan & Western Bank - Pine Street: proposed construction starting May – 1912. The central twenty-floor tower had two smaller office-wings that were linked on either side. The second blueprint had the lay-out details of the basement's footing plan.

Hooker became excited, and picked up

the cane to tap on the area containing the central strong-room. 'So that's what they're after?'

Freddie pointed at a detail caption: Chubb Time Lock - Railroad Chest - Panic Door - after Bloemfontein it is important these should be included. 'Wonder what that means, Lieutenant?'

Hooker looked thoughtful. 'I need to chat with a colleague of mine.' He carefully folded the plans and slipped them back into the attaché case before reaching over to remove his trench coat from the hanger saying, 'fancy a trip down town, Freddie?'

5

Butterfly's story: Freddie didn't seem to have time to agree before Sergeant Jugg turned his unmarked Ford into the narrow street of Pines to pull up alongside the bank, now very familiar from the blueprints they had pored over earlier. The three stared at the imposing building designed by the renowned Chas Lawson: considered pioneering for its time, having a steel structure but retaining a stylish stone Neolithic Gothic outward appearance. The complex now dominated by the adjoining modern skyscrapers pointing up to ominous dark clouds that suggested rain. A granite plaque bore the legend: "Opened Oct-1914 by Martin H Glynn, forty-third Governor of New York".

Hooker observed, 'If I remember correctly, Governor Martin Glynn didn't last long, so the owners probably wondered if that was a bad omen for their new bank.'

The right wing appeared empty with an air of neglect. Above the Main entrance hung a "For Sale" billboard. Hooker stared at the Agent's name: "Edwards & Rivera". 'That's very interesting Freddie. Rivera hangs around with your circus trio. I've heard that occasionally, Mister Rivera likes to take Dandy-Dandy out for walkies on a lead.'

Freddie sighed. *Does he ever stop wisecracking?*

A recent notice had been pasted across a ground floor window: "Ground Level – Leased".

'Um. This is getting more interesting by the minute.'

Freddie felt he had to make some comment. 'I guess you're right Lieutenant.'

Sergeant Jugg slowly shifted his irritating gum to nod his agreement.

Hooker sat silent, staring and deep in thought. Freddie sat quietly in the back, trying to out-guess the Lieutenant's next move; *the Lieutenant could do with a haircut*. Hooker suddenly took a deep breath and glanced at his wristwatch. He said, 'it's funny how Rivera, estate agent, keeps cropping up. That firm always seem to be near, or involved with buildings that get robbed. About time I gave Rivera an invite to the Precinct for some of Toby's coffee...that always seems to make them talk.' He glanced in the driving mirror. 'Freddie I have a little job for you ... and Toby ... motor on to Eldridge. Do you know it?'

'Of course I know it,' the Sergeant grumbled, as if for the rooky sitting quietly in the back. As the Sergeant weaved through the morning traffic, Hooker gave Freddie his instructions.

Sergeant Toby parked further along Eldridge just as a foot-patrol officer approached to indicate the no-parking sign with his nightstick. Hooker wound down his window to flash his shield.

The officer pushed his cap back and leaned into the car. 'Hi Lieutenant, what yah doing down this far?'

Hooker pulled his head back as he caught the officer's breath. He loudly whispered, 'you know how it is officer,' he rolled his eyes over to the Sergeant, 'I'm taking the wife shopping.'

'Sure, sure,' grinned the officer, realising he wasn't wanted. He stared hard at Freddie before continuing his saunter, swinging the stick.

'OK,' indicated Hooker, 'you're on your own.'

Freddie left the car to follow in the direction of the patrol officer who had disappeared round the corner.

Edwards & Rivera was located on the corner of Eldridge and Grand Street. A shingle board hung above the corner office: "Edwards & Rivera – Commercial Realtors since 1936". Just visible in the worn and fading entrance-mat: "Italian Fine-Art Emporium". He guessed that once it must have been a snazzy place to be seen in. He automatically wiped his shoes as he pushed the Kannel revolving-glass door that squeaked on each second turn. The large reception area greeted him with an odor of thirties tobacco, implying the Second World War had probably passed unnoticed. The reception office still retained the pre-war, arched-windows fringed with copper beading; this would allow any nosey passerby a good view of the interior still clad in its period oak-panelling. The panelling was adorned with somewhat dusty, fading prints of commercial premises to be: “leased/rented/sold”. The oak-parquet floor was partially covered by a worn Tabriz-design carpet with a large oak reception desk in its middle. Next to the desk stood a brass object that reflected a strange habit from the past: an antique brass-spittoon conveniently placed within spitting distance from the chair. On the cluttered desk stood an Underwood typewriter, a writing pad and an assortment of ballpoints and blunt pencils that splayed star-shape from a red porcelain pot. An unopened Lucky-Strike pack lay next to a red butterfly ashtray. Clamped to the desk edge, an antique Boston pencil-sharpener with its glass container jammed solid with old shavings.

A candlestick telephone had its pear-shape receiver pinned firmly to the ear of a thirty year old oriental-female that no war could possibly pass by. She wore a distant smile across her face as she sat with one silk-stocking leg swinging a red, spike-heel shoe from the toe of her dainty foot; the other shoe lay on the carpet half way across the office where she must have flicked it.

He couldn’t have dreamt her up: the long, black hair hung down past one shoulder, having a deep, iridescent-sheen that most women would kill for; her black oval-eyes encircled by corral-red mascara; pencilled eyebrows; a turned up nose that could only be described as cute; the white-powdered face emphasising the lips painted Chinese-red. To complete her image, she had a pair of red, butterfly-glasses perched saucily on her head.

Despite Freddie's entrance she continued the conversation in what he assumed to be Mandarin. Her bird-like voice was colored with an attractive Bronx accent. Her free hand nervously straightened her black Geisha-cardigan that had tiny clusters of sewn, red butterflies, and then she fiddled with the gold chain hanging from her slim pale neck; this chain had a red butterfly tear-drop matching the butterfly earrings.

She would occasionally smile at Freddie, flashing her black eyes and pointing long antenna lashes in his direction as he waited by her desk. He couldn't help looking at her long red nails on the slim fingers nervously twisting the telephone flex, round and round; *she can type with those?* She seemed a bundle of nerves, fluttering here and there like a butterfly. Then she arched one pencilled eyebrow as a motion for Freddie to sit on the lumpy, high-back, granddaddy leather armchair with its Bradley & Hubbard floor-stand ashtray; he preferred to stand and admire.

Further to the rear of the emporium, a dusty interior window looked straight into a rear office. Swivelling and leaning back into an important looking kid-leather office chair, sat a pale and flabby Mediterranean individual with Mafia-style, oiled ash-gray hair smoothed back. His broken nose was off-set in the middle of a round face balancing the cauliflower ear with his other ear that stuck out. His catalogue midnight-blue silk jacket had a large red carnation in the lapel; a lemon tiffany silk-tie looked sweet against the white silk-vest to match the display-handkerchief poking from the breast pocket. He kept gesticulating with a sweaty palm to someone hidden behind a filing cabinet, and his podgy finger waved a large nine carat stone that winked bucks at Freddie. There appeared to be a dispute, but occasionally turning his head to look through the dusty glass straight at Freddie with eyes that were deep-set, sadistic ... suspicious; this gentleman he assumed to be Hooker's Mister Rivera.

The girl's conversation finally finished with a giggle. She tried to un-twist the telephone flex, but finally gave up and jammed the receiver at a strange angle back on its two-finger cradle. She picked up the Lucky-Strike pack and tore off the cellophane before resting her chin carefully in one tiny hand to concentrate those black eyes on Freddie. At the same time, with the other hand, she flicked loose a cigarette and offered it to him. He shook his head and quickly leaned forward with his lighter. She held his hand to steady the flame; her hand was soft and warm. One eyebrow suddenly arched and the smile that followed would make an ancient Chinese golden Buddha melt with desire. He spun the wheel and ignited the flame. The cigarette lit with the end glowing until it matched the color of her lips. She took it out, flicked a fleck of tobacco from her lips before saying, 'thank you,' and in her accentuated accent, 'have you come to buy a *very tall* skyscraper?'

Freddie grinned*, must remember that line.* 'Sorry, not today. I never buy *tall* skyscrapers on Tuesdays.'

She puckered her red lips and blew a smoke curl at him. 'That's a shame because I would get a wonderful commission and buy you lunch. Hey, it's not Tuesday, you're teasing me.'

Freddie was enchanted and had to swallow before launching into his rehearsed spiel: 'I'm looking for a location to shoot office scenes and just happened to see the building next to the bank on Pines.'

On the word filming, her eyes suddenly sparkled. She leaned closer, her antenna lashes wide open. ‘And who might you be then?’

‘My name is Freddie Vermeer, and I'm working for a Hollywood production company. You've heard of Sam Spiegel I assume?’

Her face became more animated, looking at the man as if he really was her elevator ride to the top of a skyscraper; a pink flush appeared through the white powder. ‘I’m sorry, but that building is leased for six months Mr. Vermeer ... Hey, I think I will call you ... Mr. Hollywood?’

He grinned and nodded. ‘Sure, but I was hoping you might let me have the contact number of the people who've leased it, just to see if we can do a deal for this filming. The shoot will only take a weekend.’

‘Spiegel,’ she queried, her voice lowering, ‘hey, ain't he the one to do with that Waterfront movie?’

‘Sure, I worked on that, now I'm working this new movie.

Her eyes widened as her voice rose again. ‘Did you get to meet Marlon Brando?’

‘Sure, of course.’

‘Did he ever speak to you?’

'Sure, course he did.'

She leaned forward, expectantly, drawing on her cigarette, blowing another curl. 'Tell me, what did Marlon say to you, Mr. Hollywood?'

He was enjoying this banter. 'Difficult to say ... he just mumbles.'

'Does he mumble like that all the time?'

'Sure.'

'Wow!' She exclaimed, casually tapping her cigarette with one finger over her butterfly ashtray as would a sultry female in a Brando movie.

Freddie smiled back and asked, 'what do you think ... any chance of that contact number?'

This time she arched both eyebrows, shrugged her shoulders before scowling. 'I'll have to have a word with *dear* Signore Rivera.'

She balanced her burning cigarette on the butterfly ashtray, walked over to pick up the other shoe and pulled them both on before slowly tottering to the office door. She desperately tried not to catch the threadbare carpet with her spiked heels; maybe Mr. Hollywood could get her a part in the next movie? Without the spikes she was still tall for an Oriental female because of her long legs. He watched her through the window and could see that she was glamorising his request; her black, oval eyes wide and shining, her arms waving and gesticulating through the window towards Freddie. Rivera was obviously in a scowling mood; he scowled at her and turned his head to scowl at Freddie. He bit at a cigar, spat the end out and struck a match, puffing at it before suddenly shaking his head. He waved his arm for her to go away so he could continue his argument with the filing cabinet. Freddie caught the occasional flash from his expensive ring as it swung around.

Freddie glanced at a security camera on the wall behind her desk. He had experience with that make having used it in a TV movie awhile back and betting it hadn't been used for years; not much to steal in this tired realtor's office. He followed the wire coming from the back of the motorised camera-casing to continue down the wall, passing under the carpet and disappearing below the fancy "Italian Fine-Art Emporium" door mat. Reaching over the desk he felt a switch just under the top lip. Out of curiosity he picked up her pencil pot looking for marks etched on the bottom: *interesting*? He carefully put it back down.

He watched the pedestrians hurry past the arched windows; everyone's always in a hurry in New York. There were times when he desperately missed the unappreciated leisureliness of his youth in the forests of Maine. But he had to admire Hooker's careful, measured and deceiving manner. He imagining him in the car doing his crossword with the Sergeant's head rolled back fast asleep. Hooker would keep glancing at his strap-watch, getting agitated, wondering how his latest recruit was getting on, hoping Freddie would return with at least a telephone number.

He suddenly realised the butterfly girl had returned by the sound of her shoes being flicked across the office. She wrinkled her face. 'I'm sorry, but his answer is no. He can be a right jerk at times.' She glanced at the window where he was still gesticulating and scowling at the filing cabinet. She quickly removed a file from a drawer. Opening it she slipped her red butterfly glasses down on the cute little nose and quickly scribbled a telephone number on her pad, hesitated and quickly scrawled one more number. Glancing again at the window she furtively tore off the sheet and slipped it across the desk and looked at him over the top of her glasses. She was a little flustered. 'He'll go mad if he knew I'd given it to you.'

'Gee, thanks. I get the impression you don't like our mister Rivera.'

'No I don't!' Her cute nose screwed up again. 'Besides, he stinks of garlic. Typical Italian, why can't they stick to eating ice cream?'

Freddie chuckled. 'By the way what's your name?'

She went coy and shyly lowered her eyes. 'My name is Crystal Papilionoidea. My father is a very tall Greek, hence my long legs; you *may* have noticed them?' She waited for his reply and he acknowledged with a grin and a nod.

'However my friends call me Butterfly ... and if Marlon comes into town, maybe he would like to pin me in his collection.' She giggled. 'Tell him that butterflies never bite.' She looked upwards at him as if about to display her wings, her eyes suddenly filled with red reflections within her black pupils, and for a moment she looked very minacious!

'Well Butterfly, I'm sure that Marlon would love to meet you.'

A faint blush appeared again through the powdered face, and then came another giggle. *Under her pale makeup, she was very pretty and certainly a fun girl. Others would perhaps say, 'wash it off Butterfly,' but no, of course not, that would spoil everything about her.* So he just asked, 'what's the second number for?'

She sighed. 'Why, that's mine of course, just in case mister Spiegel decides to buy a very tall skyscraper.'

He nodded at the red pot containing her pencils and pens. 'Where did that come from?'

She frowned and stared at it. 'You mean this old thing? I found it at home in the cupboard. My grandmother probably brought it with her from China. Why?'

'Well don't let Rivera get his hands on it. If I'm right that's a Chinese brush pot. I think it's called Sang de Bouet. That could buy you a swarm of the most expensive butterflies.'

She picked it up. 'Really?'

He nodded. 'Careful, and get it checked. Then if it is, I'll be back for that lunch.'

Her face darkened. 'On the head of my grandmother, *please* don't let him know how you got that number.' For a moment she seemed frightened. 'Promise me? He's not a very nice man!'

Freddie nodded, took her hand and kissed it. 'My word!'

She sighed and watched him leave, calling after him, 'and if it's not a sangy-whatever-pottee, then you could always buy *me* lunch, Mr. Hollywood. I don't want to end up pinned in any old collector's cabinet.' He didn't hear, so she sighed again, drawing on her cigarette, blowing a spinning curl and narrowing her eyelids to stare into the distance; her black pupils started to reflect red again as the Kannel door continued to revolve, squeaking on each second turn... *Hollywood ... commission ... Yeah, if only*! She stubbed out her cigarette and looked thoughtfully at the pot, carefully tipped out the pencils and biros before turning it over to study the faint markings on the bottom. She looked up and found Rivera staring at her!

As Freddie made his exit, the office door opened behind him and the hidden person emerged, stuffing a small parcel and envelope into a pocket. The man was lanky and topped with a ginger toupee. A startled Freddie quickly turned his face away and hid behind an exterior recess as Ginger Snuffy Vente slunk out. He paused to pull his collar up round his large sticky-out ears, then holding his hand on his toupee as protection against the deluge of rain starting to sweep in, he glanced up and down the street, lowered his head and scurried into a bar; his drawn face troubled and pinched.

Freddie hurried back to the waiting car and brushed off the rain before getting in. 'Who do you think I saw in there? Our friend Snuffy Ginger! He was in Rivera's office and followed me out. He didn't see me and I watched him go into a bar on the other side of the street.'

Hooker grabbed the radio-phone from the front dash and requested a plain-clothes to get down fast. He glanced at his watch. 'And pass this message on to Leo ... ask Lieutenant Carver if I could see him in my office in one hour.' He looked in the mirror. 'Snuffy might recognise you Freddie ... so best stay here.' He eyed the Sergeant examining a zit on his chin. 'Toby, go up to the corner and keep an eye out in case our friend Snuffy Ginger decides to leave. As soon as the replacement arrives, I'll send him up. He can follow and see who he mixes with. Maybe he'll lead us to the dog that's wagging this tail ... or maybe the tail that's wagging the dog?'

Jugg grunted and heaved himself from the car, hurrying to the rear trunk to extract his black-rubber cape. Hooker growled and called out, 'Toby, a police cape for surveillance work? For heaven's sake man, put your coat on.' The two watched from the car as the Sergeant slipped into his trench coat and tied the belt into a knot, pulled his trilby down low over his eyes and slunk away through the rain with his hands pushed deep into the pockets.

Hooker grinned in the mirror at Freddie. 'There goes Phillip Marlowe, private tec!'

Freddie recalled his conversation in the office with Butterfly and handed over the slip of paper. 'That number is her private one if you're interested in collecting butterflies. Remember Lieutenant, I gave her my word that no way would Rivera ever find out she gave me the number. She seemed frightened of him.'

Hooker studied the slip of paper. 'OK Freddie, my word. Now you can understand why I want that villain behind bars. I've been after him for years and at last I think I might have the answer. Suggest you give Spiegel a buzz to warn him he might get a call with someone checking up on you. But don't tell him too much, and for Christ's sake, don't mention my name as the cop you're working with. He and I didn't exactly part on good terms at Waterfront. Remember, you're part of the team now ... Agent Freddie.' He grinned at his own humor and then became thoughtful. 'When I get back to the station I'm having a word with a colleague of mine, and I'll get you to put the plans back exactly where you found them. Then I'll withdraw my police presence leaving the coast clear to draw Snuffy Ginger in. Hopefully I'll drop them back to you this evening, so make sure you're home.'

Freddie nodded, murmuring, 'as long as I get my story, Lieutenant.'

Hooker chewed his pencil. 'Oh sure, you'll get your story. But I'm afraid this is what police work is all about Freddie, hanging around. Not like your movies.' He returned to his crossword. 'Hey Freddie, you should know this: ... the morning's music question. Six letters ... "it wasn't God that created rain in a monastery?"

'Have to think about that Lieutenant.'

Hooker nodded. 'Don't take too long as Lieutenant Carver bet I wouldn't get it.'

Luckily Ginger didn't seem in a hurry to leave and only interested in comparing the racing page with the radio predictions. About twenty minutes later, the plain-clothes officer arrived and their wet, disgruntled private tec, Phillip Marlowe, returned to the car. They dropped Freddie outside his apartment. Freddie slammed the car door behind him and as the sergeant put his foot down, Freddie suddenly tapped Hooker's window. The car screeched to a halt and Hooker wound it down.

'Well?' He growled.

'Chopin, Lieutenant ... your music question: Chopin composed "Raindrops" in a Spanish monastery. Get it?'

Thor

'Hey Toby, this man's a genius.' He reached for the newspaper as the car shot forward.

Hooker had important decisions to make, and do, before getting his star witness to put the attaché case with the blueprints back in the shaft void, and Freddie had several pages of typing to catch up with. But first he slowly drew a red butterfly on the character sheet pinned to the board. He couldn't help thinking of those capricious red reflections in black, oriental eyes that any man would willingly drown in.

What a girl!

6

Carver's story: It was Lieutenant Sebastian Carver who Hooker had stopped and chatted with in the Precinct. A man of few words but very astute. In the war, he had served in the Army Air Corp but seconded onto Patton's staff after D-Day as the lateral thinking General recognised the value of people like Carver with the rapidly changing situations as they headed towards Berlin. Later in the early fifties, there came an unprecedented series of bank raids in and around New York. Street intelligence would never be shared between Precincts because of the rife and historical inter-departmental jealousy. After Wagner was elected Mayor in '53 he turned to the man he had worked with in the Air Corp. He asked Carver to set up one central office to coordinate all this intelligence ... 'but leave the kudos to each Precinct.' Carver was quite happy to remain a shadowy figure and in time he gained the trust of the various departments; the raids dropped significantly and the delighted Mayor was later duly re-elected.

On Carver's desk stood a small plaque facing the visitor with one of Patton's quotes: "*The object of war is not to die for your country, but to make the other bastard die for his"*. He viewed the mafia as the new enemy. He'd lost many friends during the war and aware of the continued threat they posed to the new peace, especially as the situation in Vietnam was rapidly deteriorating, and so he found himself studying the 1912 plans of the then proposed Manhattan & Western Bank spread across Hooker's desk. He adjusted his pince-nez glasses and laid a slim finger on the strong room layout. 'This is Chubb of course, has all the latest details for that period: ... time lock ... railroad chest ... panic door. After the Bloemfontein fire it became essential for all this to be installed.'

Hooker raised his eyebrows. 'Bloemfontein?'

'Sure, big fire in a South African bank in 1908, but not one single item in the safe was harmed. So after that fire, clients wouldn't deposit unless a bank had this layout fitted.' He pulled out a thick green-colored file: "*Classified*" in red ink across the cover. He opened the heavily-tabbed file and scanned through the index. 'Yes it's all here. Chubb naturally keep records of all their bank layouts. These are the details of what were fitted and the methods of reinforcements used.'

He opened a page and squinted through

his glasses before reading out loud: 'a steel plate in the walls and ceiling, but this is what I'm looking for ... the floor ... as I thought ... nothing!'

'What's so special about the floor?'

'These strong-rooms are extremely expensive to install and this bank was a mid-western outfit trying to get into the big time by opening in Manhattan. Money was in short supply after the virtual collapse of the banks in 1907. After that time, any small town bank wanting to expand had to have a prestigious building right here in Manhattan, to be seen near the man who stepped in that year and saved them financially. J.P. Morgan moved away from the old financial enclave of Philadelphia to create one of the important financial centres in the world. This was where it was all happening, the new order here in New York. The Wall Street banking area was built on reclaimed land with a high water table, so tunnelling was not an option for criminals. This meant that many banks cut costs not bothering to reinforce their basement floors. This worked out fine, but over the years with the new anti-flood drainage systems, the water level has dropped dramatically. The bigger banks with bottomless pockets have now been reinforcing their basement floors, but not all ...' Carver then paused, '... and this bank hasn't. Customers are not aware of course, and the banks are such closed shops they keep that info close to their chests, even about their rivals. It might even cause a run on the smaller banks that could eventually cause a domino effect even on the bigger ones; they don't want a repeat of the thirties. Nowadays, if somebody could get into a neighboring building, it could be a possibility to tunnel under and up through this bank's unprotected floor.'

Hooker lit a cigarette and blew one of his smoke rings, tapping the bank's right wing. 'What if I was to tell you that this has just come on the market? Now empty and the ground floor and basement have just been leased out for six months?'

Carver waved the smoke away and stared at Hooker.

'Sorry,' apologised Hooker moving away.

'Who's leased it?'

'Don't know, but I'm hoping to find out this afternoon.'

'So what's your next move?'

They sat in silence, Hooker watching Carver hoping he would think the same as him. After a while Hooker mouth gave a hint of an impatient smile. 'I was hoping that you might be reading my mind.'

Thor

Carver continued to look at the plans, tossing ideas around in his head before prodding the blueprint. 'See here, at the rear of the strong room, there appears to have been some extra basement footings extended into the rear yard, so should they ever need to extend the strong room, they could push out behind the bank and build up.' He tapped the folder. 'The info here clearly states that the strong room extension has never been done. But this plan could be altered to show that the strong room is actually under the bank's rear yard and that's where any tunnelling would have to be done. So yes, I believe we're thinking the same, but there's not much time if you want this done by tonight.' He raised his eyes to the ceiling. 'No time to consult higher up. But then Patton once said to me: "a half baked plan put into action now is better than a foolproof plan put into action two weeks late."'

'Yeah,' Hooker replied, amused at Carver's numerous Patten quotes, 'but then this ain't half baked.'

Decision made, so the excited Carver carefully re-folded the blueprints and picked up his files. 'Oh yes, Herman, try this: ... "Greek with swollen foot marries a close relative, seven letters?"'

Hooker leaned back into his chair,

staring at the ceiling before grinning at Carver's expectant face. 'Oedipus?'

Carver growled. 'Damn, thought that would be hard.'

Hooker shrugged his shoulders. 'It will be for others of course,' he stated, continuing the grin,' use it ... it's good.'

Carver opened the door and without looking back tapped the blueprints. 'They'll be ready later ... promise.' Hooker lit another cigarette from the glow of his old butt, then picking up the phone he dialled. He could still hear the excited Carver chuckling as he hurried back to his own office.

'Hi Freddie, how's things? Have you given Spiegel a call? Good. I'll definitely see you later with the plans ... *no*,' irritated, 'I won't forget the attaché case.' Shaking his head with annoyance he tapped the phone cradle. 'Leo, get me the Manhattan & Western ... please.'

One hour later, Cornelius Swindon, manager of Manhattan & Western bank for more years than he cared, tapped on Hooker's office door. The Lieutenant opened it to a small, bald-headed, middle-aged man, who blinked nervously through large owl-shape glasses perched on a protruding thin nose: the conventional Dickensian dark suit with the silver fob-watch clipped to a dangling silver chain tucked into the vest pocket; the forties pin-striped shirt with its tight detachable collar; the sallow complexion that can come from years pouring over bank accounts; *a dying breed* mused Hooker.

Hooker studied the man from another age who carefully repositioned the offered chair and deliberately perched himself on the seat-edge to directly face the policeman. Hooker reading the man's signal that he couldn't spare much time. He sat upright, his briefcase on his lap gripped with long bony fingers, continuous blinking through the round glasses as would any owl unsure of its surroundings; a police precinct being an alien territory away from its nest, or wherever owls and bank managers live went through the Lieutenant's mind. Hooker recalling the Short-Eared Owl he once had pointed out to him as a boy, pecking at a hardboiled egg it had pinched. The species finally settled down.

The Lieutenant spoke quietly to reassure him. 'Sorry I made you leave your office, but I thought it better to meet here rather than make a visit to the bank. There may be others there that would know me and wonder?'

The manager blinked faster. 'Wonder? Oh, I see ... well I came as soon as traffic would allow. Now I'm here what can I do for you?'

He became agitated as Hooker explained the possibility of a break-in to his strong room.

'Nonsense Lieutenant ... the strong room is extremely well reinforced.'

Hooker posed the question. 'What do you have in there that would interest these people ... perhaps you're having a special delivery soon of gold or cash ... jewellery maybe?'

'I couldn't possibly disclose any information. We have strict client confidentiality, and on matters like that, you would have to speak to the board. We don't always know the contents of sealed packages we hold. There's no legal requirement.' He shrugged. 'To be honest I'd rather not know. We only rent out what we call: "AHS",' he paused, "Air Holding Space".' Then as if with a sense of regret, 'I'm only the manager, I don't make the rules. Anyway, how would they possibly attempt it?'

Hooker threw his cigarette pack across to the man which was refused; *probably an evening pipe-man, relaxing by the radio waiting for supper.* The Lieutenant took the pack back and waved it. 'Do you mind if I?'

Swindon didn't mind.

So the Lieutenant leaned back into his

chair, pulled out a cigarette and lit up before staring at the man. 'They could tunnel up through your strong room floor.'

The manager's eyes widened ... blinking ... retorting, 'impossible! Huh, that only happens in movies I believe.'

Hooker quickly leaned forward making Swindon start, his tone stern. 'Not impossible, because of your un-reinforced floor,' he snapped. 'Your company cut corners in 1914 because of the flooding and difficult ground conditions, but since then, the drainage systems have improved. It's a different ball game now. Most of the other banks have been spending bucks over the years reinforcing their floors, but you and a few others are still penny pinching. Your clients don't know this and if you had a hit they would run from you ... maybe sue?'

The manager squirmed and wrung his hands. 'I have to agree and yes, I've warned them for years ... but they won't spend any more money than they have to. No, they don't listen to me ... what would I know? ... sometimes I can't sleep at night when we have a big delivery ... I know they would make me the scapegoat—'

Hooker grabbed his pencil and quickly sketched out the basement area. He pushed it across the desk. 'My intelligence tells me that when the footings started in 1912, work was also done at the rear of the strong room, just here ...,' he tapped the sketch with his pencil, '... to extend it further under the rear yard at a later date should it be needed, like this. Was that ever done?'

The Manager shook his head. 'I've never seen any plans, but I believe the actual rear groundwork was completed, but not needed as the present strong room has proved to be perfectly adequate.'

'Well back to the tunnelling idea, have you not considered the empty building next to you?'

The manager suddenly looked ashen. 'Oh dear, oh dear, no I hadn't,' he spluttered. He pulled out a folded white handkerchief and wiped his brow.

Hooker lit another cigarette. 'Do the bank still own it?'

'No. The two wings either side were sold off at the end of the thirties after the depression ... that helped the bank from going under—'

Hooker pushed hard back into his chair. 'I see it's up for sale, but the ground floor and basement has been let on a six month lease. Now why would anyone lease part of a building in the financial centre for just six months? It's not exactly where some back-street, get-rich grifter would set up shop with damaged warehouse goods and run. That's why I asked you here. I happen to have street intelligence of something special you're holding, or going to have. I suspect a valuable consignment is coming in soon. The coincidence of next door being leased at the same time as a special delivery, is too good to be true ... surely? ... Someone's moving fast ... maybe they have inside information?' He raised an eyebrow and turned his ice-gray eyes on Mr. Swindon whose sallow complexion turned a slight pink.

The man swallowed and quickly rose to his feet. 'Are you accusing me of giving information?'

Hooker huffed. 'Please sit down Mr. Swindon. All I'm trying to do is make you see the seriousness of this. My job is to prevent it happening. Remember I'm on your side and I want to see these scum where they belong ... behind bars.'

The manager regained his perch on the chair edge, trying to compose himself. Hooker wondered about Mrs. Swindon: *a lion or a mouse? Owls eat mice.* The manager swallowed, carefully adjusting his glasses, blinking back at Hooker. He asked quietly, 'do you know who has taken the lease?'

'I was hoping you might tell me, but

maybe I'll find out later today. I've got to be careful with this as I don't want them getting any suspicions we're on to them. I'll make a phone call and you go back to have a chat, but *only* with your President, and explain the situation. I suggest he pops in here, quiet like, as the least number of people who know of our chat, the better.' Hooker stood up indicating the interview was over. 'I could obtain a court order.'

The manager swallowed again. 'I don't think that will be necessary. You are quite right of course Lieutenant. I'm afraid I'm out of my depth here and naturally I must follow your advice. I'll *try* to have a quiet word with our president, but I'd rather leave the details to you as he can be quite ... um—' He didn't finish and ran his finger around his tight collar, quickly consulted his fob watch and rose to leave.

Hooker shook a surprisingly firm hand, opened the door and watched the worried man hurry out clutching his briefcase as if he was about to be mugged in the outer office. He closed the door and picked up the phone, hesitated and put it back down deciding to use the public phone-booth in the street; he wouldn't want his next call traced back to the Precinct..

Thor

7

The Goon: The Lieutenant leaned against the street phone-booth, double checking the two numbers on Butterfly's list, making sure he didn't call her. He lifted the receiver and dialled. Above the rumble of traffic noise he heard the ringing burr, then ... 'Yup?'

He waited for the clink of the nickel as it tumbled.

'I understand you have just leased the building next to the bank on Pine?'

'What's it to you then?' The Bronx accent, thick and slurred.

Hooker put a finger in one ear to block a passing ice truck grinding through a bad gear change. He shouted, 'I work for a movie company and we are looking for an empty office location in Manhattan. That ground floor next to the bank in Pines would suit us perfect. It seems you have beaten us to it?'

'How'd yah get this number?'

Hooker had to lean further into the booth, cupping one ear to escape the damn traffic noise. 'Oh, there are ways.'

'Did the agent give it?'

Hooker played careful for Butterfly. 'No. They wouldn't play ball. Look, it's only for a weekend shoot.' He couldn't help smirking; *this goon would appreciate "shoot"*. 'I'm writing the script for this new movie, and before I speak to Sam Spiegel I need to case the location.'

'Sam Spiegel, the movie man? No yah wasting yah time. The boss won't wanna know.'

'There's money in it. Spiegel doesn't mind flashing a few dollars. If I think the location is right, then we could leave it to your boss and Spiegel to argue and sort the bucks out.' He tried to whisper, 'does your boss need to know about this first visit? There'll be something in it for you ... cash!'

'What type of *cash*?'

Hooker suggested a figure out of his head and the voice whistled. Hooker pressed home. 'Nobody would know we looked round beforehand. This is just between you and me ... hey Buddy, come on, where's the harm?'

The voice hesitated and whispered back, 'bread in the hand, before yer look round?'

The Lieutenant was enjoying the game. 'Sure! Nice and crusty like Momma always bakes. No problem.'

The voice hesitated. 'The boss would *kill* me if he found out.'

Easily arranged my friend. Where do these goons come from?

Thor

They agreed, noon next day, outside the bank's empty wing. As Hooker finished the call he shouted above the traffic, 'by the way, my name is Vermeer ... Freddie Vermeer.'

The Ulcer: Hooker knocked on Captain Mulligan's outer office door. A muffled voice echoed, 'come in lieutenant.'

He opened the door to see the back of a middle aged woman who had her head inside a steel filing cabinet. She turned clutching a dusty manila envelope, slightly red faced from the effort.

'Morning Jenny, how'd you know it was me?' he asked.

She glanced at the wall clock. 'Considering you made an appointment for this exact time it didn't take much effort.' Her Scottish vowels rolled across her sharp tongue. She blew dust off the envelope and dropped it to the floor, straightened her plaid dress before sitting at the desk. She patted her dishevelled gray-speckled hair and started to file her nails. She stared at him with suspicious eyes.'

Hooker asked, 'what mood is he in today?'

'Since you rang and demanded to chat with him, I would call it foul! In fact he sent me out for some Alka Seltzer.'

'About time he had that ulcer whipped out. Maybe I'll offer to do it for him.'

'Yeah and his left eye's playing up today so no wisecracks. Remember I have to work with him. He's given you five minutes.'

'I'll make it ten,' he replied and tapped H in morse-code on the inner, half-glass door: Captain R Mulligan jnr.

A pained voice bellowed, '*OK, HOOKER. COME IN*!'

Hooker grinned at Miss McDonald and winked. 'Love the cobweb sitting on top of your bouffant.'

'What!' she exclaimed, grabbing her handbag.

The Captain sat at his desk staring at an Alka Seltzer tablet as it danced and spun in a glass of water. He didn't look up as the Lieutenant sat down in the facing chair.

'Don't suppose you have an ulcer Hooker?'

'No Captain.'

'No, you wouldn't would you.'

Hooker stared at a vase of petunias sitting on the edge of the desk as the Captain used a pencil to prod the vanishing tablet on its final spin.

Mulligan hissed, 'no comments about that blasted plant Hooker. That's Miss McDonald's fancy idea. Infact you can put it on the filing cabinet in the far corner. Word soon gets around as I know your Floor-Three will start pushing rumors.'

Hooker picked up the vase and dumped it on the cabinet. 'Feels a bit dry Captain, shall I water it?'

'Leave it be, Hooker'. The Captain stared at him. 'Tell me Hooker, why is it I always get a *sinking feeling* when you walk through my door?'

The Lieutenant sat down and shrugged his shoulders. 'I believe those were the exact words the Captain used before Titanic hit the iceberg.'

The suffering man took a deep intake of breath, picked up the glass and gulped down the hissing mixture. He carefully placed the glass back on the desk and fixed his good eye on Hooker, the other eye half closed.

'Well?' he snapped coldly, 'make my day!

The Lieutenant told him about the noon meeting he had arranged for the next day and the bribe to look round the basement.

Captain Mulligan's bushy eyebrows suddenly shot skywards. He glared with his good eye.

'How *much*?' he squealed!

Hooker glowered back. 'Cheap at the price Captain,' he argued. 'You don't mess around with these people and there isn't much time.'

The captain drummed the fingers of one hand on the desk, his other hand clutching his stomach.

'You must remember Captain,' Hooker continued, 'I'm supposed to be a movie man and these guys think movie men are loaded. A cheap bribe would ring suspicious like.'

'And this is tomorrow at noon? You don't give me much time do you Hooker.' He rubbed a nicotine finger across his heavy jowls and sniffed; the bad eye now looking towards the lieutenant's shoulder.

'Better be worth it,' he growled. 'You always think my budget is bottomless.' Leaning over the desk he wagged the same nicotine finger at the Lieutenant. 'Problem with you Hooker, you think you're a law unto yourself, and don't respect regulations. Regulations are there for a reason. I'm supposed to make a triple application for bucks when it's ending up in some villain's pocket. You can have it but only if you handle this yourself.' The finger continued to wag. 'You will *personally* hand over the money and inspect this basement, no one else. Get it Hooker? ...NO ONE ELSE!'

'Are you suggesting that you don't trust any of my team to do it?'

The man's face seemed to pale. 'After that fiddle two years ago, I nearly lost my job, so I'm not getting into that corner again. Is that clear?'

'If I remember correctly Captain, that was a sting you personally arranged, handed over the money and had nothing to do with me or my unit?'

'Don't play smart arse with me Hooker. Besides which, I'm still waiting for your report on the Finnegan farce.'

'It's in the *new* system you implemented last year to speed things along.'

'Well I still ain't received it, so the system ain't working.'

'Precisely Captain.'

He went red. 'Don't twist my words. What I mean is ... the system's not being *implemented* correctly!'

The Lieutenant decided to keep his mouth shut as he had no intention of doing the report. In the dead silence, whilst the Captain considered his options, there came the sound of rapid typing from the outer office; Hooker casually used his hand to cover his grin.

The Captain suddenly resigned himself to the demand and hissed between his clenched teeth, 'the hell with you Hooker and your Floor-Three.' He snatched open a desk drawer, took out a pad and reluctantly slipped carbon between the sheets. He licked an indelible pencil and kept glancing and hissing at the Lieutenant as he filled in the details. He grunted and tore off the top two sheets, carefully checking before handing them across.

'OK,' he snarled, 'make to admin and get the money before I change my mind. And remember ... it'll be *you* handing over and doing any *basement inspection*! OK?' He quickly put his hand up to his mouth.

Hooker nodded and put them in his pocket. This was the best time to leave before the tablet worked, and glad he decided not to mention that a civilian, called Freddie, his star witness, was going to be the front man in the operation. As Hooker opened the door, the Captain suddenly burped and bellowed, 'on your head be it, Hooker!'

Out of respect for the Captain and his ulcer and the strange eye, he quietly closed the door before grinning at Miss McDonald who was now painting her nails. Her rapid typing for the day appeared to be over.

Hooker leaned over the typewriter and whispered, 'he wants you to go and rub his stomach.'

Thor

She flicked his ear with the paint brush and giggled!

As he was about to close the outer door he look back. She still had her suspicious eyes on him. He said, 'the Captain told me to move your plant *off* his desk.'

Her eyes flashed as she stood up, automatically straightening her plaid dress. 'We'll see about that!'

Returning from admin with the bribe money, he met Carver walking to his office clutching the precious blueprints. Carver spread the now altered bank plans across Hooker's desk. Before pointing out the alterations, he tried Hooker's patience by cleaning and re-adjusting his pince-nez glasses on the bridge of his nose.

Hooker eagerly studied the drawings. He was impressed and commented, 'unbelievable.'

Carver grinned, obviously delighted with his work, and as always with Hooker, recalling the past. 'Just after the landings, we came across a metal container full of German military papers in an abandoned farmhouse. We re-cooked the plans and had a fighter plane lose the case near their artillery. Result, the Germans started shelling their own lines.

Later in his Mulberry apartment, Freddie watched the Sergeant trying to park. He lit a Winston and counted the time for the smoke ring to drop on the floor before picking up the phone. 'Hi Sam ... did your secretary explain to you ... good ... I told you I'm working with the cops to get a good story line ... look, in case anybody should ring to check that I'm genuine ... someone has already?. I see. Your secretary told them yes. OK ... good ... soon Sam. Yes I'm working on it right now.'

As Freddie waited for Hooker's expected knock on the door he mulled over the day's strange events. Suddenly the entrance Tannoy buzzed, it was Hooker with a change of tactics.

Freddy opened his door and he came in clutching the attaché case.

'I was expecting you to tap on the door lieutenant.'

'Oh, why would I do that when you have the Tannoy?'

He looked out the window at the Sergeant now leaning against his car sipping a Deno coffee. He tutted to himself and patted the case as he placed it on the desk. 'Perhaps you'd like to see the alterations before you put it back ... exactly as you found it.'

The duly impressed Freddie left his apartment to return the case, while an equally impressed Hooker studied Freddie's pin-board. The characters had been coded with different colored crayon marks, one in ginger; obvious who that was? The plot sheet became clearer to Hooker: the roof killing, the hidden attaché ... the chat at the Precinct ... the bank and the estate agent and then tomorrow morning with a red tick at the bank? *Freddie couldn't know anything about that arrangement he'd made*; *but it was there.* It had been set out as if predicting an unfolding pattern, day by day ahead. It was clever and fascinating, as if Freddie was one or two days ahead of events and maybe he was even ahead of Hooker. A ginger crayon mark next to a half moon predicted Ginger would be back at dusk that very evening? Moving his finger further down the line he came to a full moon alongside two circles: planets maybe; two circles drawn again but now merged as one; a full moon in the middle; an alignment? Freddie had chalked and underlined a red cross. Hooker had a growing respect for his witness. He jotted down a few notes describing the system ... it was clever. He knew Carver would want to study it.

On the sidewalk Freddie adjusted his backpack that now contained the attaché case and crossed to the entrance directly opposite his apartment. He nodded at the duty uniform cop standing there. Sergeant

Jugg continued to lean against his car and looked the other way, obeying Hooker's instructions not to watch.

Hooker stared across as Agent Vermeer appeared on the roof.

Freddie thinking again the roof looked smaller than the view from his opposite window where he could easily make out the Lieutenant. The girl's laundry hung still in the calm air as he made his way to the third ventilation shaft. He paused for a moment to stare at the chalk outline of Charlie Chaplin. Raising the cowling he slid the attaché case back into the void exactly as he'd found it; w*as that only this morning?* He made his exit and noticed Hooker was now training the binoculars on him.

As Freddie emerged back into the street, the duty cop left the entrance and climbed into the back of the Sergeant's car. The Sergeant moved it further down the street to await the Lieutenant. Freddie returned to his apartment and poured himself a drink, offering the bottle to Hooker who shook his head.

'I don't want you getting *inebriated* tonight Freddie. The next part belongs to you. I want you to keep a beady eye on that roof. Ginger will be back as soon as possible now the police presence has cleared off. He's desperate to get his hands on those drawings just to keep alive. You've got my number so keep me informed.' He glanced at Freddie's pin-board prediction. 'Oh by the way, I've another little job for you tomorrow midday. I've arranged for you to meet this goon who's agreed to show you around the ground floor of the empty bank wing. When you're in there, I want you make an excuse to go into the basement on whatever pretence to do with filming. See if they've been up to anything down there already or if there have been any alterations over the years. You know the original lay-out from the plans.'

'Can't you get one of your undercover pals to do it?'

'We can't take any chances. He'll probably have your description from Rivera after your visit to the office. I pretended to be you ... I gave him your name. You can confuse him with your movie jargon.'

Freddie sighed and nodded. 'Thanks. It seems as if I'm already up to my neck. Spiegel said that somebody's already rung his office and his secretary confirmed I'm working for him.'

'Good, it's working out fine. We'll pick you up in the morning and if Snuffy Ginger hasn't come by then to pick up the attaché case, I'll stay here and keep watch and the Sergeant will take you down to Pines to meet this goon. But I'm convinced he'll come when it's dark as he's aware of nosey neighbors looking out their windows.' He paused to scratch his head, scowling. 'Ginger's not as dumb as we like to think. Annoyingly the agent lost him at the bar. He recalls a bald head coming out in a group with several others. Perhaps Ginger guessed he was being watched and removed his wig?' He opened the door. 'Be careful Agent Vermeer, these people can be quite ruthless.' He closed the door with a smile.

Freddie growled at the door. 'Thank you Lieutenant, it's not a game. I'll sleep better knowing that!'

He went over to the board and sipped his drink; studying his plot predictions ... they seemed to be working out fine. He picked up a yellow crayon realising he hadn't drawn a circle for that morning visit to the Precinct. Who was the street girl with the yellow bandana ... why was she there? What was it about the street girl that he found intriguing? Even the scar had an appeal. He tried to forget her and concentrate on his typing, but it was difficult; he couldn't get her out of his mind.

Thor

8

Ginger's return: That evening he put down the half empty Daniels bottle and pushed his glass away. *No! I must stop drinking - Loretta's right – just because I'm under pressure.*

He returned to the window to stare from his darkened room into the dusk for the hundredth time. Suddenly he became aware of a shadowy movement. He rubbed his tired eyes, grabbed the binoculars and had trouble focusing in the gloom, but there was Snuffy Ginger lit by the flashing neon, with his arm in the ventilation shaft. He pulled out the attaché case, quick glance inside before hurrying back to the exit, clutching the case as if his life depended on it, which it probably did according to Hooker. He gave a last glance behind him and disappeared through the roof door. It happened so quickly. He picked up the telephone and dialled.

Hooker's familiar voice responded, '*great news Freddie, well done ... you can go to sleep now. See you in the morning.*' Freddie turned his desk-light back on to pour that drink he had refused himself earlier.

Thor

Grand Central: The lanky, bald headed man, dressed in a shabby trench coat, cautiously entered the left-luggage door situated on the lower ground-floor-level. A self-rolled cigarette hung sideways from his thin lips as he placed an envelope and one small parcel on the counter. His edgy eyes flicked side to side as he waited for the resentful youth to enter the two items into a desk ledger. A uniformed female manager scowled at the sullen rookie as he tore off two receipt-stubs and tossed them across the counter. She whispered sharply in the youth's ear, 'don't be so bloody awkward, he's a customer.'

The man picked up the two stubs and slipped them into an addressed, stamped envelope. With the cigarette drooping from his mouth, he stuck his tongue out sideways to lick the flap. Then without a murmur he left the office, catching the woman's acid remark to the youth, 'if you don't pull yourself together boy ... you're out on your ear!'

The man dropped the envelope into a mail-chute as he made his hurried exit onto East 42nd Street. He wiped his brow with his coat sleeve. He was nervous.

9

Grand-mamma's crusty bread: It was mid-morning when Freddie slipped into the back of Hooker's unmarked car. They wound their way through the heavy Manhattan traffic towards Pines. The Sergeant parked away from the suggested meeting point where they could sit and observe. Hooker watched in his mirror as a uniformed council street-sweeper slowly swept his way to them. He dropped his cart down and brushed round the car.

As the man swept past his door, Hooker wound his window down and commented, '*Yer* doing a good job there, Nathan. I'm impressed. *Yer* look a natural with that broom. '

'There's nothing to report, Lieutenant ... nobody here that shouldn't be.'

Hooker nodded and Nathan continued his brushing. Hooker looked in the mirror at Freddie. 'He'll be checking your back.'

Hooker glanced at his strap-watch as a baby-pink, open-top Cadillac Eldorado coasted up Pines and squeezed into a non-parking bay. The engine was cut with a last defiant roar by the tanned, muscular ginzo sitting behind the wheel. His powder-blue chin perfectly matched the powder-blue suit, and the oiled-back hair and obligatory dark shades made him look like an Al Capone recruitment poster-boy. His image was completed by the Rita Hayworth look-a-like car accessory, who sat next to him dressed in pink. Her tiny cigar-box hat floated in a wisp of netting and pinned at a saucy angle on the flowing red hair. She tried to project an aura of sophistication by pointing a long, ivory cigarette-holder in the air, whilst admiring her face in the car's vanity mirror. He swung his legs over the car door and sprung out to impress; but she had seen it all before and now concentrated on her eye-brows. He bounced up the bank steps to hide behind one of the stone pillars at the entrance.

Hooker chuckled. 'This is the clown that insisted we kept all this low key Freddie.'

Suddenly his head popped out from around the pillar to glance up and down Pines before quickly withdrawing.

Hooker laughed. 'Reminds me of when a kid, watching rabbits popping their heads out the ground.'

He folded his newspaper. 'Well that's your man Freddie. You couldn't make this up could you? Wish I'd brought my airgun for practice.' He handed over an envelope. 'You know the drill. Here's the money. He's bound to check it out before he lets you in, but it's all there as agreed

... and this,' he handed over a paper bag and grinned, 'he'll love this.'

Freddie looked in the bag. 'A loaf of bread?'

'Sure, tell him it's a crusty Pane Crostoso, just like grandmamma used to make. You'll have a friend for life there, Freddie, I promise. And don't forget it was you who spoke to him yesterday. I'll give you thirty minutes, if you're not out by then, I'll *follow* Toby in.'

The Sergeant glared. 'Why do I have to go in first?'

'You're a born leader Toby. You lead ... I follow – remember?'

'Oh hell,' exclaimed Freddie, 'it's Ginger!'

The three men stared in disbelief as Ginger suddenly appeared from an opposite bar clutching the attaché case. He hurried across the street to stumble up the steps and start talking to blue-suit. They watched him hand over the now familiar case. Blue-suit opened it to check inside before Ginger scarped back down the steps into the safety of the opposite bar.

Hooker growled, 'that's a piece of luck seeing the hand-over. However I don't think this has anything to do with your meeting Freddie. If Ginger looks out of the bar hopefully he won't know you if you wear this,' he removed his Fedora, 'and these.' He whipped off the Sergeant's shades! Freddie pulled the hat down and slipped on the shades. He muttered to Hooker as he got out of the car, 'this is ridiculous. Hope Sam appreciates what I'm doing for him.'

The two cops watched new agent Freddie Vermeer as he hurried along the sidewalk before crossing towards blue-suit hiding on the steps. They watched with interest the hand-over ceremony taking place.

'Don't laugh,' exclaimed Hooker, as the man gave Freddie the attaché case to hold as he turned his back to count the money. He nodded and looked inside the paper bag. He flung his head back and roared with laughter before giving Freddie a hard slap on his shoulder. Still laughing he unlocked the big glass door. Freddie couldn't help a quick glance back at the car before going in rubbing his shoulder. Blue-suit looked hastily around and followed.

Hooker checked his watch. 'Thirty minutes Toby. Don't know why I bothered to wipe Freddie's dabs off the case. I've a feeling that goon is the son of the de Vince family. Old man baby-face de Vince runs that scrap metal yard over in Brooklyn. Bet he doesn't know his Cadillac is being used to impress some broad. Wonder who she is?'

They watched Nolan suddenly appear with his cart to park behind the pink Cadillac. He unhooked his stiff brush and started brushing vigorously around the car. The red head started waving her hand trying to push the dust away. She turned her head and opened her mouth at Nolan. He shrugged his shoulders and returned to his cart, carefully clipped the broom back in position, before wheeling it to the other side of Pines.

Hooker and the Sergeant roared with laughter. Nolan then strolled into a nearby drug store. When he reappeared, he was carrying a coke and bagel.

Hooker wound his window down and called out, 'Nathan!'

Nathan walked to the car with a silly grin on his face.

Hooker said, 'that was the weirdest chat up I've ever seen. What's she like?'

He leaned on the door. 'Put it this way, she looks better at this distance than close up, especially when she unzips her mouth!'

'What did she shout at you?'

'That Lieutenant, I couldn't possibly repeat to a man of your sensibility.'

Hooker said, 'OK fun guy, but I want you to keep close to that bar opposite the bank and keep an eye on the man with the ginger wig in there. I want him picked up and brought in *after* we've left.'

The two occupants waited in the car and watched the coming and goings of a busy banking street. Hooker became interested in the bank uniformed security man who came out the Manhattan entrance. He looked up and down the street as he lit a cigarette, for a second his gaze seemed to rest on their car before crossing to the opposite sidewalk. He made a quick call from a public phone-booth and as he finished, he stared across at the red head in the car before grinding the cigarette with his heel. He hurried back into the bank. Hooker muttered to himself, occasionally glancing at his watch as he studied the Sergeant looking somewhat odd without his shades.

'Toby, all these years I've had to put up with you, I've never seen you without your shades. Has my sister ever seen you without them?'

The Sergeant grunted and continued clicking his gum louder to annoy his brother-in-law.

Hooker grinned. 'Do you wear them in bed?'

'Yep ... if I can't sleep! That reminds me, your sister's been nagging ... she reckons you could do with a haircut ... as if it's *my* fault!'

Hooker looked in the mirror and flicked his hair. He glanced at his watch. 'Hey I've given them an extra five minutes, better go in.' Freddie and blue-suit suddenly re-appeared and started talking earnestly.

'Looks hopeful Toby,' exclaimed Hooker, 'he's shaking hands. Such a gentleman is our new boy. Whenever I shake hands with villains, it's usually with cuffs.'

Freddie tried to casually stroll whilst blue-suit hurried to the Cadillac clutching the attaché case and his bag of bread. He dropped the case in the back of the car and tossed the bag of bread onto the woman's lap. He then smoothed back his oily hair before swinging his legs over the car door and dropping into his driving seat. He started the engine, reversed out and roared away as if a man on a mission. His companion continued to study her face in the vanity mirror.

As the car disappeared Freddie quickened his steps still rubbing his shoulder. He slid into the rear seat with a grin on his face and handed the shades to the Sergeant. 'I've promised him a walk-on part in the movie ... he's a keep-fit fanatic and wants to play a heavy,' he laughed out loud with a sense of relief, 'and the bread really cemented the arrangement.'

Hooker sniffed. 'I told you he'd be pleased. Shame he's not in a cage, you could have fed him through the bars. Let's go home now Toby.' The Sergeant drove slowly pass the cart as Nathan called out, 'all OK Lieutenant, he's only interested in the gee-gees ... his ears are stuck solid to the radio.'

Hooker nodded, 'thanks for your help.'

Detective Nathan, sometimes council street-sweeper, grinned and pushed his cart round the corner straight into the back of an unmarked truck. As they drove away, an unmarked prowl-car pulled up and two cops went into the bar to unglue Ginger's ear from the radio. They escorted him down to the Precinct to discuss the theory, as to why the scantily dressed Themis would be sitting blindfolded on a cocktail stool in the lobby.

Whilst the car crawled through heavy traffic, Freddie related events in the building. '... and did you see him give me the attaché case to hold as he checked the money? Couldn't believe it ... all he's interested in was being in the movie. I knew that if I didn't get away you'd come bursting through the door and ruin it.' He handed over several small photos.

Hooker frowned. 'Where did you get these?'

'Would you believe he had a Polaroid camera and thought it would be good to show Spiegel some photos. He thinks he's in for more cash as well as a part in the movie. I was worried when we went down to the basement ... but look,' he pointed to a picture of the basement clearly showing tools stacked in one corner, 'there's a pneumatic drill, shovels, pickaxes and a stack of wood planks probably to shore up the roof of the tunnel. When I asked about them, he looked uneasy and said the boss was planning some alterations. From what I can see, the basement layout is exactly the same as on those drawings'

'Good. Did he say why they leased the building?'

'I asked him, but he just played dumb.'

'*Dumb*! Bet that was easy. Well done Freddie, so all we need is some info from our friend the bank manager and his boss, and then we'll have a better idea when all this is supposed to happen.' He rubbed his hands together with pleasure. 'Swell! Toby, tell my sister I didn't have time to get my haircut today!'

10

The Cowboy: Hooker sat typing and thinking. He cursed and pulled the half finished report from the machine, screwed it into a ball before tossing into the trash-can. He put his last cigarette in his mouth and the empty pack followed into the can. He lit up and glanced at his strap-watch. 'Come on Mr Spooler, what's keeping you? Bet if I was late with a payment you'd be sitting on my doorstep.'

Suddenly there came a rumble from a deep voice in the outside corridor and a large shadow appeared on the door's frosted glass - heavy tapping. Carefully putting his last cigarette on the ashtray, he opened the door to find a six foot six, Stetson-wearing cowboy, out of breath and glaring. He stood there mopping his pink face with a large red silk-handkerchief.

'Is this Hooker's office? He growled.

Hooker made a point of staring at his name tag on the door. 'Looks like it. I take it you're Mr. Spooner?'

'Spooler,' he growled.

A worried Cornelius Swindon appeared from behind the cowboy, smiling nervously. 'Hello again, Lieutenant.'

'Gentlemen, please come in.'

Thor

The cowboy walked past the Lieutenant, ignored the offered hand and stood swaying in the middle of the room to eye up the sparseness of a cop's office. Swindon immediately settled down on the edge of his chair, blinking ... watching. Hooker motioned Spooler to sit and the man eyed the offered chair for a moment before lowering his bulk. His wide hips squeezed between the arms as the chair started to creak.

He glared. 'It's most inconvenient Lieutenant ... most inconvenient.'

'Sorry Sir, but that's the only chairs they issue.'

The man glared back. 'No, not the chair! We had to walk up two flights of stairs. Damn elevator out of action ... most inconvenient, Sir. Most inconvenient!.'

Hooker flicked his finger and thumb. 'Of course the elevator's annual fumigation of missing felons. I forgot. Sorry about that. Yes, *even I* had to walk up this morning ... most inconvenient.'

Chuck T. Spooler the Third, president of Manhattan and Western Bank, stared at Hooker with thick lips pulled back to grip an unlit Cuban cigar in perfect dental-white teeth. Hooker observed the large bull-neck Texan: in his sixties, gray-speckled blue eyes almost hidden by deep craggy eyebrows, hair that had been groomed and dyed a rusty brown. Hanging across the forehead was a lock of hair that had been combed into a cheeky curl as if to distract from the bourbon-veined nose. His complexion was of a life outdoors and complete with a jutting chin skilfully framed by snow-white mutton-chop side-whiskers. His cream Stetson rested on one knee, clutched by thick manicured fingers stained nicotine.

The cream hackneyed suit with contrasting red silk shirt; the black silk necktie clipped by a gold Texas-Star. He lifted and crossed a thick leg that sported the obligatory dude cowboy-boot with its deeply- engraved leather. Hooker viewed the two contrasts seated in his office with some form of casual amusement: Swindon unusually cool and composed, and the Texan suspicious and agitated, sweating and ready.

Spooler ran a finger around his collar and mopped his face again. 'Sure am hot in here Lieutenant, sure am hot.'

Hooker stood up and muttered quietly as he opened the window a notch. He sat back at his desk and offered to light the man's cigar but was refused with a wave of the manicured fingers. Hooker took his last cigarette from the ashtray and deliberately blew a smoke ring towards the cream suit.

He spoke to the cowboy, 'I'm sure Mister Swindon has filled you in with all the details.'

'Yah doggone right Sir.' The words slow, drawn out, Texas style. 'Sure ... but ah wanna hear it from you ... *direct*.' The manager tried to ignore his President's bullying manners.

But the unfazed Hooker, having spent years dealing with bully-boys of the low and high ends of society, calmly went through the details; the Texan just growling occasionally, chewing his cigar as he became further agitated, mopping his red face, squinting at the man opposite.

'Sir, yah wanna me to break confidential matters. How do I know this ain't some kinda con?' He nodded at the manager. 'He might be easily fooled, but yah canna' get one over old Chuck T. Spooler the Third.' He sat defiant, weighing up the Lieutenant.

Hooker could feel the adrenalin start to pump and he retorted back, 'Mr. Spooner—'

'Spooler!'

'Of course ... Mr. Spooler. I take offence at your suggestion that this is a con. I wouldn't be doing my job if I ignored this threat to your bank, but if you wish me to do nothing, then you must take the consequences and I wash my hands of this whole affair. I'll put that in my report to the D.A. *and* the Commissioner. I'll also state that Mr. Swindon took the report seriously.'

The manager glanced nervously at his president but nodded in agreement. Hooker rose and offered his hand. 'Well Sir, I'll say good bye as I'm very busy.'

Chuck T. Spooler the Third waved his Stetson at the Lieutenant. 'No sir, ah donna mean that. Yah must understand ah must be cautious. We have very important *cliental,*' he drawled the word, 'it wouldn't do to make them feel as if we were lax with their confidentiality. News soon spreads here in Manhattan. Yah must understand Lieutenant; ma great grand-pappy founded the bank when he hit an oil strike on our ranch way back. Ah don't want it to go under. Means a lot to me. It's family ... yah understand ... family? Who would be privy to any information yah require?'

Hooker stared with the coldness he had perfected over the years. 'I'm the only one that needs to know. I have intelligence that suggests there could be an attempt on your bank, so there must be something you have, or are going to have, in your strong-room they want.'

The Texan chewed and wiggled his

cigar, made strange groaning noises as he contemplated the Lieutenant. The chair creaked. He furrowed his brow and peered from under his craggy eyebrows. He cleared his throat and drawled, 'sir, do ah have yah word as a gentleman ... as an officer of our government ... that yah will treat this as classified ... err ... classified as to the bank's business?'

Hooker managed not to smile, deciding time was right to call him by his proper name and not deliberately antagonise. 'Yes sir, as an officer of our government, Mister Spooler, you also have my word as,' he drawled, '... *a Northern gentleman*.' Hooker deciding it was time to test his theory ... *once a reluctant interviewee thinks he's important enough to be included in your inner circle ... he's putty in your hands*". He looked side to side, as if checking for listening ears, leaned forward confidentially before speaking quietly, 'you must also realise, Mister Spooler that this operation has a Section 2D notice slapped on it by the Commissioner.' He leaned back.

The two stared. The Texan looked worried. 'What does that mean, Lieutenant?'

So Hooker leaned forward again and with the same quiet voice, 'well, classified of course! Naturally we had to do a check on your background to clear you for a Section 2D, otherwise I couldn't reveal details of this operation.' He raised one eyebrow, with lips gripped together trying to appear serious, waiting for the man's reaction which immediately warmed towards the lieutenant.

Spooler nodded and glanced at his manager. 'Ah Section 2D, hear that Swindon, just yah an' me know. Sure Lieutenant ... Swindon here will give yah any help yah want. Appreciate yah concern with ma family, Lieutenant.'

The large Texan pulled himself from the chair, at first slightly unsteady on his high heeled boots as he stuck out his fist to shake the Lieutenant's hand. Swindon glanced at the floor to avoid the pantomime of his superior. Hooker just smiled and took the large manicured paw. He stood and opened the door. The two men trooped out with the cowboy growling through his clenched cigar, 'ah Section 2D notice Swindon, Just yah an' me know. So keep your mouth shut. Well, well ... who'd believe it?'

Hooker shut the door, stony faced, lips still tight. He closed the window and sat back at his desk. He leaned back and blew a last smoke ring before stubbing out his cigarette, brooding. He couldn't contain himself anymore and burst out laughing, quickly wiping his eyes as Carver looked in.

'You OK, Sherman?'

Hooker giggled. 'Hey, you didn't see a horse hitched up in the yard?'

Carver shook his head and grinned. 'I don't think so. You and I need to have a chat Sherman.' He came in and sat down. 'I think we're treading on each other's toes.'

Hooker wiped his cheeks and tried to look serious. 'Explain!'

'For the past year, I've been collating intelligence about Nazi loot being smuggled into the States from Europe and a particular trail comes straight from Switzerland, would you believe. Well we've known of course that even before the war, looted gold, paintings, jewellery, you name it, was allowed to be deposited by the authorities into Swiss bank accounts as a holding bay before being smuggled down to the South Americas, particularly Argentina. This is denied of course by the Swiss government or cantons as they call themselves. Because of diplomatic pressure from Eisenhower, and the presence of our navy, the authorities down there have laughingly closed some of these routes. Now a new route has emerged bringing precious jewellery items and paintings into New

York before being taken overland into the South Americas, right under our noses; audacious and clever, eh. I've had a team working at the docks for the past year and it occurs to me your suspected bank robbery and this loot is connected.'

Hooker started taking notes. 'Carry on.'

'We understand this loot goes into the bank system here, then moved on to another branch, and so on until it works its way down south. The banks have no idea as to the contents as the packages remain sealed until it leaves our jurisdiction. Once it gets over the border into Mexico its open house down to Argentina. It coincides with your case as the Manhattan is the bank they are going to use for a new consignment. My intelligence suggests that local villains have cottoned on and want a slice of the action. Their intention is to get their hands on it before it leaves the city. They don't realise just what they're letting themselves in for. This is a big racket and the people ruthless; they don't tolerate small-fry Mafioso.'

Hooker nodded. 'And I suspect small fry Jose Rivera wants his grubby hands on it. Yes it makes sense. Maybe this will give me the chance to nail him once and for all—'

Carver nodded his head in agreement. 'Yes and if we pool our resources, you can nail your man Rivera, and I can close this particular route going back into Europe. The authorities over there are ready and waiting for our signal.' He leaned forward. 'This is how they're getting the loot in ...'

Hooker continued taking notes. 'Right, let's go and have a chat with the Commissioner.' He reached for the phone.

Thor

11

SummerWind: The two Lieutenants sat side by side in Commissioner Dennis Washington's office and stared at the back of the tall man as he stood at the big, half-opened window. His bald head glowed pink from his recent trip down to his launch "*SummerWind*" moored on the Florida Keys. He used one finger to bend down one of the blind slats and gazed through to take in the whole of the dock area. The sun was beginning to dip and cast long shadow fingers. The Commissioner watched the cranes in the distance unloading goods brought in from foreign lands that would be on the shelves the following morning. He could see the unmistakable three funnels of the Queen Mary that had docked earlier, busy preparing for its rapid turn-around departure back to the UK. In the distance he could just make out the tall thin bow of the "SS. United States" heading in to dock alongside her great rival. He let go the blind with a snap and tried to tap the black springy tobacco down in his briar pipe with a pencil. Hooker stared at the window's low positioned stone-cill; handy if the job's getting you down he supposed.

The lads below on Floor-3 refer to them as suicide windows after the accident of an assistant commissioner, who later turned out to be up to his ears in debt to the mob.

The panelled walls were adorned with oils of the past Commissioners, empty eyes as if bored with it all. Hooker fixed his gaze on the empty space at the end wall he assumed was waiting for the present incumbent; he glanced at the suicide window. But the Commissioner's mind now concentrated on more pressing matters so he moved back to his swivel chair and at the same time ran a hand across his baldness to smooth imaginary hair. On his large mahogany desk stood a framed photograph of a determined looking woman standing next to a tall girl dressed in mortar board and gown; Hooker noticing they shared the same hooked nose. Another picture was of "*Summer Wind*" hitched to the jetty of an expensive looking, white clapperboard yacht-club called "Admiral's Retreat"; Hooker betting the picture was taken from the cocktail bar window.

Lined up in front of the spotless blotting pad were two copper Florida alligators. One looked friendly as a cigar-lighter, and the other alligator had a lethal-looking tongue to open letters. The Commissioner picked up the lighter, flicked its wheel and lit his pipe, drawing before blowing his tobacco ash off the desk with a cloud of dark smoke. He waved his pipe around. 'Managed to get some Mexican tobacco from a friend who lives on the Keys. He swears by it. What do you think? Do you think my good lady Mrs. Washington will approve?

'Yes Sir ... very smooth Sir,' they both said in unison.

Carver unfolded copies of the blueprints to explain the alterations he had forged that morning. The Commissioner pulled open a drawer and took out an alligator-skin spectacle case. He slipped on his reading glasses and followed Carver's finger as he indicated his work before asking, 'so, you're both confident with your plan?'

They both nodded in unison and Carver continued. 'The delivery the bank is expecting will be quietly swopped with a dummy package of identical wrapping and weight.'

The Commissioner drew on his pipe, turning his face sideways to blow the black smoke away. 'How do you know the packaging?'

Carver said, 'it could go wrong of course but we are tracking two separate crates en route south at this moment. They seem to use identical packaging so we're taking a chance this third will be the same. As soon as we make our move here, then those two original crates already en route will also be picked up.'

'Have you confided with the Manhattan bank?'

Hooker's mouth pulled at the corners as he pictured the Texan. 'I've only told the manager and their president, Mister Chuck T. Spooler the Third, that there's a possibility of a raid. Not about the Nazi loot or our proposed plans. I've stressed that this is highly confidential and covered by a Section 2D notice you've slapped on it.' He blew a smoke ring up to the ceiling.

The Commissioner frowned. 'What the heck is a Section 2D notice when it's about?'

Hooker grinned. 'Nothing actually Sir, just my sense of fun, I often like to quote that as it seems to keep talkative mouths shut tight. Customers like to have labels and it makes them feel they're involved in secret operations; especially to someone like, Mister Chuck T. Spooler the Third.'

Both Carver and the commissioner looked at each other and chuckled.

'I like it,' said the Commissioner.

Hooker continued, 'there has to be an informer in the bank, so it's prudent to keep this to ourselves. My information suggests there's a special delivery next week, but the bank have no idea as to what it is. They often handle and store packages without knowing the contents.'

The Commissioner frowned. 'Why not just take them before letting the delivery get to the bank?

Hooker leaned forward, excited. 'It's my chance to get a certain local villain behind bars where he belongs. The Lieutenant here gets his route closed down and I shut the file on a homicide at the same time.' His eyes gleamed. 'We'll let them start tunnelling under the bank to actually catch them on bank property before we take them, which makes it a federal crime and a longer sentence. I wanna be there and enjoy his face after he's been sweating for hours underground and that moment he realises he's been rumbled ... Can't wait!'

Carver folded the two plans and put them back into a folder. He paused for a minute cleaning his pince-nez glasses. 'My intelligence suggests that this looted consignment, which we believe to be of unique jewelled religious items, together with three small iconic paintings by Raphael, are being smuggled into the country today. We don't know for sure but have a good idea how this is being achieved. Our Coast Guard keep a watch on the liners coming into the country and they know that just outside territorial limit at night, the liners dump all the food stores not used on the voyage into the sea ... sides of meat, butter, cream, flour ... you name it ... out it goes.'

The Commissioner stared at Carver, pulling hard at his briar pipe. 'You're telling me that all this food goes to waste?'

Carver nodded.

The Commissioner shook his head and tutted. 'Whilst Europe starves?'

'Sure ... because their turn around is so fast they have a set quantity of provisions waiting on the docks. They dump what's left over from each voyage then take on the new stock. It doesn't quite go to waste, because the trawlers wait for them to off-load, then in they go, picking up all the meats and anything else. Doesn't do any harm in the salt water, keeps them in provisions for weeks!'

Hooker blew another smoke ring. 'So they can dump items overboard without raising any suspicions.'

Carver started coughing and agreed. 'Sure. We work with the Coast Guard to keep an eye on what's going on out there. They've loaned us a covert trawler under a Captain Kinston. He's a good man and nothing gets through under his nose. The liners like to do this in the blackness of night so the passengers don't see the dumping. We suspect one trawler called "Pandora" that waits for the designated liner and moves in quickly. It picks up the sealed bag containing the loot and gets away long before the other trawlers come in looking for any discarded goodies.'

The Commissioner tapped his pipe and tried relighting with the pet alligator. 'Surely they can't do this to the paintings?'

Carver shook his head and smiled. 'In today's delivery they're small enough to be in one package but normally that's even easier. In the "SS. United States", they have a restaurant called *The Impressionists and Masters.* The walls are covered in copies of the great masters—'

Hooker beat him to it, asking, 'and all they have to do is replace the copies with the originals—?'

Carver replied, 'sure, as simple as that. Forgers in Europe make copies so good that only an expert would notice and anyway these pictures are changed around all the time.'

The Commissioner added, 'so when in dock, the pictures are changed back to the copies and the priceless originals slip through security?'

Hooker frowned, 'I can see the ease of dropping items overboard, but how about the weight if it's gold?'

'They use inflatable rubber bags that the Navy Seals use to float heavy arms from submarines. You can pick them up from any military store. They inflate when they hit the water and rise to the surface. They're camouflaged and difficult to see ... particularly at night. This is the consignment we believe is going to Manhattan & Western Bank. But this time we're doing our swap—'

Hooker cleared his throat. '... and my local gang has got to hear of this, so we're convinced they are going to tunnel in to relieve the present owners—'

Carver coughed again with the smoke getting to him. '... it all ties up. The banks are not obliged by law to know what they're storing. The customer seals the packaging and as long as that seal remains unbroken, then the customer is responsible and the bank washes its hands of any suspect goods. They get the storage cost; sometimes in cash ... would you believe. These banks tread a very narrow line but they're not breaking any law. The loot finds its way into our country and then transferred bank to bank until it becomes difficult to trace. When it passes through each state it becomes virtually impossible for us to follow as the interaction with the banks, state to state, is nigh on impossible. Truman was under pressure by the UN to change the law, requiring all the banks to declare the contents, supposedly supported by a posturing Hoover who threatened to resign if it didn't go through. However it was defeated by powerful business interests, and also, shall we call them, political shadows who really run this country. Big business for the banks you see. So the banks carried on and of course Hoover never carried out his threat.'

Hooker lit another cigarette and turned to Carver. 'And you believe this is being delivered to our bank next week?'

Carver nodded. 'These guys work in a calm unhurried way, so this raises no suspicions. But I reckon the action will happen very soon. So this ties in with your information Lieutenant, next week sometime—'

The Commissioner broke in. 'And this weekend is when we can expect some actively in the building next to the bank, preparing for their hit?'

Hooker nodded. 'Yes sir.'

The Commissioner swung round in his chair and studied Hooker. 'And this is when your plan comes into action.' Hooker nodded again. The Commissioner discarded the alligator and returned to using a match. The match was successful and he continued pulling for a while before commenting, 'you mention an informer, what are you going to do about him ... or her?'

'I want an order to tap the public phones within the bank including the booth outside on the day they take this delivery. Our informer is bound to confirm the goods have been delivered but daren't use a bank phone to make his call. I guarantee he ... or she, will come out in their lunch break and use the public booth just outside. I doubt they would use the public phone in the bank as it would look unusual when they have access to the bank phone. My hunch is the bank's security personnel.' He shrugged. 'It usually is!'

The Commissioner pulled at his pipe, frowning before waving the dark smoke away, then asking, 'you now have this witness who led you to these plans and so shouldn't he be protected? It doesn't take long for word to get round?'

Hooker nodded. 'Sure! He's off to a concert this evening so we're keeping an eye out for him there, and as a caution, I think tomorrow morning I'll get him to spend a few days back in his own place in Brooklyn.'

Thor

The Commissioner nodded and studied the two men who appeared to be so enthusiastic with their plan; he had nothing but admiration for them: *Sometimes it was better not to know what they were up to. Good team!*

In a way, he envied them their freedom; but also guessed they were treading on dangerous toes.

Hooker discretely ground his fallen cigarette ash into the thick fibres of the dark green carpet, comparing the floor with the mustard linoleum in his office. Still, the detectives in the outer office only had wooden boards; at least he had moved up a notch.

As they started to leave, the Commissioner suddenly asked, 'you didn't say what you have called your joined-up operation ... I ought to know.'

The two Lieutenants stared at each other. Hooker started to, 'um,' as Carver coughed and quickly said, 'well we're calling it: "Smoke-Screen" sir ... "Operation Smoke-Screen".'They quickly made their exit, leaving the Commissioner to tap out his pipe before throwing his Mexican tobacco pack into the trash can. He hurried over to open the window wider and took deep breaths.

As the two Lieutenants went their separate ways, Carver called back over his shoulder, '... and you didn't help with your smoke rings.'

Hooker roared with laughter, shouting, '*Operation Smoke-Screen!* Fast thinking.'

Carver had a concert ticket to deliver.

Thor

12

The concert: Freddie made his way into Carnegie Hall through the gathering concert goers and headed straight to the bar where he ordered a double Jack Daniels. He loved the buzz of anticipation at these concerts: all the punters in their best clothes; the ladies at their most glamorous and the men at their most importance. He wandered away from the bar and leaned against a wall to survey the laughing crowd from a distance. As a writer of people he would observe all their characteristics and mannerisms, mentally tuck them away in pigeon holes, from where he could pull them out when needed.

At the far end he noticed a young woman talking to a man in his fifties; had they been looking over at him? The man looked a typical academic, dressed in a light blue-suit with a red bow tie ... but familiar? *Where have I seen him before ... and her*? She now had her back to him and he took in her elegant appearance with her light-green shift-dress and a matching jacket; her blonde hair hung loose across one shoulder and the high heels making her much taller than her companion; *where, oh where had he seen the man before? ... Something familiar about her too?*

Suddenly there came an announcement ... 'five minutes to the concert'. He swigged down his drink, watching as the man handed over what appeared to be a concert ticket before patting her on the shoulder and hurrying for the exit. She studied her ticket turning towards the curious Freddie; he guessed in her mid twenties? She was attractive, and moved with an assurance that suggested self confidence. He then lost sight of her in the milling concert-goers trying to find their seats.... *where, oh where had he seen her before?*'

The usherette girl asked to see his ticket and glanced at her clipboard. She smiled. 'I'm sorry sir but there's been a mix up with the booking and you are now in seat thirty-one, row H,' pointing over to the side, 'it's still the same area sir and actually a better view. Hope you don't mind?'

Freddie shrugged and looked for the aisle seat in a short row of five. The four remaining seats to his left were empty. The lights dimmed and the hall quietened to an expectant buzz. The arrival on stage of the maestro Artur Rubinstein drew a wave of enthusiastic applause from the audience. He acknowledged the welcome and walked to the Steinway Grand. He adjusted the stool and immediately went into Chopin's Ballarde No.1 in G Minor ... Freddie relaxed into the sweeping movement. As his eyes grew accustomed to the dim light, he became aware of one person sitting at the far end of his row. He would occasionally sense the head turning as if to look his way; he realised it was the young woman in the bar.

Elisabet Stella Bergstrom studied the man she was told to keep an eye on at the concert. Since that morning when she had first seen him in the Precinct trailing the Sergeant, he had often crossed her mind, wondering what he would have made of her dressed in her other persona she called Thor, and then the assignment sprung on her to keep a watch out on Hooker's Mulberry Street witness at the Carnegie concert. She couldn't believe she was unexpectedly going to see her hero, Artur Rubinstein, the world famous pianist. Weeks before, she had stared with frustration at the Carnegie poster having worked out that she would be on duty that evening, and now she here she was with a free ticket; she couldn't believe her luck.

Who was the man she had to keep an eye on? She always did her homework before an assignment; leave nothing to chance. She had wondered if his name

Maliseet really did derive from the American Indians. This intrigued her, so that afternoon on her way back home from the docks, still dressed as the street girl Thor, she paid a visit to the New York Public Library and headed straight to the North American ethnic-studies catalogue section. The middle-aged, female attendant in charge of the index section gave the appearance of deliberately scrawling her frizzy hair tight back as if to emphasise the long nose and thin lips to suggest some authority. She peered with anxious eyes over her half-framed glasses to watch the young street girl thumbing through her precious index cards. When she was handed a request for two books, she asked for some form of identification, coolly raising her eyebrows when presented with the police I.D. Her thin top lip curled slightly as she sniffed: *a cop doing research*? She grudgingly handed over a desk number and told her to wait in the Rose reading-room. As Thor moved away the woman anxiously studied the index cards for any smudge marks.

Thor entered the Rose reading-room and caught her breath with its sheer size and grandeur: the high, gold embossed ceiling with the theatrical-painted billowing clouds in the centre; the resplendently arched high windows letting the honey-colored sunlight in as if to add luminosity to the beautiful hanging chandeliers: she counted eighteen of them; the reading-room back home was just a simple annex.

She looked around for her numbered desk, spying it halfway along an aisle and found herself tiptoeing because of the mandatory silence libraries have built into them during construction. It appeared that she was sharing part of her desk with an elderly-looking, bush-bearded academic who glanced up as she pulled the opposite chair out. He sighed with irritation and stared through his heavy-rimmed spectacles at her appearance before reluctantly moving his clutter to make room. Thor coolly ignored his manner and sat down, trying to work out the upside-down titles of his books: "Lenin, Carl Marx, Chairman Mao and his Red Book". He scribbled furiously in pencil on lined paper as if frightened of being late for the next revolution; he certainly wasn't afraid of bully-boy McCarthy.

Suddenly her two books appeared on the desk and she sensed her bearded companion's immediate curiosity as he too tried to read her upside-down titles, and at the same time continue to scribble with his pencil.

An image began to emerge as Thor delved into the "Chronicles & Cultures of

Passamaquoddy/Maliseet Heritage"; she read: "*...descended from the inhabitants living alongside the Penobscot River that flowed down from the upper reaches of Maine to tumble into the Atlantic sea. They lived on the East coast and were called the Wabanaki (People of the Dawn), as theirs would be the first eyes to see a sunrise each day";* she loved the conjecture behind that paragraph. Becoming even more intrigued she came across a Molly Mathilde, born in the mid-seventeenth century who married a French Baron. Of course, these intermarriages would explain his intense blue eyes.

She glanced at her watch realising the time had flown. She had to shower and make Carnegie before 7.30 to collect her ticket from Lieutenant Carver. She made a note of the books, determined to come back and continue her research. She closed her books and stood up. Her companion scowled and spread his clutter back across the desk as a gesture to clear off. She leaned over the table and whispered, 'come on Che Guevara, you and me, let's start a revolution right now!'

He went purple and the pencil slipped across the paper. He furiously tore the top page from his notepad, screwed it up and threw it into a waste bin by the desk. Thor laughed and tiptoed to the exit, pausing to take in once more the grandeur of the Rose room: *room they call it, I really must return.* Her encounter with the revolutionary seemed to put her in a good mood so she smiled at the catalogue female, who returned the gesture with a curled top lip. She walked round to the back of the library building, through Bryant Park to where she had parked Harvey, realising the man she would be seeing tonight was becoming more fascinating with every step: a facet of America she hadn't given much thought to, and with the feeling that a part of history was wantonly being neglected.

From her seat she was able to study Freddie's face ... she now understood those blue eyes, and yet they looked tired; maybe he had been working too hard; why was he living in Mulberry when the file gave his address as Brooklyn? There was little in his file apart from his army war record and working as a writer; nothing ... such as ... was he married? She was determined to get to know him on a personal level. She had to keep reminding herself why she was there and not to be drawn to her hero Rubenstein and his playing.

The maestro came to the end of the first half with warm applause from the appreciative audience, leaving the stage with the announcement there would be a twenty minute break. By then she had slipped out of her seat waiting to see if he would go to the bar.

He pushed through the crowd to the bar and as he sipped his drink—

'Hello Mister Vermeer, Are you enjoying the concert?'

It was the girl sitting near him of course. He immediately felt the intensity of her eyes as she studied his face. Her accent had a slight, sing-song lilt. The scar on one cheek looked familiar.

'Or may I call you Freddie?'

He returned the gesture. 'But only if you tell me *your* name.'

'Stella.'

'Stella. It suits you ... there's an ancient Greek expression: "She who bears the spirit of Stella will wander amongst the stars".'

Her expression warmed at his remark.

'I did notice you in the bar before the concert,' he said, 'and I know I've seen you before ... but where?'

'Try the Precinct the other morning. You were with Lieutenant Hooker and he stopped to have a chat in the corridor.'

'Yes of course, the man with the red tie talking to you before the concert. I couldn't place him ... or you?'

She started to grin. 'Did you not notice

that seedy looking female with him in the corridor? The one with a yellow bandana round her head?'

'Yes I did!'

She started to grin. 'Is my other persona that good?'

The penny dropped ... the scar on her cheek. 'Hey I can't believe that was you.' He looked her up and down. 'But you look so different. I'm amazed.' He shook his head and grinned. 'I remember thinking that I wouldn't want to get involved in a scrap with you. But why were you dressed like that? I reckoned you were just another Hooker suspect dragged in for questioning.' He pulled a face. 'Just like me.'

'Yes, Lieutenant Hooker can be quite daunting.' She nodded at his drink. 'I was hoping someone would buy *me* a drink?'

'I'm sorry, of course.'

'Well as it's a special occasion, I'll have what you're drinking.'

She watched him at the bar, feeling a sense of pleasure in his surprise.

He returned and they raised glasses.

'Special occasion?'

'Well to me it is, as I'm seeing my hero Athur Rubenstein.'

'Ah yes! So you're saying that you're connected with the police?'

She pulled at a strand of her hair as if

unsure with her reply. 'Sort of—'

'OK. Who's the man you were talking to before the concert? Is he police?

'Yes, I work for him.' She changed the subject in her lilting accent,' 'but listen to me Freddie, are you enjoying Rubinstein? ... Isn't he wonderful? Oh imagine being able to play like that.'

'Do you play an instrument?'

She nodded. 'Yes. As a teenager, I dreamt of being a professional pianist. I went to Music College to study the piano and also the violin as I had to have two instruments to get in. Then I realised that I would never reach the high standard needed to make a career, so I now enjoy playing for myself and others.'

'Then you must play for me some time.'

'Yes. Yes, I would like that.'

With the second-half announcement, they hurried back and this time she sat with him. He became aware how completely she involved herself in the music; the way her eyes responded. He recalled once writing dialogue ... how did it go? ... *"Eyes are windows into the soul"*. He could have written that for her.

During a break in the music her thoughts were on the man next to her ... *his file didn't mention if he was married.* Then that guilt feeling made her swallow as she thought of Charlie. It must have made her start because he turned his head to look at her.

'You OK?'

She nodded, but it took a while to get back into the music with that crazy thought; reminding herself she was also supposed to be on duty. Tonight she couldn't hide her feelings behind Thor; tonight she wanted to be Stella, to enjoy being here in Manhattan with this man.

At the end of the concert they found themselves in the foyer entrance watching the concert-goers grabbing cabs or just disappearing into Seventh Avenue under an assortment of bobbing umbrellas. There was an awkward silence between them, as if waiting for the other to make the first move.

Freddie lit a cigarette and suggested going somewhere for a drink.

She pointed to the Carnegie-Soda-Fountain just opposite. 'I would love to go over there and have a *"knicker-bocker-glory".'* She laughed. 'I love saying that strange American *"knicker-bocker-glory"*. Since I've come to Manhattan, that's all I live on ... well almost.' *I'm supposed to be on duty, not enjoying his company.*

The rain suddenly stopped, so they joined the crowd hurrying across the pedestrian walkway. The parlor was packed and buzzing from excited concert-goers, but they managed to grab the last two stools in the far corner. They brushed the rain from their coats and Freddie pushed his way to the bar. As she watched him, she wondered, did she really have that crazy thought in the concert ... *was he married?* She was suddenly aware he was returning.

'A dime for your thoughts Stella of the stars?'

She found pleasure in his teasing and guessed she must have blushed.

As she spooned into the ice cream, Freddie sipped his coffee which gave him the chance to study her. Despite the outward show of confidence, he sensed fragility. She felt his gaze and her hand went to her cheek. He leaned over and gently pulled it away saying, 'don't hide that scar from me.'

He was the first person to say that. For a brief moment his fingers remained on her cheek with a sudden tingling which made her jerk.

He commented, 'that tingling is a good sign. I promise.'

She didn't need an explanation and from that moment the scar didn't matter. He suddenly picked up his coffee spoon and asked, 'may I have a spoonful of your ice cream?'

She instantly pushed it towards him. 'Of

course, share it with me.'

'Just a taste, thanks.'

'Next time, I'll have the coffee and you the ice cream Freddie.'

'A deal! Will there be a next time?'

'I hope so,' she murmured quietly.

Over the crowd-noise of chatter and laughter, she relived the concert. He found himself watching her face as she discussed the Maestro's interpretations, particularly the Rachmaninov sonatas. She was speaking a music language he didn't quite understand, but so enjoyed sharing her excitement.

After a while the crowd suddenly grew quiet with many leaving to go home, so she queried, 'I understand you were made to go into the estate agency for Hooker ... that was cheeky!'

He was surprised that she knew. 'So you know all about that visit?' He thought of Butterfly and grinned. 'Actually that was fun. But there's something I forgot to mention to the Lieutenant.'

'Tell me ... I can pass it on.'

'Above the desk, there is a Leica camera pointing towards the entrance door. It's motorised and treading on the mat triggers it.'

'That's very observant Freddie. I think the Lieutenant would be interested.'

'Well it didn't whirr when I came in or

when I left, so I guess it's not turned on. I noticed the control switch is just under the desktop. We once used that in a TV movie. It used to be a fashionable art gallery called the Italian Fine-Art Emporium, would you believe, and I doubt if the security's been used since then.'

'OK, I'll let Carver know in the morning. I'm sure Hooker will be interested.' She looked at her watch and wrinkled her nose which he found delightful. 'Listen to me Freddie, I'm sorry but we really must go, tomorrow I start early.'

As they made their exit from the parlor, Freddie was bothered enough to ask her. 'I've enjoyed your company Stella, but you didn't appear by chance, and I guess it had something to do with my seat being changed. Why are you here and why was your boss with you before the concert?'

'He came to give me my ticket.' Her eyes lit up. 'My free ticket Freddie would you believe? Lieutenant Hooker should explain all this, not me. But it was decided when he knew you were coming to the concert tonight. After all you're his only witness.'

Freddie wasn't sure he liked her explanation. 'So you're saying he sent you to keep an eye on me?'

She nodded. 'Yes that's why I'm here. My boss knows my musical background. But you intrigued me when I first saw you in the Precinct and I wanted to meet you. That's why I said hello in the bar. Listen, I couldn't believe my luck in coming.' She giggled. 'Somehow I suppose, he couldn't see Sergeant Jugg enjoying himself.'

He took her arm. 'Look, I must get you a taxi.'

'You don't have to worry about me as my dear friend Harvey is waiting.' Noticing his look of disappointment, she gestured with a toss of her head. 'Come with me ... I'll introduce you.' He had a feeling of disappointment as he followed her across the busy avenue into Central Park. There were still a few cars dotted around and she headed to her Harley-Davidson slightly hidden by bushes.

She made a grand gesture of sweeping her arm. 'May I introduce my friend Harvey, and Harvey, this is Freddie.'

Freddie stared at the bike. 'I can't imagine you having the strength to handle it.'

Her eyes flashed and she sniped back, 'Why ... Because I'm a woman?'

'No, but it's such a heavy machine. OK, now I want to show *you* something.' He took her arm and teased her by repeating her phrase, 'you must listen to me. Come with me. Come!'

He led the intrigued Stella along a path to one of the huge boulders left over *from the Laurentide Glacier period. He scrambled up the wet rock to turn and* look down at her. 'Give me your hand,' he asked.

'Freddie I have high heels.'

'Well kick them off, I want to show you something.'

She kicked off her shoes and grabbed his extended hand. As he pulled her up she cried out, 'that's my best nylons ruined mister Freddie ... listen, you owe me a new pair.'

'Never mind your nylons, turn round and look.'

She held onto his arm to steady herself as she turned to look through a gap in the trees. Seventh Avenue was busy and humming with traffic ... the never-ending carpet of red stop-lights reflecting off the puddles, splashing in the light rain. Further on in Times Square, crowds of people were jostling like moths. Their excited expressions lit up in the moments of flickering, colourful, ugly in-yer-face neon adverts. Just beyond, the colourful theatre-land of Broadway beckoned with a floodlit skyscraper rising into the night: a thousand glowing windows as stars from a musical back-drop.

By tomorrow morning, the night people will awaken into the cold light of yet another day. They'll discover the mirage of theatre lights have been turned off. There'll be the sound of road-cleaning machines and the whistle of the bell-hop on his early shift. This is the hour when parts of Broadway will be ugly and shabby: the colourful neon's glowing the night before, now as abandoned skeletons screwed to some theatre front. Buildings neglected. But there will always be other buildings still wearing their elegance with a promise for that night to come. But for now, it's that time to climb on board the Broadway Carousel.

She gripped his arm tighter. 'Wow, isn't that amazing! I would never have thought of coming here. How did you find it?'

'By chance: I was returning from a concert in Central Park. That night had one of those crystal, clear starry skies. So I climbed up this boulder to see if I could get a better view through the trees and suddenly caught that scene down the Avenue. It was one of those special moments you just want to share with someone.'

She had her special childhood dream of walking over Brooklyn Bridge. She was determined to do that before leaving New

York. In another time she would have been with Charlie.

She sighed. ‘Well thank you for sharing it with me Freddie. It’s been quite a dreamy evening all round—’

‘Well I guess that’s what Manhattan’s been built on... *dreams*.’

She wanted to linger. But he reminded her, ‘don’t forget you’re starting early, remember?’ He slid down the rock, turning to catch her as she stumbled at the bottom.

Her voice sounded excited as she asked, ‘maybe we could do that another time before I finish my work here?’

‘And when’s that going to be?’

She didn’t answer as she looked for her shoes in the darkness. They walked in silence to her beloved Harvey. She unlocked the pannier box and he helped her into her bomber jacket. She then pulled on waterproof leggings before fastening her yellow bandana tight around her head.

All this was suddenly cut short when a shadowy figure jumped from the bushes, waving a gun, shouting in crazy, broken English, ‘Money! Quick, yer Money!’

A startled Freddie pulled back, but she reacted instantly, thrusting a wallet at the figure who reached his hand out in a snatch movement. She deliberately dropped it, instantly confusing him. As he bent to catch the wallet, she gripped his neck, thrust him forward and kicked the back of his legs. He gasped with surprise and fell to the ground. She dropped and pinned him with her knee, pulled one of his arms hard across his back. He screamed in pain.

Freddie couldn't believe what happened! She now had a gun hard against the man's head: suddenly she was the girl from the Precinct!

'Quick, grab his other arm,' she hissed.

They hauled him to his feet. He didn't resist, he was just a kid who started blubbing. She put her gun away and picked up the stick the boy had used as a gun. She shook him and pulled his frightened face to her. 'Listen to me, what the hell are you doing, you stupid child.'

They stared at the dusky Mediterranean face, the baby stubble on his chin, the curly black gypsy hair. Freddie felt a rising compassion for the youth, making no sense as he sobbed.

Freddie glanced at her. 'What are we going to do with him?'

She glared into the boy's frightened face. 'Answer me. Do you understand English?'

The boy nodded. 'Yes. I understand little.'

She opened the wallet and waved her badge. 'Look, I'm a cop. You must listen to me. I could take you in for what you've just done. Where do you live?' she demanded.

He nodded his head to the park, sobbing. 'Here. This is my home.'

Freddie gripped his arm tighter, 'where's your family?

The boy shrugged his shoulders. 'I have none.'

'What is your name?' she asked.

'Alix.'

'Alix what?'

'Alix Palos.'

'So you're Greek? How old are you?'

The youth nodded. 'I be sixteen.'

'Do you have any papers?'

He shook his head. 'No. I have none.'

'So you're in America illegally. You have no right to be in this country?'

'No.' His face dropped. 'No I came with many people. We come from Canada.'

Freddie looked at her and grimaced. 'There are so many kids like him in New York.'

She shook him again. 'When did you last eat? Have you eaten today?'

He shook his head. 'But I have friend in restaurant that gives me food left over when he can.'

Freddie whispered in her ear, 'what are

you going to do with him? This is your territory not mine.'

She looked hard at Freddie, her eyes boring into his, her mind racing. She hated the situation ... *oh hell, what would Charlie do*? She glared back at the youth and took a deep breath. 'You must listen to me Alix, I should hand you over to the authorities and you could be deported or even sent to prison. This is not the way to start your life in this country, when that happens you'll have a criminal record.' She shook her head. 'Then you've got no chance.'

Freddie thought of the young Deno Spiro in Hooker's photo album. Was he picked up as an illegal like this kid, getting his face recorded?

The frightened kid stared at her. She shook him again. 'Do you understand what I'm saying?'

He nodded and tried to wipe his cheeks.

'I must be mad but I'm letting you go.' She opened her badge-wallet and took out a folded ten dollar bill. 'Take this, go and get yourself a good meal. You must listen to me ... you do *not* spend it on alcohol, but on *food*. Do you understand what I'm saying?'

The youth's eyes widen and he hesitantly unfolded the bill to stare at the picture of a stern Alexander Hamilton.

Thor

He nodded and looked as if he couldn't believe his luck. 'Only food, I promise.'

Freddie took a biro from his pocket. He grabbed the lad's arm and wrote "Deno Spiro".

He asked, 'do you know Mulberry Street in Greenwich?'

The youth nodded.

'Deno's another Greek and he owns a bar there. Everyone knows him. Go and find him and say Freddie sent you. Be honest with him and tell him everything. Say you want to find work. Do you understand?'

The youth answered. 'Yes! I find him in morning. Tomorrow I go ... I promise.' He looked hard at the name on his hand. 'Yes, I find Deno Spiro.' He started to go but suddenly turned back to the woman whose face he would always remember. He took her hand, opened it and kissed the palm. He looked up to stare into her anxious face and

vowed, 'I promise one day I find you to give back. Your face reminds me of my mother. She was beautiful like an angel ... I *never* forget you.'

He suddenly straightened himself upright, put his thumb, index and middle finger together and made the sign of the cross ... then disappeared ... swallowed by the night as quickly as he came.

Thor

They stared after him into the darkness. She whispered, 'listen Freddie, did I do right giving him that money? Was I mad?'

'You took a chance. Sure, you could have handed him in. He has good taste and as he said, you have a face like an angel, so he deserves a good start. I have a good feeling about him. But I still can't believe how quickly you reacted. Supposing it *had* been a real gun!'

She pulled herself away, as if irritated. 'I know the difference between a gun and a stick, he just happened to choose me.'

He picked up the Carnegie concert program she had dropped on the ground. 'I can't believe all this happened tonight of all nights.'

She pulled the bike free and sat astride it, studying his concerned face. 'Listen to me ... sometimes you have to believe in people. Tonight it was his turn Freddie. Come on, don't let it spoil a super evening and don't worry, I can handle myself.'

She kick-started the engine and its deep throb echoed across the lot. 'I've been riding these since I was knee high. My father was a biker so I've never known a life without one.' She nodded to the pillion behind her. 'Jump on ... don't look so startled, you're going home. The rain has stopped so you shouldn't get wet and at least I know you'll be safe.' She laughed. 'I was told to look after you...remember?'

'I've only ridden horses before,' he protested.

'Just relax and put your trust in me ... and Freddie,' she turned her expectant face towards him and smiled, 'you must hold me tight.'

He heaved himself onto the bike and willingly held her exactly as she had asked; at that moment he would have done anything she wanted of him. She roared from the lot to corner expertly into Seventh Avenue. A strolling couple turned and paused as they watched the couple on the motorbike roaring into the night.

Above the smell of wet tamacadam, Freddie became more aware of her perfume. Two streets away, a youth sat in a 24hr-Eater studying the menu, clutching his ten bucks. He glanced into the street as he listened to the fading Harley-Davidson. He was thinking of the angel who wore a yellow bandana, the one with the friendly face that briefly touched his solitary life; it felt good to be in the Big America. Suddenly, the street outside lit up with a flash, followed by a distant roll of thunder that echoed ominously across Manhattan.

Thor

***

Chicago: Earlier that evening, a slightly built woman in dark tinted glasses, entered the General Delivery Counter of the Central Post Office. She was about forty years old with long flowing auburn hair and wore a red classic knee-length coat and flat loafer shoes. The office was busy, so she hung back as if to study posters until the counter became empty. She gave her usual smile as she handed over an identity card to receive the envelope from the young assistant. To him she was a regular caller and over the past few years he always made a point to acknowledge her as she always dropped a ten dollar bill into the children's charity box screwed to the counter. As she walked away she studied the envelope and smirked at the hand-written name: *Mrs. U. N. Nown.* Heading for the railroad station she boarded the overnight Amtrak train, first class for New York. She carried no luggage.

On her arrival at Grand Central early the following morning, she discarded her used ticket into the trash bin and purchased an open single ticket for Syracuse which she tucked into her wallet. She would normally walk, but as the rain was heavy that morning, she headed straight to the

Metro to make her regular visit to the Church of the Holy Conception.

***

At that same time in Mulberry, Freddie stared through the rain splattered window across to the empty roof, mulling over the drama of the past few days. The heavy rain clouds still hung like a wet blanket over Manhattan. Another rumble of thunder, the squelch of rubber on wet tamacadam sounding above the morning rush-hour, the same sound he recalled sitting on Harvey; a journey he just didn't want to end: an evening of music and female companionship he had forgotten until her unexpected appearance and that twang of jealousy he felt when she said, 'my friend Harvey'; the pleasure of sharing her excitement with that view down Seventh Avenue, and then the drama with the youth. For her to give that money when the lad had tried to rob them moments before, was intriguing: one moment she was the street girl he first set eyes on in the precinct, able to look after herself, and the next moment the woman Stella who played the piano; *must get her to play for me sometime;* he then had an idea. He smiled at hearing her voice in his head with her delightful vocabulary: "*you must listen to me Freddie*". What an unusual female she was turning out to be.

He grabbed the phone and dialled.

'Hi Deno ... has a young man called Alix been to see you this morning? He has!' Freddie laughed. 'Been eating you out of house and home, thinks your coffee is the best in the world. Well I could have told him that.' He nodded as he continued to listen. 'Thank you Deno, I know a certain young lady will be delighted.' He slowly replaced the receiver, *good for him.*

He noticed the puddles forming where Charlie Chaplin had lain during his last moments on that roof; the sky becoming darker, another sudden rumble of thunder now getting nearer, his radio crackled and the over-excited announcer droning on with the upcoming World Series final: "*would Johnny Podres pull it off for the Brooklyn Dodgers?*" 'Not a chance.' His thoughts returned again to last evening and their ride back home through the streets of Manhattan. She was right, she could handle that bike and after the first half mile he relaxed into the journey. He had felt safe in her closeness and her perfume still lingered in his nostrils; *must find out the name?* He made a note to ask her. He gave a sigh and sat down at the Remington to continue his typing as the lady in the next apartment started her violin scales: the clear sound coming through paper-thin walls, starting off the Italian family opposite his door with their usual noisy ten minutes of shouting. Sam was on his planned trip to London, so the phone should be quiet for a couple of weeks. Sam had wanted, no he had demanded, a script update of the story sitting on his desk for his return the following week. Freddie was getting pleased with the draft's progress but his mind kept returning to Stella and their evening together. He found her strangely unsettling. But, would they meet up again?

He picked up her concert program he had forgotten to give back and grinned when he thought of her reaction with the torn stockings when he pulled her up the boulder. He tapped the program and wondered, *Sam owes me a favor, and apart from money ... I wonder if he would?* Scribbling a note he clipped it to the program and slipped it into an envelope together with the draft script waiting for its ending. He then turned his thoughts back to the next part of the script. Later, he stopped typing to straighten and stretch his shoulders as his neighbor turned her attention to Barbar's Adagio: her playing was confident, the calibre of a professional and somehow the sound of the solo violin created tension to his writing. He felt restless and rose again to look out the window. The past few days and now Stella, or was she Thor? An interesting double character for the movie; do I dare? She seemed a bit prickly at times!

The rain decided to stop and the leaden sky started getting brighter as the nervous young laundry girl came on the roof carrying her full basket. She glanced quickly as if looking for Charlie's ghost but turned her back to wipe the dripping Cola support cables ... c*ouldn't have been easy for her, but work is work, especially when it puts food on the table.* For a while he admired her dark Latin beauty before returning back to his typing as the phone rang ... damn, it was Hooker!

Hooker's voice was cool and questioning, '*enjoy the concert last evening, Freddie?*'

'Yes, thank you—'

Hooker's voice broke in. '*I liked the idea of the security camera Freddie. You forgot to tell me about it, glad I've got you in the team. I gave her the nod. I'm going to have a camera outside as well and your idea would be a bonus.*'

'What do you mean, you gave her the nod?'

'Only that she is taking care of it. Don't

forget Freddie, this is her job. She's aware of what she's doing.'

'You're not putting her into any danger are you?'

'*She's a big girl, Freddie.*'

'Maybe, but I'm still concerned Lieutenant ... Remember, I suggested it?'

'*Hold on Freddie, not so fast. For now, I want you to lay low. I don't want you going out; you didn't choose a very good neighborhood to witness a mob killing—*'

This annoyed Freddie and he snapped back, 'don't go out! I've got to live Lieutenant'

Hooker growled, '*you've got a better chance of living by staying*

where you are, believe me—'

'I'm short of provisions, Lieutenant.'

There was a pause and Freddie thought he'd put the phone down. Suddenly Hooker said, '*OK Freddie, I'll see what I can do, leave it to me,*' another pause with voices in the background. Hooker continued, '*by the way, your friend Ginger just been found floating under Brooklyn Bridge ...*' a longer pause ... '*the Sergeant's still out there with his rod, fishing for Ginger's toupee.*' He laughed as the phone clicked dead.

'That's great!' Freddie shouted. 'Don't be concerned! Damn you Hooker.' He slammed the phone down.

Thor

'What have you got me into, Sam Spiegel?'

Thor

13

Bubble's story: Hooker had remarked to Carver, 'I suggested getting your Thor to play the part of a broad, not a tart.' This was his observation when Thor appeared at the unit before making her way on to Rivera's office as Butterfly's replacement.

She sat at Butterfly's desk, popping gum-bubbles and watching Rivera through the street window as he crossed Eldridge to enter the bar opposite for his morning black coffee and brandy labubumba; regular as clockwork! He was known for this ritual which lasted thirty minutes on the dot, every single morning. He seemed to be a man obsessed with punctuality ... which can be one's downfall of course!

Thor checked her watch: she had two tasks to complete within the thirty minutes. She pulled on cotton gloves before inserting two Hudson serrated metal-strips into the lock on Rivera's office door. She pushed until the tumblers clicked, and then with a hard twist the door opened. She ignored the filing cupboard and headed for the desk, quickly flipping through a pile of papers before working her way through its drawers.

There appeared to be nothing of interest except a box of illegal Cuban cigars. She held one to her nose ... *papa would love one of these* ... this went into her pocket! But in the bottom deep drawer she found a .38 snub-nose revolver, together with a torn manila booklet:

"US Military Corps of Engineers.

Tunnel Construction within varying geological formations.

The theory of manual excavation and essential shoring materials to contain and support drainage.

Issue WD E-248a - US War Dept 1942"

The inside pages had line drawings of supports needed for shoring-up in different soil conditions. She scribbled down the name of the manual and checked her watch ... twenty minutes left.

She took the gun back to her desk and tore off a strip of clear Scotch-tape which she carefully pressed to one side of the handle. Carefully peeling the strip away, she stuck it to the shiny back of a carbon copy-sheet. Then repeated the process on the other side of the handle; hoping forensic could recover any prints.

She looked up ... Rivera was outside chatting to the mailman. She checked her watch. *Hell still ten minutes to go, what's he up to?* But he turned on his heel and walked unsteady back to the bar. She returned the gun to the desk drawer with the booklet and shut the office door.

It was now or never. She quickly pulled her chair to the wall and climbed up to lift the camera from the motorised casing. She unlocked the back, inserted a film and then dropped the camera back into the casing. Suddenly Rivera appeared in the window on his way back to the office. She jumped down, pulled the chair to her desk and pressed the button under the desk. The camera made a whir as the mechanism switched on. She quickly sat down and started typing as Rivera walked through the revolving door and trod on the security mat. The camera clicked and whirred and the door squeaked. He paused as if to regain his balance, and then made for the internal office. Thor caught the whiff of brandy. He fumbled trying to insert the key in the office door. Suddenly the door shot open and he stumbled in. He yelled with a slurred voice, 'hey sweetheart, make to get coffee going.'

She couldn't stand the ill tempered clown so delayed the coffee. As she put the tray on his desk, he tried to focus his eyes to leer at the office-temp in her short skirt and the low-cut top. Thor had outlined her eyes with Hawaii Palm-leaf mascara and wore large, square, gold-rimmed glasses. A large bubble emerged from her glossy red-lips. He watched as the bubble grew and grew and popped to shatter her enigmatic witchery. He giggled and sneered and hic-cupped brandy fumes across the desk.

He tried to lower his intoxicated high-pitched voice, 'you know sweetheart, if yer make with the right gear and my connections yer could fly, my how yer could fly. Did the agency say why Butterfly couldn't, or *wouldn't,*' he slurred, 'make to come in ... hic?'

She shook her head and wiggled her nose. 'No honey. Ah had this call to get down fast as she wasn't up to feeling good.'

She noticed the desk bottom-drawer was open. Rivera pulled at the cigar-drawer and fumbled as he tried to grab a cigar. He automatically pushed the bottom drawer shut as his lecherous eyes concentrated on her cleavage. He bit the end of the cigar and giggled as he spat it out, hissing, 'yer mean she was out all night, flapping her wings and making a nest with some dumb sucker in a crumby night joynt.' He sniggered. 'What makes with yer name sweetheart? Yer didn't say ... hic.'

'Ah guess Ah didn't honey!'

Her sharp reply with the sing-song

accent seemed to tease him.

'Ok miss nameless, play yer cards right and the job's yer's. I kinda like yer. Yer know sweetheart, yer got class ... Butterfly kinda makes me nyvous. She buzzes around and yer never know where she's landing next ... hic.' He leaned forward, hissing with laughter and smacked her arse.

Thor gritted her teeth, containing her urge to punch and flatten his sticky-out ear. Taking a deep breath, she managed a ventriloquist smile to mutter through clenched teeth, 'were yer serious about me having the afternoon off?'

'Sure.' He waited for another bubble. 'Yeah that's what I'll call yer ...Bubbles. Make yerself off to the movies with yer boyfriend, *Bubbles*. Ah got a meeting this afternoon and donna wanna be distybed.'

Thor tried to look excited and looked at her watch. 'OK. Ah'll leave at one, honey.' She opened a box of matches on the desk and leaned low across the desk to light his cigar.

He eyed her cleavage, swallowed and took several quick draws on the glowing cigar. 'Sure Honey ... Sure! He flipped open a silver cigarette box and pushed it across. 'Help yerself.'

She looked at the light brown Mexican cigarettes and shook her head. 'Ah don't smoke, honey.'

He hic-cupped and stared at her cleavage, giggling. 'Ah can't see any problems with yer lungs, Bubbles?'

She shook her head. 'That's because I've never smoked.'

He frowned, confused, trying to work her out. 'Ok, but when yer go ... hic ... leave the door unlocked, and make to put the closed sign on the door ... *Bubbles.*' Hissing with laughter he blew a cloud of smoke at her and tried reaching for the phone.

Thor smiled demurely, wiggled her nose and suggestively popped another bubble in the clown's direction. She returned back to her desk trying not to cough, her heart pounding. Rivera continued to leer and giggle through the office window.

Thor deliberately kicked the desk and sat down, popping and swearing in Swedish in the direction of the window. *I'll give him Bubbles.* She tried to pass the time by reorganising the desk-top. She dusted the typewriter and emptied the red butterfly ashtray. Then she emptied the Boston container, jammed solid with pencil-shavings before cranking the handle to sharpen Butterfly's blunt pencils; now kept in a cracked shaving mug. She looked at her watch yet again, thankful to pack up at midday and get away from that clown, grab a few hours rest before her evening shift at the docks, wishing she hadn't passed on Freddie's idea with the security camera ... supposed to be her day off.

But they had other plans for her that evening.

14

Kottbuller: The evening sky started with a crisp, cold light, suggesting a full moon. Freddie watched the shadows starting to lengthen across Mulberry. He felt his tummy rumble, he was hungry! He left his staring out the window and moved to the kitchen to grab a coffee and see what food he could muster.

The Tannoy buzzed. Sergeant Jugg's drawling voice sounded tinny: '*Say, I got provisions, Freddie*.' Freddie eagerly pressed the entrance button and minutes later came the expected tap on the door. He opened it to look into her smile. She had a bulging satchel over one shoulder and carried two large paper bags that started to topple ... he looked surprised and grabbed them off her.

'Stella!'

'Hello mister Vermeer. I thought you might have been pleased to see me ... especially with goodies.'

She was dressed as the girl in the Precinct with the yellow bandana, the bomber jacket and the torn jeans.

'Sorry, I just wasn't expecting you. Where's the Sergeant?'

'I was asked to get you provisions and

the Sergeant happened to be parked outside Deno, so he rang the bell for me.' She laughed. 'I think the Sergeant was playing a little fun with you.' Her eyes took in the uninspiring room.

He followed her gaze and ran his fingers through the uncombed hair. 'Oh what a mess this room is.'

'So this is your office?'

Now in her presence, he regretted his appearance and the run-down room. 'No. It's not really my office.' He felt his unshaven chin. 'I'll explain—'

She touched his lips as a friendly gesture, smiling. 'Listen to me Freddie. I know you live in Brooklyn in a very nice apartment. In fact I rode past there today just to have a look.'

He felt uncomfortable with authority probing his private life; even her.

'Look, I've already prepared a meal. Show me your kitchen and see what I've come up with.'

'Kitchen you call it?'

He led her into the walk-in cupboard and put the two bags on the worktop. She opened her satchel, pulled out a covered dish and placed it on the stove, then emptied the two paper bags onto the worktop.

'Look, I bring you buttermilk, bread, cheese, butter-spread, coffee, breakfast flakes and a special treat for you, some buttery croissants.' She turned asking, 'how am I doing? Do I look after you?'

'I must say it's a lovely to be spoilt. Thank you. I did wonder if we would meet again as you were working last night.'

'I wondered that myself.' She studied his face. 'Would you have made contact?'

'Yes! I thought I might have to ask Hooker to pass on a message.'

Her face lit up. 'I did want to see you again Freddie. I overheard Hooker saying he had to get provisions for you as he didn't want you going out, so I volunteered. I hope you're hungry as I'm starving.' She removed the bandana and tidied up her hair which was tied back. As she took off her jacket, he glanced at her shoulder holster.

'Hey Freddy, I'm dressed for duty and going from here to the docks.' She paused. 'That's why I'll have a soft drink if you have one. Mind you, as I'm not actually on duty at this very minute, it doesn't say anything in the rule book that I mustn't do this.' She went up on her toes and kissed his cheek.

He was experiencing so much pleasure in her company and with her obvious warmth.

'OK,' he asked, 'but who are you

tonight ... Stella or Thor? I get confused.'

'I'm always Stella with my friends. Pity we had that encounter with the young lad. I couldn't help thinking about him and the money I gave him. Maybe foolish, but I didn't want to spoil a super evening.

'Well don't worry on that score, I rang Deno and he *did* turn up this morning and was busy washing dishes to pay for eating a hearty breakfast—'

She stared at him. 'Say listen Freddie, I just knew he would—'

'...and Deno is having a word with some newspaper guy about work for him. Apparently the lad called you his night angel.'

'Really! The point is Freddie, you must understand what I say, we hit them over the head with a stick, we throw them in prison and wonder why they turn out the way they do ... there must be a better way.' She quickly changed the subject. 'Yes I must tell you, the man at the concert was Lieutenant Carver ... he's actually my boss and working with Lieutenant Hooker.'

'But first explain, is your name really Stella or is that another cop field-name?'

'My name of course!' she exclaimed. 'Stella Elisabet Bergstrom. Elisabet was my grand-momma's name.'

He took in the color of her hair, the deep

green eyes and her charming Nordic accent.

She prejudged his next question. 'We came here from Sweden just before the war.'

'Tell me about Thor. What's she all about?'

She turned to face him, put one hand on her hip and waved the spoon. 'Freddie you must listen to me. When I dress like this I'm Thor. But first I must tell you, as a teenager I was very, very shy, finding it most strange coming to the big America from our small country. I was trying to learn the language and such a different culture to Sweden: everyone here dressed in jeans and the T-shirts and the baseball caps. I'd only seen that in the movies. I felt completely wrong here. I dressed maybe old fashioned, and then a gang started picking on me. Huh, you know how it is with kids; take it out on someone new, laughing at my accent.' She shrugged her shoulders, 'I had accent then, but have no accent now of course, so it annoys me when people say I have the accent, even today ... you understand?'

He grinned, he understood.

'These kids frightened me so I stopped going to school, and when this came out my father told me that I had to think of a way to make the leader lose face. Well my teacher knew what was happening and told me that she taught martial arts at a youth club. She promised to teach me how to stand up for myself. We didn't tell anyone, not even my parents, they thought I was having extra English lessons after school. So I put up with the bullying and then one day when I was sick of them and had enough confidence, I stood my ground. Instead of running away, I confronted them, showed defiance by not running. I held my ground and stared straight into the bully leader's eyes. This put *him* on the defence. He didn't know how to react.' She waved the spoon at the imaginary bullies. 'And that was when Thor was born.'

By now Freddie was fascinated. 'So what happened?'

Her eyes glared as if she was back in the schoolyard. 'Listen Freddie, I tell you, I was pretty scared, my knees were shaking, but I teased the leader of the bullies. I shouted at him, so all would hear me. I asked if he was brave enough to take on a small, weak little girl. Her voice rose. 'He had to react to my challenge in front of his gang, so he came rushing towards me all cocky, laughing and went to push this stupid girl over. I stepped sideways, put my foot out, gave him a push and he went flying; it was so simple; he lost face so he had to try again. This time I had him pinned against a wall with his arm across his back. He started crying. Freddie listen to me, he was *crying* like a baby. I couldn't believe it. He was frightened of *me*! When I let him go, he ran away and I shout something about, "running home to mummy", most of it in Swedish, but he got the message.'

'What did the rest of his gang do?'

'Do?' Her face expressed it all and she laughed. 'Freddie listen, I charged at them and they ran. It was a very good feeling.'

'Did they ever trouble you again?'

'No. They didn't even want to have anything to do with the bully leader and always avoided me. And that was when Thor was born.'

'Why, the name, Thor?'

'My teacher watched it happen. She was thrilled and said I was just like a female Thor ... you know, the Scandinavian God of Thunder? As you can imagine, it didn't take long to get round the school and the name stuck. When the Academy taught us the art of creating another persona for field work, I naturally adopted the name,' her eyes danced, 'and that's when Thor *grew claws*!'

Freddie suddenly went to his desk to scribble on his notepad. He pinned it on the board. 'I love that. "The girl who

Grew Claws"! What an amazing title.'

She laughed. 'You're crazy.'

He came back to lean against the doorway. 'That's how titles are born ... off the cuff. Now what happened after Thor *grew claws*?'

'I learn to walk and strut as a boy ... like this.' She swivelled her hips, and he tried not to grin. 'Then I noticed the Thor's of this world, at first, always kept their eyes down. But when they want to make a challenge, then they must make straight eye contact to show their defiance. You understand me?'

He nodded. 'Yes and when we first met in the Precinct, I did find you had a defiant look in your eyes, as you call it.'

'I'm sorry Freddie. I certainly wasn't expecting to see someone like you. Strange but you seemed to catch me off guard, making me feel vulnerable. I had just come off duty so I was tired. I can't just turn her off until I've had a shower and changed out of these clothes.' She frowned and studied his face. 'You must listen and only think of me as the woman at the concert called Stella. That's the real me'

'And the perfume you were wearing?'

'So you noticed.' She enjoyed his embarrassment in asking.

'Well, I didn't have much choice riding

on Harvey. Perfumes are of unknown territory to me.' He now noticed the blush coming to her cheeks. 'You don't mind me asking?'

She shook her head. 'Do I sense a chink in your armor, Freddie? It's *Cabochard.* It's French and a little expensive ... a gift from ... someone—' she hesitated.

He changed the subject. 'Stella ... is that a Swedish name?'

She concentrated on the meal before answering, 'listen, my mama told me one night she had this strange dream with a voice telling her that she would have a girl called Stella. So she told everyone about her dream and they thought she was a little crazy. But she loved the name and had to call me Stella.' She laughed. 'Maybe I'm a little crazy, eh Freddie. My Papa demanded Elisabet as my first name, but in the end mama won.'

'What dish are we having tonight chef?'

'It's very popular in Sweden, called Kottbuller ... a meat dish. Oh dear, you're not veggie are you?'

He grinned, shaking his head.

'I had already prepared it just for me of course, but there's plenty for both. I only need to warm it.'

He groaned as she opened the oven. 'You can only use one ring, and the oven is very temperamental.'

'I have a good idea Freddie, I'll see to our meal and you give the Super a bell to sort out this cooker.

'Well at least Spiegel's paying for this so called apartment. But I think a miss bossy boot, called Thor is exactly what I could do with. I'm so involved with my work I just don't seem to have time for normal living. I'll do it now.'

She couldn't help grinning as she heard him talking firmly into the phone. He returned and leaned against the doorway.

'Tomorrow morning he promised. I told him, "If the electrician doesn't turn up, I'll send my Swedish moll down to practice her marshal art techniques on him".' This made her laugh.

'Stella, tell me, so you work for this Carver guy then?'

She nodded. 'Yes, but it's only temporary. I've been loaned from the FBI for a short while and I really do come from Minnesota. This past year Carver managed to infiltrate an organisation smuggling Nazi loot in from the war. Usual things like gold, jewellery, art work. It's building up to a climax now. That homicide you witnessed the other day had a link with this smuggling and that's why Hooker and Carver have set up a joint team to co-ordinate: "Operation Smokescreen".'

He gave a nervous laugh. 'So I'm now part of this "Operation Smokescreen"?'

'It seems to me you're already doing Hooker's dirty work. The Maffiamedlem must know the police have a witness and I'm here this evening to feed you and make sure you're OK.'

'Maffiamedlem?'

'In Sweden we call Mafia the "Maffiamedlem", or Dark Forces. Those nasty people out there, Freddie.' She lightened the conversation. 'Of course it could have been Sergeant Jugg here preparing this meal. But I volunteered. Listen, have they told you, that you're going back to your apartment in Brooklyn in the morning until this is all over?'

'No. And what does, all over, mean?'

'It means picking these Dark Forces up in one swoop, even their contacts in Holland.'

'And when's that?'

'I don't really know ... but Carver says it is soon.'

'Hooker told me you'd set the security camera up with film.'

'He managed to stop the normal receptionist called Butterfly from going in,' she laughed, 'I think she's a little crazy ... a-crazy like me—'

Freddie thought of Butterfly fluttering around Rivera.

Thor

'Mind you, she needs to do some dusting and keep her pencils sharp. I went in as a replacement from the agency. This guy Rivera always goes out every morning for his coffee and brandy. I had things to do as well as put a film in. I only just managed to get back to my desk as he came back. I heard the camera whirr as he trod on the mat. He arranged a meeting in his office for the afternoon so told me to clear off lunch time and didn't want me around. I'm going in again in the morning so I'll get the film and we'll see who they are.'

She put one hand on her hip and pulled an angry face. 'Listen to me Freddie. I felt like slapping his ugly mug. He smacked my arse, and suggested that I should play my cards right and make to work for him. Damn greasy pig! It's not funny, Freddie.' With that she turned back to the stove trying not to smile.

Freddie thought of the people she had to deal with, but as Hooker said: "it's her job Freddie".

She glanced at the pale mark on her wedding finger, 'I'm not married any more Freddie, I don't wear my ring when I'm on duty, but I do normally.'

Freddie knew he would have to be patient, wait until she wanted to talk. They moved back into the sitting room. As if to change the subject she leaned over the Remington. 'I've never seen a real movie script before.'

He watched her face as she read softly to herself, her lips and her expression changing to the rhythm of the dialogue. She grinned at him watching, but suddenly noticed the Russian poster on the wall. She moved to the poster and placed her hand on the writing. 'Do you understand what this means Freddie?'

He shook his head. 'No. But I'm assuming it's Russian.'

She nodded. 'Yes: "*Go, plough, sow and harvest all that awaits in other lands*".'

'You speak Russian?'

'No, but this is on the first page of my grand-momma's family bible. She came to Sweden from Russia in the twenties. She taught it to me as a toddler. I've never forgotten it!'

'That was left here with the clock. Maybe they decided that they didn't want any reminders of the old world in this new Promised Land!'

'Yes. I think you're right. How strange Freddie that you have this here, and I've known it all my life. As if—'

'As if what?'

'I don't know. How unpredictable ... but maybe not.' She stared at him for a moment before looking through his pile of records: 'Shostakovich, Purcell, Beethoven,' he noticed she seemed to hesitate, 'Chopin of course.' She studied the Chopin sleeve, before continuing, '...and Liszt, Barber, Copland, Mahler ... my goodness Freddie, quite a selection!'

'I had to bring some with me to keep me sane. I'll explain, Sam rented this place for me to get a feel of the Italian quarter and come up with some big ideas for another movie. When I first came here, I spent a couple of weeks trying the bars, wandering around Chinatown and getting to hear the way they talk. Just hanging about watching the characters like Runyon did for his short stories.'

'Talking of Damon Runyon, did you know they're doing extra performances of 'Guys and Dolls? I saw that show in Minnesota and want to catch it again.' She closed her eyes and sang:

'"When the smell of the rain washed pavement
Comes up clean and fresh and cold
And the street lamp light
Fills the gutter with gold,
*That's my time of day!"'**

She opened her eyes and grinned. 'I love the dawn so I try to have an early run every morning along the East River where I live, and I sing that song to the seagulls that wait for me. I tried to get a ticket for the show but they'd all gone,' murmuring hopefully, 'hey, you could have come with me.'

He tried to look serious. 'I would love to, but only on one condition—'

'Oh.'

'You won't wear that damn shoulder holster.'

She suddenly shrieked and ran into the kitchen to pull a smoking dish from the oven.

After they had eaten and drinking the tea she had insisted on brewing, he became aware of her eyes on him, surprising him with ... 'why did you try my ice cream after the concert?'

He frowned and shrugged. 'It looked nice.'

'It was, but no, another reason. Tell me.'

'I was testing your first thoughts about me.'

'Testing?'

'Yes. When you first meet a stranger in the situation we were in, then asking that stranger to share something as silly as an ice cream, tells me— well you passed the test because, without thinking, or any hesitation, you wanted to share it with me. The gesture was sincere, from you to me.

And I liked that.'

'But I wanted to share it with you—'

'Precisely, and it spoke volumes about you.'

'Oh dear, does my cooking past the Vermeer test then?'

'I can't possibly make up my mind on the first meal.'

'I think it's your turn to tell me about you.'

'I'm bit of a mixture. My mother is Dutch, her name is Sibylla. My father descended from the Maliseet people in northern Maine. His birth name is Madockawando but calls himself Maliseet as he wants to keep his people's name to go down through his descendants.'

She knew some of this of course from her trip to the library, regretting that she had mentioned her earlier ride past his apartment. She studied his face. 'That explains your blue eyes. You have such strong features Freddie, you must be very proud of your heritage?'

'Yes of course, it's very important to me.'

'My grand-momma would call them, intelligent eyes.'

He gave a glimpse of a smile as he continued, 'my mother met my father when she was doing an article covering mixed marriages on the early settlers who first came to America. She was a junior reporter for the Boston Globe and the editor sent her and another reporter up to Maine for research. His idea was that the article would have opposing points of view. She was young and had strong anti-views on these marriages, and the other reporter was very liberal. They did their interviewing and research, and the evening before they were due to return back to Boston, she met my father Joey: end of story, she didn't return to Boston, and the editor didn't get his article. So here I am, living proof she changed her ideas.'

'What a lovely story. Who do you take after, apart from your eyes?'

'Oh, my father I'm told.'

She grinned. 'I think I can understand why she didn't return.' She blushed and looked away.

'She was offered a job as assistant editor on our local paper which, according to her, she grabbed as an excuse to stay.'

'So that's where you get your interest in writing.'

He nodded and stared at her. 'Your turn now. I want to hear about when you first came to the Big America, as you call it?'

She sighed. 'I could make it a very long story, but I was born in a town called Malmö not far from Copenhagen. I was a naive teenager to really understand the problems brewing in Europe, but my father and mother were very adventurous, and when he had an offer to open and manage an import branch for his firm's Swedish tractors in the Big America, he jumped at it.' She shrugged. 'So that's how I come to be cooking Kottbuller for you Mister Vermeer.'

'Do you miss your early life in Sweden?'

She nodded firmly. 'Yes there are many moments. My favourite time was staying with my uncle Vida at his log cabin in the forest of Dalsland. It is beautiful there and we would go swimming and fishing in the lakes, and also for the hunting. That's where I learnt to handle a gun and Hella hunt.'

Freddie frowned. 'Hella hunt! What the hell is Hella hunt?'

She laughed. 'I am sorry, I forget, but I think everyone in America would know Hella. You must listen to me as I explain.'

He was enjoying her vocabulary.

'Back in the ice age there was this big volcanic eruption and it was so cold that the spitting lava immediately froze, and with the velocity, you understand when I say velocity?'

He nodded and smiled to assure her. 'Yes I understand and I'm listening.'

He noticed a grin on the corners of her mouth as she continued, 'the pressure shaped the flying lava into flat heavy discs called Hella. They're about ten inches wide ... like this,' she held her hands apart. 'The discs have a slight curve as the Frisbee shape.' Her eyes flashed. '*We* had the Frisbee before *you* had the Frisbee in America, except we call it Hella.' She started to giggle. 'This is serious Freddie. The first inhabitants found they could spin and throw them straight, so they learnt to use them for hunting. Well, my uncle Vida taught me the skill and soon I could hit a target at sixty walks—'

'Paces.'

'Pardon?'

'You said walks. You mean paces.'

She shrieked with laughter. 'Sorry, I mean paces ... your funny language. Yes, the early people learnt to grind the edge down to make them sharp as an axe. I could slice through a young sapling tree. Doubt if I could do that now.'

He loved the sound of her laughter. 'My father would like to hear about your Hella ... he would be intrigued.'

'I think I would very much like to meet your father.'

'And what time are you supposed to be on duty tonight?'

She looked at her watch. 'In a couple of

hours. Why?'

'Tell you what Stella, we'll leave the dishes and I'll take you into Chinatown. My cleaning lady Loretta is in tomorrow morning and she'll deal with it. She'll be surprised at two plates and what will appear to have been a proper meal.'

'No, I don't think so,' she said, shaking her head. 'You've been told to stay here.'

Freddie gestured with his hands. 'It's no problem. I'll wear different clothes ... we'll slip out the back.'

She pulled a face and took a deep breath. 'If anything goes wrong I could be in trouble.'

'Nothing will go wrong. I'll take responsibility. There's somewhere I want to take you and it's not far from here.'

She bit her lip at his suggestion, torn between duty and yet wanting to share his enthusiasm; understanding why his mother didn't get round to write that article. *What the hell,* 'OK!'

Waiting for him to get ready she realised she hadn't laughed like that for a long, long time, it felt so good! Giggling again when he emerged from the bedroom wearing a large over-shirt with "YALE '39" across the front, and heavy tortoise-shell glasses perched on the end of his nose. He poked his fingers through the glassless frame. 'Movie Glasses. Do I pass ... would you know me in the street?'

'I would know you anywhere Mister Vermeer.' She pulled out a Dodgers cap from her bag and pulled it over his head. 'Here, try this.'

He studied himself in a mirror. 'Wonder if my mother would recognise me?'

'I just hope Carver or Hooker don't find out.'

'Aren't you going to wear your bandana?'

She shook her head. 'No. With you I want to be myself as Stella.'

'But I want to go out tonight with Thor, and she isn't right without her bandana.'

She hesitated and tied her bandana back on. 'She can be quite prickly Mister Vermeer.'

'So I've noticed.' He opened the door and said, 'by the way you have a smudge on your nose.'

She grinned. 'Yeah, well Thor would wouldn't she.'

He went to switch the light off. 'Come on Thor, let's hit the town.'

She shook her head. 'No, tonight you leave your apartment light on.'

He shrugged his shoulders and followed her, closing the door and sensing an air of adventure being with this unusual girl when she calls herself Thor. They made their exit through the rear entrance into a side passage, keeping away from Mulberry.

***

Deno stood for a while in the entrance to his bar watching the night people pass by. He glanced at the stranger who was drinking coffee and scanning a newspaper at a shadowy end-table. His trilby was pulled as if to obscure his face; Deno was used to oddities in his bar. He suddenly turned as he was called inside to a customer. The stranger kept glancing up to the light in Freddie's window; he also kept an eye on the Ford parked further down the road with one of Hooker's men in plain-clothes looking too obvious as a cop.

15

The Flower Vender: Freddie and his new companion Thor, wandered down Bowery which led into the area called Chinatown. He became aware that the swagger of Thor gradually disappeared, and occasionally she would look at him with the eyes of Stella at the concert. Soon she became captivated by the unfamiliar sights and smells of unusual spice aromas, the surreal illuminations, strange tongues and oriental eyes; the seemingly endless rows of gaily painted restaurants with subdued lighting and stringy music; elaborate stalls with unfamiliar vegetables and fruits, alongside fishmongers fighting for the couple's attention. She laughed as the vendors bowed, calling out, '*hello missy, velly sheepy missy ... bye-bye missy.*' They paused by a bar where four elderly men sat huddled at a low table on the sidewalk concentrating hard over a game of colored tiles. An overhead lantern swung reluctantly in the warm night air, its rose-colored light shining through their coiling tobacco smoke that smelt sharp and exotic. The players suddenly looked up, their eyes suspicious, but returned back to move the tiles with excited sharp clicks!

'This game is called mah-jong,' whispered Freddie, 'please don't ask me to explain, but it seems to get them excited.' He moved on, eventually steering her into Hester Street to stop at a softly lit restaurant entrance. A piano tinkled over the hum of the diners inside and a waft of cooking mingled with the sweet scent from a nearby flower stall where a tall man arranged his display with one hand; the other coat-sleeve empty and pinned up.

Freddie motioned her through the open door into a room of paper lanterns, dimly lit tables, and faces that glanced up at their entrance but quickly returned to their own private world. Two young girls in traditional dress came forward to greet them with hands pushed together and a slight bow.

Thor automatically returned the gesture. She gripped his arm. 'Oh Freddie this is lovely.'

They followed one girl to a spare table. As they sat down Freddie removed his hat and glasses. Just then he was spotted by the pianist who was playing a white baby-grand in the far corner. He was a distinguished looking Chinaman with snowy hair and a round face that broke into a wide boyish grin. He quickly finished with a keyboard flourish and rose to greet them. As he came over, he frowned at the way they both were dressed. He acknowledged Thor before turning to Freddie. 'Good evening Freddie.' They shook hands and Freddie introduced Thor as, 'my special minder.'

'Thor, this is my dear friend Ling, and those two delightful young ladies are his daughters.'

Ling beamed his pleasure. 'Please Freddie, may I offer you both a drink to welcome your young lady *minder* to my restaurant?'

'That is very kind Ling. I particularly brought Thor here for a special reason.' He leaned over to whisper in Ling's ear. Ling nodded his head and raised his eyebrows. 'But of course, especially for the young lady.' He returned to sit at the piano, smiled across at Thor before playing Gershwin's "Walking the dog".

Freddie watched her face, unsure of her response, but she turned to mouth, 'thank you.' One of the daughters brought drinks and Ling immediately continued into a further melody of Gershwin songs. As he finished, a beaming Ling acknowledged the applause before coming back to rejoin them at their table.

Thor smiled at him. 'Thank you Ling that was beautiful. I love Gershwin and you play so well.'

'Thank you Miss Thor. Now there is something you must do for me. I understand you are also a pianist.' He took her hand. 'Come. You must play for *me*.'

She glared at Freddie, reluctantly protesting. 'I shouldn't be doing this, especially dressed like this ... you know why.'

Freddie grinned and shrugged his shoulders as Ling led her to the piano. She sat for a while gazing at the keys, then started to play. The buzz of chat and laughter gradually died away as all eyes turned to watch the girl in the yellow bandana playing Chopin. Freddie knew the music so well and recalled her pausing to study the title when she had earlier looked through his collection. As she played, her eyes would occasionally look over to him. Nobody in the restaurant stirred, their eyes became fixed on the unusual girl at the piano. Ling sat down with Freddie, his eyes bright, watching her hands.

Outside, the flower vender turned his head as he heard the music from his homeland. He moved over to stand in the open doorway and stared at the young woman who played such familiar music. His eyes became distant as if lost in another time: he was back in Poland listening to his mother as she played to him as a child. For the Kraków University Professor, and then as the wounded soldier, it had been a long, cruel journey to be here in America with no possibility of returning to the land of his birth; but he could still indulge his dreams; the music seemed to soften the deep lines etched into his tired features.

As Thor finished, she lowered her eyes and laid her hands in her lap. She had only looked at Freddie, no one else; that guilt feeling again: *Charlie's music?*

For a moment the restaurant remained silent. Ling glanced at Freddie's face and then to the girl at the piano. Nobody wanted to be the first to break the moment, but then suddenly the place broke into applause with Ling clapping and grinning. He looked at the excited faces; the flower vender standing in the open doorway; all caught in a moment to remember and talk about for a very long time.

Thor became anxious to return back to Mulberry Street, concerned with the attention she had drawn to herself, so they left Ling still bowing and smiling his goodbyes with her promise to return and play again. As they started to walk away, the flower vender approached Thor to hand her a small bunch of wild flowers.

His eyes were still embracing another time as he explained quietly: 'tonight you play the music of Chopin, the music of my homeland, Poland. Tonight you remind me of my family, my friends, my country and all that I've left behind. But tonight you remind me that they may have crushed my country, but through our music they will *never, ever,* crush the soul of Poland.'

He kissed the back of her hand and made the sign of the cross, quickly turning away as if to re-arrange his flowers, not wanting to reveal his inner emotions to a stranger: it's not the Polish way.

They walked back in silence; the encounter with the man and his gift of the flowers they found deeply moving. Freddie aware the music also had an emotional link to her past and respected her reluctance to talk about it. The full moon that evening made play with the dark shadows and their thoughts. As they rounded a corner, he paused to look up at the southern sky, witnessing the drama in the heavens. She slipped her arm through his, whispering, 'a dime for your thoughts Freddie.'

He remained quiet for a moment before answering, 'when I was a boy in the forests at home, my father would teach me the language of the night sky. It speaks of predictable events and we must listen and try to understand.'

'And what does that mean, those two bright stars almost touching?'

'Those are planets. He pointed. 'That one is Mars and the other is Venus. When they align with a full moon, they are saying ... "be careful".'

'Careful of what?'

'Just be careful, because Mars represents anger and danger ... Venus represents love and beauty and that means there's a conflict coming. They warn us to be on our guard.'

'Do you believe all that Freddie?'

'Yes, of course,' he replied firmly. He paused as he noticed the cool moonlight emphasising her striking Scandinavian features. 'I can feel it.'

She glanced anxiously behind them and shivered. Noticing her sudden disquiet, he queried, 'what's the matter?'

She shook her head and pulled his arm. 'I don't know, I think you should get home.' She turned her wristwatch into the moonlight. 'I should be on my way. Come Freddie, come.'

As they neared Mulberry he said, 'I had no idea you could play like that. Apart from me, you have a fan in Ling, and of course the man selling the flowers. Ling was a professional pianist in China before he had to leave. I was watching him and he couldn't take his eyes off your hands. He'll be talking about you far into the night. You played for me, didn't you?'

She nodded—

He continued, 'tonight seemed somehow special ... thank you.'

'No, thank you for showing me Chinatown, I adore it, and of course Ling and his two lovely daughters. If there's a next time Freddie, then no surprises as Thor doesn't play the piano, only Stella.' She frowned at him, 'I mean it.' She lifted the flowers and smelt its perfume. 'And that man from Poland ... his eyes said it all. That's why Thor and music are so important to me.'

The Super still wasn't in his office as they slipped through the rear entrance. She collected her things and Freddie picked up an envelope. 'This is the draft script so far, could you get someone to drop it off at Spiegel's office as it's now urgent?'

She studied the address. 'It's near to me so I'll drop it off later.' She glanced at her watch. 'Look I really must get going.'

'How are you getting there?'

'I've got Harvey round the back.' She suddenly leaned up to kiss his cheek. 'Thank you Freddie, I agree, it *was* special. Just hope Carver or Hooker doesn't get to hear we went out. Just imagine if something had happened.'

'Well something did happen tonight. You pleased a lot of people. But you must take care. Thank you for the meal and the goodies.'

'And thank you for the English tea Freddie. It was fun.' Clutching her flowers, she stared at the poster before picking up her satchel. She opened the door and didn't look back: Thor wouldn't.

Freddie went to pour himself a drink. He stopped and thought of her playing especially for him. Glancing at the Winston pack he shook his head and ran his hand across his unshaven chin. He pushed the cork back into the bottle and put it down on the table next to the empty glass.

Pulling out the LP with the music she had played earlier, he laid it on the turntable and gently lowered the needle: Chopin's "Nocturne in C sharp minor" would forever belong to Thor and the flower man. He then looked out of the window hoping he would hear the sound of Harvey fading into the night away from Mulberry. In the evening sky the moon continued to align itself with Mars and Venus as if watching over the city. He recalled his father's voice: *"you must be careful" ... and* Thor playing Ling's piano: *something did happen tonight ... what did that young Greek lad Alix call her? ... "Angel" ... yes, an Angel who wore a yellow bandana!*

He touched the cheek she had just kissed and chalked another yellow circle on his pin-board.

16

03:25hrs. 12 miles off the New York coast: 25.4 knots/37^0 38' 43.09 N - 71^0 58'54.71 W

The giant transatlantic liner ploughed a continuous milky path into the Atlantic. High up on the raised lookout bridge, the duty officer peered intently through his night goggles and caught the colored lights of New York's skyline just breaking the darkness ahead; the mist confusing his tired eyes, making those disembodied shore-lights dance. Within a few hours he will watch those same lights fade as the monster returns into the same dark curtain on its rapid turnaround trip back to Southampton, UK.
Suddenly a side cargo-door opened and objects of all sizes tumbled into the waters below: carcasses of beef, lamb, pork, big hams, bags of flour, tins of butter, cheeses, jams, vegetables, fruits etc. The list seems endless but soon the task is done, the leftover provisions from the crossing cleared to take on board fresh provisions already waiting on the dock. The side cargo-door slammed shut and the unaware passengers slept on in their comfortable cabins; any waking thoughts

on their arrival in a few hours time will be with the excitement of another land, when the side cargo-door will open again and fresh provisions that are waiting on the New York dockside will be loaded on board for its return journey.

A small boat cuts through the gloom heading to the bobbing provisions. It slows down, drifting with the outboard running. Two shadowy men stare intently at the dark sea as they rise and drop from the heavy swell left by the liner; now just a ghost. Suddenly a large camouflaged rubber bag reared up through the surface, its side gas cylinders spluttered and died: sealed-bags normally used by the navy seals to transport weapons and supplies from submarines to an enemy shore. It rolled in the swell as it waited to be collected. The man controlling the outboard steered alongside. They grabbed the handles and with difficulty hauled it into the small boat, cursing its weight. The outboard roared into life, turned and headed towards "Pandora", a trawler that waited one mile to the East.

Two miles westward, on a covert trawler owned by the US Coast Guard, Captain Kinston observed the bag recovery through his powerful night vision goggles. He followed the returning small boat and watched as the two men attach a hook from the trawler's jib to the recovered bag that contained the Nazi loot. The bag was lifted up and the two men climbed on board. They hitched the small boat to its stern and "Pandora" turned to head back to the distant New York docks. He reached for his radio and briefed his land controller. Various innocent trawlers suddenly appeared through the gloom and swept in to openly recover the carcasses and tins that still floated and bobbed in the sea. Some will feed their families and some will be sold on to the "Manhattan"Mom & Pop" stores ... a regular occurrence.

14

Pigman: It had been a long night and Thor was feeling tired and ravenous. She entered the lobby entrance of her apartment block and picked up a welcome letter from her parents.

The scrubwoman was already in, busy mopping the floor and she gave Thor a hesitant nod. The woman assumed there were identical twin sisters living in the apartment on the third floor. Both even had a birthmark on the same cheek. One was smart and sophisticated, but this twin seemed strange and out of place. Still she was always polite; each to her own!

Last evening, after leaving Freddie, she had done three hours as a waitress in the dock snack-bar, before getting that message from Carver: go and relieve the pigman sitting in the warehouse. Pigman was Thor's name for one of the agents the FBI had also sent when responding to the mayor's request for help. She was aware Carver didn't seem to have much faith in him, and probably his own unit were glad to lose him for a few months.

The disused warehouse overlooked part of the dock where the small trawlers offload their night's catch. She walked up a flight of wooden steps and quietly knocked on the locked door. She heard footsteps inside but no request for an ID before the catch clicked open. The footsteps faded so she pushed the door and entered the dimly-lit attic, the only light coming from a low wattage bulb hanging through a curtain of cobwebs. The bull-neck pigman had returned to sit hunched at a small table where he was tidying up a hand of cards. A tripod and camera had its powerful telescopic lens poking through a cut in fabric that draped a blacked-out window. He looked up at her and scowled as she waited for him to move. The gloomy light accentuating his close-shaven skull with its Teutonic features. He glanced at his wristwatch and signed himself out the surveillance book before turning to stare with fish eyes at the newcomer and her Polish flowers.

He hissed through clenched teeth, 'so he sent you with some flowers for me ... how sweet! I thought you were down the snack-bar washing up?'

Her hackles rose, but she chose to ignore the intended barb and signed herself into the book. He skilfully swept the cards into a pack and stood up, nodded at the camera and again turned to her. 'Do yah know what this is for?'

Thor couldn't help thinking how the dim light made his strange droopy eyelids appear Mongolian, but she smiled sweetly and stared him out, her adrenalin starting to rise. 'I think so ... I have a box brownie at home.' As he went towards the door she pointed at the empty coke bottle, the orange peel and the squashed cigarette butts on the table.

'What's all this then?' she demanded.

His eyes now turned provocative, the whites looking yellow, and even in the dim light she noticed a flush climbing his neck. A shadow across his chin made his dimple look like a squashed fly and despite his irritation, she found it funny.

He snarled, 'so that's why Carver sent a woman ... do the clearing up ... know what I mean love?' and gave a throaty laugh.

Thor placed her flowers carefully on the table and slowly turned to face him straight on as she had learnt to do with those playground bullies. She moved one hostile step forward, just wanting him to react so she could whack his piggy face, but checked herself as she caught the body odour.

'You know the rules,' she snapped angrily, 'you leave as if you've never been here, not a trace. If you can't be bothered, I'll have great pleasure leaving a comment in this book, especially as you couldn't be bothered to ID me. How about a photograph of your mess? That's if I'm able to use this *manly* camera.'

The flush was beginning to creep and his heavy jowls were changing into a satisfying purple.

'I didn't need to ID you,' he snarled, 'I smelt yer perfume.' He clenched his fist and swept the rubbish into a trash bag. He grabbed his hat and coat before kicking the chair over. He swore as he made his exit, storming out and leaving the door swinging as a victory gesture!

She glanced at his initial in the book ... "A". She grabbed the door and hissed after him, 'Hi pigman! What does "A" stand for ... *APE or ASS*?' She closed the door and untied her yellow bandana, waved it around to vent his presence, feeling more relaxed that creep had gone; thank God she was on her own. Switching off the light she pulled aside the drape to get her outside bearings and watched him openly stride along the dockside, making no attempt to use the shadows. She shook her head with disbelief and tried to forget the pigman.

The trawler "Pandora" came in long before the others were due at dawn; the captain was in a hurry and eager to finish and be on his way. This suited Thor as she didn't want a long night in that old rat-infested building. It had been a drawn out day and then having to finish with that ignorant pigman; she still found the prejudice she encountered in the service infuriating, doing what some men considered their prerogative! She thought of Freddie and the prejudice he must have encountered over the years; *maybe we have more in common*. Thor paid particular attention to the faces of individuals, trying to ID them for the on-going investigation. She cursed as they would suddenly turn away from flood-lights into shadows. She photographed the jib as it lowered the large rubber bag onto a flat-back truck. The men quickly surrounded it with boxes from the night's catch until it couldn't be seen from the ground. The men were familiar from the Snack-Bar crowd: one small and wiry, quiet, kept to himself; the other, a bully boy always looking for a fight and complaining about the food; but really one of Carver's men. A third man wore an ill-fitting partisan cap and appeared to be the leader. She knew him as Vikentiy Chubinskii, a Russian immigrant, bully-boy and not a man she could warm to: built like a tank with a permanent scowl through his bushy beard. He remained in the wheelhouse with the captain and continued to berate the sullen men; he was nervous and on edge with this part of the operation. As the truck drove away towards the dock gates, she spoke into her handset to alert the driver of an old battered Ford pickup waiting outside the dock gate. He cursed and tucked his western comic behind the rear view mirror, tossed his cold coffee out the window and started the engine. Thor took out the film, closed down the surveillance gear, switched off the light, locked up, and headed home. Job done!

The truck drove towards the Fulton fish market with the agent following in the old Ford. Suddenly the truck diverted down a narrow, unlit cobbled-alley that still bore its historical street sign: "Tobacco Alley". The agent quickly switched off his lights and watched the truck backing through a dimly lit doorway into an old wooden warehouse half-way down. The heavy-timbered door hurriedly slid shut. The agent spoke into his radio and peered at his watch. Ten minutes passed when the wooden door slid open. The fish-truck drove out to continue further down the old cobbled-alley before it turned right behind the last building; the warehouse door slid back. The agent waited, knowing the lane became a horseshoe and would lead back to the main road further along the block. The trunk re-appeared and this time the boxes had been repacked and the rubber bag removed. He radioed in, turned his lights back on and returned to base where he would change into New York fire-fighting gear.

***

Back in her apartment, Thor found a jug and arranged her flowers, thinking of the wounded Polish man with his sad eyes and all that he must have been through, compared to that pigman agent. She scoffed a bowl of cereal and drank a glass of fresh orange juice. The prospect of a welcome shower and to get her head down for a couple of hours would be very attractive to Stella, but not what Thor had in mind: she needed to clear her head and forget pigman. Changing into track-bottoms and a fresh T-shirt, she pulled on her running shoes, retied her yellow bandana, adjusted her back-pack and left the apartment.

Dawn was just hitting Tompkins Square when she left for Marginal Street and the East River. She breathed in the fresh brackish air as she ran alongside the river with its over-night mist, now pink and lacy from the rising sun. She sang to the world:

'"*When the smell of the rain washed pavement*
Comes up clean and fresh and cold,

And the streetlamp light
Fills the gutter with gold,
*That's my time of day!"'**

Adjusting her pace, she approached Turtle Bay and checked her watch ... fifteen minutes for two miles ... *not good*! As she sat for a rest in the UN Plaza she ate a banana and sipped water from a bottle. She gazed at the UN Headquarters and its tall, flat-walled monolithic office building; the ski-slope assembly hall with its member flags drooping in the clinging damp air. Even at that early hour, activity was happening. There were several competing groups of Vietnam War protesters already there carrying their assortment of banners. One bearded hippy, who wore a flowered body-warmer, decided he was in charge and started positioning the group to make the best impact for the expected cameras. The office lights started to flicker in the hundreds of blank windows. Then the long black cars with their dark windows started arriving for the big debate that would fill the airways across the world as Vietnam descended into an international black hole; the US talking of sending yet more advisers; the Middle East still a mess and memories of Korea still raw with violent memories for so many! A few years back she probably would have been standing with them, but now she was working on the other side of the coin, fighting those same Maffiamedlem; but nearer home.

'*MADNESS!*' she wanted to scream. Suddenly there came a sudden movement of air along the river which set the 76 member flags stirring. She set her watch and started to run home.

As she arrived outside her apartment she checked her watch: twelve minutes, *that's better*. Her heart was pounding. She was drenched in sweat and looking forward to having a welcome cool shower with a couple of hours rest before her piano lesson at the Julliard School, where she could be Stella again.

A breeze started to come up from the river, enough to stir the trees in Tompkins Square and make their leaves rustle; she suddenly shivered.

***

The Reluctant Youth: The early morning Amtrak connection from Philadelphia pulled into Grand Central at Track 90a. Even before its metallic grinding brought the train to its final halt, the carriage doors were already banging open, allowing the mass of commuter passengers to start pouring out and dash for the track exit. Within the confusion and shouting, one slightly built man had waited on the platform with his dark trilby pulled down as if to hide his thin face; tinted glasses hiding expressionless eyes; his long, dark overcoat and matching trousers in contrast to tan elevated shoes; kid-leather gloves hiding slim hands. The man moved unnoticed into the surging crowd as if he had just alighted from the train. His ferret eyes darted round the platform looking for a discarded clipped ticket-stub with that day's date in the bottom corner. He picked one up and slipped it into his wallet and seethed at modern society with its filthy litter manners. Making his way through the marble concourse, he headed straight down steps to the lower-level and entered the Baggage Deposit Office. He leaned against the counter, agitated and starting to sweat. He couldn't stand the crowded claustrophobic railroad terminals; or an inefficient service! He kept banging the desk bell. After a while he heard coughing and the sound of a mug being clunked down on a hard surface.

A tall red-headed pale youth appeared through a rear door to stare at the man. He slowly lit a cigarette before slouching to the counter, chewing and blowing smoke with a deliberate lack of interest.

The man's thin lips started to tighten as he studied the scruffy youth: the dirty jeans; the Chi Guevara Tee shirt and the long un-kempt red hair. The man carefully laid two ticket stubs on the counter. The youth sniffed and coughed, making the man quickly turn his head away and hold his gloved hand across his mouth. He scornfully watched as the youth slowly ambled away, staring at the stub numbers before disappearing behind an end screen. He listened to searching noises coming from behind the screen, becoming more agitated at every sound. He suddenly lost patience and banged his clenched gloved fist on the counter. He screamed, 'hurry up,' his voice becoming almost effeminate.

The youth re-appeared and laid one envelope on the counter.

'Where's the other package?'

'Can't find it ... can't be 'ere!'

The man shot forward, grabbed the youth's shirt and pulled him half over the counter. 'What do you mean ... can't find it?'

The boy was now frightened.

The man yelled, 'show me ... show me!'

'I can't,' he howled ... you're not allowed back here—'

The man let go and flipped the counter-lid open. He knocked the cigarette from the kid's loose mouth, grabbed his long red hair and hauled him struggling back behind the screen.

'For Christ's sake what's this,' he screamed, waving a small package. The panicking youth kept howling with pain, trying to pull the man's grip from his hair. The man's face turned manic and he stared into the eyes of the youth before violently thrusting the heel of his open hand up into the youth's chin ... the head jerked back with a loud crack as the vertebral snapped!

He drew back, alarmed, astonished at his uncontrollable rage. The youth dropped to the floor ... the head at an odd angle, the eyes bulging. The killer pulled out a handkerchief to wipe the perspiration running down his face; he had blown his cover—

'Rusty, I'm back.'

A woman's sharp voice came from the reception area with the sound of a kettle being filled with water.

'Rusty, I'm making coffee. Where are you, *boy*?' shouted the voice.

His mouth tightened as he peered round the screen trying to control his rapid breathing. He crossed silently to the staff-room doorway and looked in at the back of a uniformed female as she fiddled with a kettle. She started to turn, but moved back to open a cupboard. He silently opened the counter lid and slipped out the exit door.

Passengers hurried past, far too busy with their own lives to notice the unpretentious individual as he quietly closed the office door behind him; even if the passing crowd had heard the scream, it would have been ignored. He kept his head down and headed to the terminal exit where he opened the door of the first available cab and climbed in the back.

The cab-driver, called Chuck, threw down his newspaper and picked up a sweat-stained borsalino to place it at a jaunty tilt on his head. He looked in the mirror.

'And where to ... *Sir*?' he drawled.

As Chuck waited for a reply, he slipped a fresh wad of gum into his mouth and studied the hunched figure in the back. The man had his trilby pulled low as if to hide his eyes. He seemed out of breath, traces of sweat started to trickle down colourless cheeks as he studied a slip of paper. He mumbled, 'Little Italy.'

'Didn't quite catch that ... *Sir,*' complained the patient driver.

The man raised his face to glare into the mirror and coldly snapped, '*I said ... Little Italy, Driver*. Get a move on!'

Thor

Chuck swore under his breath and pulled out into a u-turn before heading to the United Nations building where he turned to run alongside the East River. A black prowl-car shot pass with flashing lights, its siren whining. The passenger turned and watched from the back window as the prowl-car turned left into 42nd Street as if heading for Grand Central.

Chuck glanced in his mirror and found his passenger staring at him with a look that made him feel very uncomfortable.

***

The Fire: Halfway along Tobacco Alley, inside the old wooden warehouse, two men finished sealing the crate they had just filled with packets removed from the inflatable rubber bag. One man carefully rolled up the empty bag before binding it together with cord. He pulled it to one side as the other man finished attaching labels: Manhattan & Western Bank – Pine Street – New York. He twitched his nostrils and glanced at his companion. 'Gee, can you smell burning?'

The other man suddenly pointed at the far corner. 'Hell, there's smoke over there!'

They stared transfixed as thick fingers

of black smoke started to burst through gaps in the wood-planked wall.

'This place is a tinder box. We've gotta get out before it goes up!'

'We can't leave this,' the second man screamed, pointing at the crate as he started to cough from the acrid fumes.

'Sod the crate!'

Just then they heard a clanging fire-bell as a vehicle turned into the Alley. It stopped outside, followed by heavy banging on the timber door. A voice bellowed, 'anyone there?'

Further banging and yelling, 'Fire! Open up ... anyone there?'

Dense black fumes began filling the warehouse. The two men panicked, their eyes now streaming. One stumbled blindly to the door gasping for air! As he pulled the door open, a fire-fighter wearing breathing apparatus burst in and grabbed the choking man. He pushed him out the door and gestured for the other man to get out. The two men were roughly bundled down the alley away from the threatened building and made to wait round the corner ... out of sight!

The fire-fighter soaked the end wall with water as a third fire-fighter pulled himself over into the nearby yard to kick and stamp on a burning smoke-cartridge, grinding it into the dirt before dropping it into a metal container to take away. He threw a half burnt bag of rubbish against the side of the wooden building and sprayed it with an extinguisher; charred remains as evidence for inquisitive minds. At the same time a Rescue-Truck pulled up and three men jumped out and opened the rear door. They pulled out a crate with identical wrapping and carried it into the warehouse. The bank-addressed labels were quickly removed and tied onto the substituted crate before the original crate was carried out and shoved into the rear of the Rescue-Truck. The three firemen climbed in and the truck quickly reversed back along Tobacco Alley followed by the Fire-Tender. The two coughing men rushed back up the alley into the warehouse to examine the undamaged crate.

They both sighed with relief, with one making the sign of the cross.

***

The Priest: Hooker sat at his desk in rolled-up shirt sleeves which was most unusual for him. His coat hung neatly on a hanger next to his trench coat and Fedora. He drew on a cigarette and brooded as he gazed beyond the open window. The morning was decidedly uncomfortable with damp pavements drying from the over-night storm and humidity drifting up to reach the third floor. The harbor still obscured by a mist that clung across the face like a cobweb, Manhattan inhabitants heading into yet another warm day, longing for a sudden breeze to roll in off the sea and clear the air. His thoughts were pitched away, collating events from previous days, particularly Freddie's pin-board: fascinating. He was pleased that he and Carver were working together again. They stimulated each other, being of the same mind, he supposed. He chuckled to himself with Carver's quick witted "Operation Smoke-Screen". Strange how the murder of that little hood Broccento led him to the proposed bank robbery ... his reluctant but eager witness Freddie Vermeer ... and then it all tied in with the separate investigation Carver had been working on for over a year.

The telephone's sharp ring made him start. He picked up the receiver to listen to the familiar monotone voice. He grimaced and sighed. 'Sure if you have to Leo, send him up.' He stubbed out his cigarette and rose from his desk to wait at the door for Father Battelli of the Church of the Holy Conception. The priest entered and devoutly shook Hooker's hand with a hand that was warm and damp. The man's fine white hair protruded wizard-like from under his biretta cap as if to compliment the shaggy red eyebrows. He adjusted his cassock before sitting down on the offered seat. Hooker discretely wiped his hand on a handkerchief to perch on the front edge of his desk before offering his visitor a religious smile and a cigarette; the cigarette was declined with a forgiving wave.

The priest looked anxious with perspiration on his brow. He gripped his hands together and then rubbed them hard before looking at the lieutenant from beneath his strange eyebrows; he glanced wistfully at the Lieutenant's rolled-up sleeves and his own heavy cassock cape.

He coughed. 'Lieutenant, you'll probably say I'm wasting your time. It's just that we've known each other for many years and I felt that I should have a chat to ... well someone like you.'

Hooker's continuing smile seemed to re-assure the priest, so he moved back to sit behind his desk; his gut feeling this wasn't a social visit with a tin collection box. He made it look as though he was interested in the visitor by flicking open his desk-pad, indicating with a pencil. 'Carry on Father. Take your time;' not that Hooker had time on his side as events were starting to move in from all directions.

Thor

Father Battelli hesitated at first, coughed and then started: 'I'd like to present you with a hypothetical conjecture to illustrate the difficulties that confessions can put us priests in. A pure example,' he rubbed his hands even more, 'if I had a wild confession which had profound implications for another soul, then I would be torn between my obligation to *my* God and *my* duty to *my* fellow man.'

Hooker nodded, waiting, trying not to drop his smile. Wondering what was coming? He forced himself not to glance at his wristwatch or the eyebrows.

'If this hypothetical person came asking forgiveness for carrying out God's will to *kill* a person, I'd ask him or her, to explain how God would make such a request. He might reply with,' he rolled his shoulders, 'shall we say he had direct correspondence with God through the Washington Post.'

Hooker perked up and bit his lower lip, declining to comment: *rule one - silence draws the person - never break the flow with a superfluous question. Rule two - just stare.*

The priest stopped rubbing his hands and held them together as if in prayer. 'You must understand Lieutenant that we get all sorts. I hesitate to call them ... no, let's just say, they're *...lost souls*.'

Hooker nodded and deliberately dropped his pencil on the desk. 'I understand Father ... goes with the job. We get them all the time. We call them fruit cakes!'

The Priest smiled. 'That's the difference in our *calling* I suppose. We use the carrot, and you prefer the stick.'

Hooker's attention was ahead of the priest. 'You said, for example, he might mention the Washington Post. What made you think of the Washington Post?'

The priest sighed. 'The suggested paper doesn't matter of course, but people are very consistent Lieutenant. His story is always the same.'

Hooker sat up and stared at the man. 'You mean this same *lost hypothetical soul* comes often?'

The priest nodded, surprised at Hooker's abruptness. 'Yes, didn't I say? Well that's why I mention this in passing; hypothetical of course.'

Hooker started to show his frustration with the man's religious dissembling. 'Why come to me now?'

'Well yesterday, I received one of these strange confessions which reminded me to call in and see my friend Lieutenant Hooker, especially as he's been invited to an upcoming wedding in my church. I've been meaning to chat with you before, to discuss the difficult corners that we servants of the church can find ourselves in with such confessions ... hypothetical of course ... but you know how it is, a large flock to look after—'

'... this was yesterday he came?'

'Oh I didn't say this is a real person, Lieutenant—'

Hooker deliberately looked down, picking up the pencil as if to jot a note on his desk pad, quietly asking, 'no of course not. What's his hypothetical description?'

The priest caught off guard, shrugged. 'Oh we aren't allowed to see the person. Mind you, I did quickly look out yesterday—'

'... and!'

'But he'd gone—'

Hooker threw down his pen. 'Damn. Do you keep a record of the confessions, dates etc.?'

The priest was irritated that he had been tricked by the Lieutenant; *shouldn't have said all this.* 'No!' he answered, standing up, 'of course not. I really must go.' A crumpled off-white handkerchief suddenly appeared from his cassock like a conjurer's sleight of hand. He mopped his brow.

Hooker rose up to join him. 'I want you to think of those dates when he *may* have come to your booth, and anything he *may* have said that you *may* have written down. Would you do that please? It's very important. In fact I suggest it's extremely urgent. Pity you didn't come to me yesterday. Maybe someone's life could hang on it. I'm sure your God would want to help.'

'Not *my* God Lieutenant ... he belongs to *all* mankind,' he snapped!

'Well that's reassuring Father, I'll try to remember that next time I need him.'

'I think I've said more than I should Lieutenant. We're always anxious to help the police of course, but naturally you must understand, confessions are sacred between two people.'

Hooker opened the office door and regained his smile, trying to reassure the man. 'I like to think that we're all on the same side ... including God.' He indicated his office. 'Sometimes I feel this room is my confessional and naturally my lips remain sealed, like yours. And you've just reminded me ... must get my hair cut and collect my shoes for the wedding.'

The man frowned and stared at Hooker. He croaked, 'shoes?'

'Yes. I must have smart shoes for the wedding.'

Father Battelli raised his bushy eyebrows and chuckled. 'Of course ... smart shoes ... hair cut ... yes the wedding.'

The confused man swept out trying to brush his wild hair down with his clammy hand. The Lieutenant paused to lean against the open door and watched the priest disappear from the outer office.

You may use the carrot but I definitely prefer the blackjack. He shouted, 'Toby ... where's the hell is Sergeant Jugg?'

Back came a distant reply, 'gone to get a coffee, Lieutenant.'

'Well find him and tell him to get his fat arse back here ... at the *double*!' He slammed the door shut and returned to his desk with immediate tapping from the door.

'Since when have you started to tap on my door Toby?' he growled.

The door opened and one of Carver's technicians cautiously entered Hooker's confessional.

'I've a package for you. Lieutenant Carver said to get it to your desk fast.' He handed over an envelope.

'That's great Tommy ... quick work.'

Tommy grinned and pinched a cigarette from Hooker's pack, quickly closing the door behind him to block out any protest!

Hooker tore open the envelope and suddenly sniffed the air ... incense and mothballs! He lit a cigarette, blowing and waving the smoke around, tipped the envelope and two sets of grainy black and white photos fell on the desk. The first set clearly showing faces as they walked through the door at the agency after treading on the famous trigger-mat. The other set were taken from the street showing the same men going through the revolving glass door and more of the same group coming out later. 'Great,' he exclaimed to the room: the only reply from a distant dock-hooter signalling a work break. He returned to the inside photos and giggled at the picture of Thor dressed as a tart. 'Well done young lady or whatever you call yourself? And well done Freddie?' He mused. 'Maybe they would make a good team?'

He immediately put names to faces, particularly those on one print showing three men grouped together: two tall and one short. Dandy-Dandy and his twin brothers just had to be the three Freddie had seen on the roof when Broccento died. One of the tall twins was probably responsible for the killing of Ginger. *Bet that's the same gun that dealt with Broccento. If I had pulled Ginger in and held him, he'd probably be alive today. I must get Freddie to cast his eyes over these prints.*

Just then the door opened, Sergeant Jugg carefully entered balancing two coffee mugs. He slammed the door shut with his rear and slowly put the two mugs on the desk before sitting down with his feet splayed on another chair. He sniffed the air. 'Is that the aftershave I gave you for your recent birthday? Smells nice and sexy. You must get me some. Remember that Christmas present you still owe me?'

He half-closed one eye to aim and toss his hat at the spare hook next to Hooker's Fedora. The hat was on target but fell to the floor. He removed a wad of gum from between his clenched teeth, took aim and flicked it straight into the metal trash-can with a thud. He nodded and yelped, 'hey, that's worth ten points if you're counting?'

Hooker shook his head and grumbled, 'you have some disgusting habits Toby, can't believe my sister puts up with it.'

'She doesn't, that's why I do it in your office.'

'Toby, I want you over at Mulberry right now. It's urgent. I need Freddie back in his own Brooklyn apartment. Don't let him argue. If you have to, use the cuffs and drag him. OK?'

Sergeant Toby Jugg sighed and slowly nodded. The Lieutenant took a sip of coffee and opened the morning paper to scan the crossword. 'Toby ... who discovered comfort for the feet and potential militancy by the hand under a rock ... seven letters?'

He watched his brother-in-law furrow his eyebrows, counting his fingers, scowling, 'the garbage man ... dead easy ... garbage, seven letters.'

Hooker grimaced. 'Carver will be impressed Toby,' and pencilled in the crossword. He glanced at his wristwatch. 'Come on Toby, get going and pick Freddie up. I want him away from Mulberry ... NOW!'

The Sergeant gulped down his coffee, picked up his hat and popped fresh gum into his mouth. He opened the door and Hooker called out, 'actually it was Theseus.'

The Sergeant paused and frowned. 'Who?'

'Theseus ... he lifted a rock and found sandals and a sword hidden there.'

The Sergeant grunted and shouted back as he started to close the door, 'OK ... Theseus ... as I said ... Theseus the garbage man.' He slammed the office door shut and Hooker shouted, 'you're not at home now!'

The door immediately opened and Carver poked his head round. 'Hey, are you shouting at me or your tame gorilla?'

Hooker laughed. 'Come in Sebastian. Don't look so worried—'

Thor

Carver appeared agitated. ‘Can you come with me to Grand Central? I’ve just had a call from Captain O’Connell. There’s been a homicide, and although it’s out of your area he feels we should still take a look. I suggest you come with me. We have to go, *now*! ... I think our hit-man’s in town.’

Lieutenant Hooker suddenly felt a sinking-feeling in the pit of his stomach. He grabbed the phone. ‘Leo, radio Sergeant Jugg and tell him it’s even more urgent to get Freddie away. Got that ... it’s urgent!’ He slammed down the receiver, pulled open his desk drawer and took out his .38, checked the chamber before pushing it into his waistband. He reached for his hat and coat.

The siren-wailing police car expertly cut a path through the Manhattan traffic. The two passengers gripped the side of the lurching car, jumping lights and cursing jaywalkers. Carver shouted above the siren, trying to recount his earlier telephone conversation with Captain O’Connell and what the man had said: "... at first this seemed a run-of-the-mill murder, but I remembered our chat at the conference a few weeks back when we discussed this hit guy you’ve been chasing for so long. There’s something about this that fits in with the pointers you suggested when there isn't an obvious motive ... I think this fits the bill. Hope I'm not wasting your time but I think you should come ... now ... I think he's blown his cover".

15

The Ferret: After getting Hooker's message, the Sergeant had moved fast getting to Mulberry and waited in the middle of Freddie's apartment. He stood with his legs firmly wide apart and flicked his hat round and round in one hand, eyeing Freddie as he collected his belongings. Freddie put his last bag down near the door and looked around his home of the past few weeks. He suddenly remembered to hand the Sergeant a slip of paper with some dollars. 'Hey Sergeant, as I'm going to be confined to barracks for a while, would you do me a favor and see if you could get these two items for me?'

The Sergeant looked at the paper and scratched his chin. 'Sure. But I think I'll have my old lady get them.'

Freddie walked over to the clock and wound it up as the sergeant held his wristwatch in Freddie's direction, tapping it.

'Come on Freddie, never mind that clock, the lieutenant wants you out of this building fast. He told me to cuff and drag you if I have to.'

'Oh Sergeant, one more thing, on our

way out, is there any chance of calling in to the Julliard Music School?'

'Yup I guess so. But not for long, I've had my orders,' was his exasperated reply, his jaws clicked wildly. The Sergeant was getting on Freddie's nerves. He shook his head and wondered how the Lieutenant could put up with the man for all those years. He was soon to find out. As he went to pick up his bags by the door, there was a knock and a voice from the corridor called out, 'ELECTRICIAN!' Freddie clicked the catch and pulled the door open in one movement as the Sergeant screamed, 'DON'T OPEN THAT—!'

The door opened to a short man with tinted glasses. He wore a long brown overcoat and trilby. He smiled and went to shake Freddie's hand. But the other hand held a .38 snub-nose special at Freddie's head. The trigger-finger whitened as it squeezed ... *sudden blinding orange flash ... two loud bangs ... the Ferret's face jerked violently backwards.* Freddie shot sideways from an impact on his right shoulder, caught his head on the edge of the door and collapsed to the ground.

***

Over at Grand Central, the two Lieutenants joined rough-neck Captain O'Connell who was rolling an unlit panatela cigar in his thin lips. By his side stood a pale-faced Lieutenant Hammerton who confessed to a cold and a temperature as soon as they arrived; his constant sniff helped to break the silent atmosphere as the four men stared at the body of the youth sprawled face down on the floor. Hooker's mind went back to all those other young faces with blank and staring eyes he had seen on the road to Berlin eleven years before; at least they thought they knew what they were dying for.

Hooker muttered, 'he didn't deserve this Sebastian, young kid only just left school. Who would have thought working here he would have crossed paths with that bastard. No ordinary person would know how to kill like that. That's one of the methods taught to the marines ... or the Seals! That's definitely military. Just has to be the Ferret.'

Lieutenant Hammerton held up a transparent forensic bag containing two ticket stubs and sniffed. 'We found these under the body. Reckon that's what our killer came in with to collect something.'

Carver agreed. 'But why harm this lad? Why draw attention? According to those tickets he's only collecting two items, so what happened?'

Hooker asked, 'what time was he discovered Lieutenant?'

Hammerton went as if to sneeze, but controlled it and replied through his blocked up nose, 'ten minutes past ten this morning to be precise. The woman in charge went out for cigarettes and this is what she found on her return.'

The four turned their heads and looked through the open door at a woman dressed in railroad uniform. She sat clutching a glass of water with a sympathetic police female supporting the woman's trembling arm. Her drawn face was pale and frightened as the realisation had probably just kicked in ... it could have been her.

'She'd been to the cigarette stall. She reckons probably ten minutes, but absolutely insists no longer, so she almost walked in on him. We could have been looking at two homicides.'

Hooker pondered. 'So working backwards ... he was in here until 10.05 ... in the office for ten minutes, so that means he entered at 9.55. We must assume he came by train ... say 9.40. We must find out which train came in about that time.'

Lieutenant Hammerton sniffed and called out to a uniformed officer who looked bored as if having nothing to do but prop the doorway up and pick his teeth. 'Pop over to the info desk and find out if a train came in about 9.40.' The officer nodded and pulled himself from the door to scurry away. The Captain rolled his panatela and growled through clenched teeth, 'they only keep a record of the type of package deposited and the ticket number, no name or address, not that would have made any difference as it would have been false. The deposit book says these stubs relate to two items left two days ago, one was an envelope and the other a small package. They're not here now so he's got them, whatever they were.'

'But why did he come round the back of the screen?' asked Carver.

Hooker studied what the kid was wearing. 'Did the woman say what type of lad he was? By the look of his clothes and scruffy shoes he was probably resentful working here.'

Captain O'Connell removed the panatela from his mouth and growled, 'you're right. He was on this six week youth job scheme the Mayor's running. She says he resented doing everything, particularly his attitude to the customers and that's why she came back fast as she couldn't trust leaving him. Apparently he was on his last warning and certainly wouldn't be getting his uniform if she had anything to do with it!'

The counselling police woman appeared at the door. 'Captain, the woman said that she definitely closed the counter lid behind her when she came in and now recalls it was open when she discovered the youth.'

The four men looked at each other and then out to the woman.

Lieutenant Hammerton sniffed. 'God she was lucky. He must have been behind the screen when she was in the staff room. There's no way he would have left a witness.'

Hooker concluded. 'We can guess what happened, the killer comes in, the kid's on his own, takes his time out the back, and of course we're dealing with a sociopathic mind here. I know these people, they appear calm and in control but sometimes one little aggravation will cause them to explode and lash out. The killer was desperate to get his packets and go. Everything they do is precise and to the clock. They can't stand slackness. I bet he kept banging that bell and shouting to hurry the lad up. He goes round the back of the screen to find him and the poor lad probably didn't feel a thing.' Hooker wagged his finger. 'He must realise he's blown his cover and we'll be on to him. So now he's acting fast, kinda desperate and dangerous.'

The now worried Captain rammed the panatela back between his clenched teeth, scratched his head and growled, 'so what was he collecting?'

Hooker shrugged. 'Probably picking up instructions in an envelope, together with a weapon in a separate package placed here by the mob. He would never use his own gun of course. After the job, he'd discard it probably in the Hudson. If it was ever recovered, there wouldn't be any trace back to him. These stubs would be sent to a Delivery Counter of his choosing, where he, or a duped innocent, would pick them up; therefore no link at all.'

Just then the returning uniformed officer tapped on the door and stared at the group. 'It's the 9.45 from Philadelphia ... on time, Lieutenant.' He resumed his propping up the door to pick his teeth.

Carver nodded at Hooker. '...and he would have gone straight out and grabbed a cab.'

The captain struck a match to light the panatela. 'We'll send someone out to question the drivers and if —'

Hooker broke in. 'Would you mind if we do that with him, Lieutenant?'

'Be my guest, Lieutenant. The forensics have now finished so if there's nothing else here for you, I'll get the young lad moved and they can open up this place for business.'

Thor

Hooker stared at the ticket stubs in the bag. 'Interesting to see whose prints are on them. The lad's will be there of course but not the killer. He would have been wearing gloves and I bet there is another set of prints of the man who sent them to the killer. I doubt if he would have bothered; probably an innocent earning a dollar. I have a feeling we already know who that'll be. If I'm right then he should lead us to the man who did the arrangement.'

They all stared at the kid on the floor for a moment before shaking hands. The two lieutenants left with the uniformed officer, leaving Captain O'Connell now to enjoy his panatela cigar. Lieutenant Hammerton suddenly started to violently sneeze.

The Captain snapped, 'for Christ's sake Hammerton, get off home!'

Outside at the taxi rank, Carver looked at the long line of cabs. 'Sherman you take that front end and we'll work towards each other.'

It wasn't long before Hooker indicated success to Carver. The driver was almost at the head of the taxi line-up. He stared them with hostile eyes and pushed his sweat-stained borsalino hat to the back of his head. His rotund body fitted into the padded seat like an old friend.

Hooker leaned through the cab window

and fixed his cold eyes on the edgy driver. ‘What time did you pick this guy up then?’

The driver lit a cigarette and threw the spent match past Hooker into the street. He blew the first puff towards him, shrugging. ‘Probably gone ten this morning ... maybe?’

Hooker calmly picked up the match and handed it back to the driver. ‘Next time put it in your ash-can ... otherwise I’ll book you for street litter. OK?’

The driver scowled as Hooker asked sharply, ‘what does *maybe* mean cabbie? Be precise?’

The driver pulled out a clip-file, glancing at the customers pouring from the station; the waiting cabs started moving past him to the front. He scanned down the list with his finger. ‘Say, 10.15 ... yeah it was 10.15. I remember him ... strange guy.’

‘What was so strange? Would you be able to identify him?’

He shrugged again. ‘Weird. He had a trilby pulled low over his face which was thin and gaunt. He wore tinted glasses ... had horrible eyes, know what I mean officer? He kept them on me all the way, staring in the mirror.’

Hooker pressed him. ‘What was his manner like ... was he agitated ...

sweating?'

'Yeah, that's it, and out of breath. When we got there, he was out like a shot.' He snarled, 'glad to get him out of my cab.'

'And where is *there,* driver?'

'Little Italy—'

Hooker glanced at Carver. 'But where precisely ... the address driver!'

The driver lifted his hat to wipe his brow with a tissue. 'On the corner of Mort and Prince Street ... by the church.'

'What was he carrying, and did he have to find the address?'

'Yeah, that's right. All he had was a brown package and an envelope. He seemed to be a bit confused and had to read from a slip of paper he took from the envelope ... yeah that's right. Something else I thought strange—'

'What was that?'

The driver indicated behind him. 'He then started walking back to Mulberry. Why didn't he ask me to drop him there? I got the feeling he didn't want to be seen, covering his tracks like they do in the movies. Yah know what I mean Lieutenant? What's this guy done then?'

'Homicide, driver ... Old fashioned murder!'

'Holy cow! And he rode in the back of my cab!' He stared at Hooker. 'Yah never know who you're picking up, Lieutenant, yah never know. Say, when we were heading alongside the river, one of your prowl-cars passed like a bolt out of hell and turned into 42nd as if towards here. Flashers and bells ... real crazy. That explains why my pickup was real interested. Wait till I tell my missus.'

Hooker nodded. 'Sure. Life is full of flashers and bells in Manhattan driver. We'll want to contact you again, but in the mean time you can make a statement to this uniform here. Where's your licence?'

The driver handed over his registration. Hooker nodded and handed it back. 'OK Chuck, we'll keep in touch. If you recall anything else give me a bell ... OK?' He handed over a card. 'That number will get me. Thanks for your help and next time watch the litter ... Mayor Wagner's getting angry.'

Just then their overweight driver came panting along the pavement. 'Lieutenant ... you're wanted,' he hissed, 'Leo just called on the radio ... it's urgent!'

Stella felt uneasy as she repeated the set-piece music on the Steinway. The elderly woman sitting next to her tutted, showing her displeasure, 'Stella, what is it? You can do better than this. Your mind is far away. You must concentrate more.'

Stella stopped and rubbed her cold

fingers. 'Sorry, but I feel that something is wrong this morning.'

'Tell you what young lady,' the woman took the music away from the piano, '... ignore that music and play whatever you want, pretend you are playing for someone you love, not for this ancient woman sitting next to you. Play with your heart.'

Stella stared at the keys, her thoughts far away. She then started to play the music she had played for Freddie.

Her teacher smiled, now showing her approval. 'That's better my dear.'

Stella suddenly became aware of Sergeant Jugg standing in the doorway ... He stared at her! That sudden numbness in her stomach she knew only too well. She gasped, 'oh no ... not again! *Behaga Gud, inte igen!*'

16

Sergeant Jugg's story: The two Lieutenants cast their eyes over the second body they had seen that morning. This time it wasn't a youth, but a middle-aged male sitting perfectly upright on the corridor floor and leaning against the opposite wall to Freddie's apartment door; the small hole in the middle of his forehead had a small trickle of blood that told how his life had ended. The tinted glasses hung down as if a comic gesture from one ear; the trilby hat was wedged hard against the wall behind his head from the sheer force of the slug.

Hooker glanced at the Sergeant who leaned against the door frame staring at his victim; the wad of gum moved cheek to cheek.

'Well done Toby, you must have moved fast.'

The Sergeant grinned. 'Yeah! Straight between the eyes.'

'And how's Freddie?'

He pulled a face. 'Ok. He'll live, got it in the shoulder, I've seen worse. He fell over with the impact from the slug and banged his head when I shoved him out the way ... probably a touch of concussion, but he didn't really know what happened. He shouldn't have opened that door. They never listen. One of the passing prowl-cars took him straight to hospital.' He shoved another gum in his mouth.

Hooker took a pencil from his pocket and inserted it into the barrel of the revolver still gripped in the Ferret's gloved hand. He wiggled it free and examined it closely ... 'Snub-nose .38special ... the Enforcers favorite! Wonder if this was used on Broccento and Snuffy Ginger? Get a feeling this is the break we've been looking for. Forensic might be able to tie this up with other homicides Toby. What do you think?' He started going through the pockets and pulled out a leather wallet. He opened it and counted three, one hundred dollar bills; one calling card had a line-drawing of a ferret; one rail ticket timed 14.00 to Syracuse for that afternoon and one clipped-stub from Philadelphia dated for that morning. 'So that's where he came from.' He handed the card to Carver. 'No mistaking who he is, our friend the Ferret. This is the card he always leaves on the victim just in case we didn't realise it was him; so called professional pride. Hell, they're so vain these people.'

Carver studied the drawing on the card. The only other item was a brown envelope containing a sheet of lined paper with Freddie's Mulberry apartment address scribbled in pencil and a group-photo of men dressed in dinner jackets, raised glasses, grinning glassy-eyed at the camera: one face ringed in red pencil. 'You can't mistake Freddie. It must have been a reunion of some kind. How would they get their hands on it?'

Carver nodded. 'I wonder, but forensic will love all this.'

Hooker became curious, staring closer at the Ferret's face. He suddenly leaned forward to pull the trilby away. The head tilted sideways, dark curly hair tumbled down.

The startled Lieutenant exclaimed, '*It's* a dame!'

He pulled the coat open. The inside was red gabardine. 'Look, even the coat has two sides, and look at these.' He lifted one of several clips hanging from the inside jacket. 'I guess the trouser-leg bottoms are hitched up to hide them under the coat. She's wearing stockings and the shoes could be male or female. Before the job she arrives as a man, and afterwards she turns her coat inside out, clips up the trouser bottoms, lets her hair down and walks away as a woman in red. After all these years we've been asking for sightings of a man, not a damn dame.

Now then ... how cleaver is that? No wonder we've never had any luck.'

Carver shook his head side to side. 'I hate to say it, but she gets top marks for ingenuity. Damn clever.'

Hooker growled, 'yeah but the press ar'gonna have a field day with us. These people eventually make one mistake and hers was to meet Toby here.' He looked up and grinned at the Sergeant. 'Ain't that right Toby?'

The Sergeant shrugged his shoulders, subdued, thinking of another time, another place.

'Thank God it was you Toby. Otherwise Freddie wouldn't be finishing his movie.' He suddenly asked, 'where's your Thor girl, Sebastian?'

Carver looked at his watch.' Well she was on all night, so this morning she's ...,' he shrugged his shoulders, 'maybe at her apartment.'

The Sergeant shook his head, looking slightly embarrassed and coughed. 'After dealing with Freddie, I went straight to the music college and took her to the hospital. I knew she was there because Freddie told me. I left patrolman Jenner here until I returned.

Hooker stared at him, irritated. 'What made you do that Toby? You should have stayed here.'

The Sergeant shuffled his feet. 'Don't know. Guess I didn't like the idea of her finding out by accident. I reckoned that's what you would have done. Ok, I should have waited, but sod the rules. After all,' he looked at the body, 'she wasn't going anywhere.'

Hooker rose and put his hand on the sergeant's shoulder. 'You're right Toby. She certainly wasn't going anywhere. Sure, I would have done the same. I'm going back to the Precinct and you can deal with forensics. Cheer up, don't look so glum.' He slapped the Sergeant's back. 'Freddie owes you.'

The Sergeant turned away. 'Yeah, but it don't seem right ... shooting a broad.'

The Forensic team arrived led by a young Asian technician. For a moment the Sergeant stared at the Oriental features of the young forensic before turning to the poster of Jesus. He began thinking of that other time:

C*ombat-medic Toby Jugg noticed the blood-stained figure of a Japanese soldier sprawled down the side of the shell crater; he thought he saw the hand move. He walked over and looked down into the frightened face of a young Japanese girl; the flour-white oval face with black pupils stared back terrified; the American devil was coming to kill her. He knelt down and* *moved as if for his gun. She prayed to her Kami, make it quick. ... he gently held her head up and put his water bottle to her mouth. She tried to swallow ... it was difficult ... she choked and coughed. Through fading eyes she glimpsed his blue eyes ... the Yankee was human. He lit a cigarette and held it to her lips. She pulled on its strength; the strange Yankee taste was good and for a moment she seemed to relax and smile at him, then her sight faded as she died in his arms. Her torn uniform revealed her tiny undeveloped breasts; oh God she was just a child. He pulled the top across to cover her nakedness. The war-weary medic made the sign of the cross as a tear ran down his cheek; the first tear he had shed in the past three years of hell.* He felt his arm being shaken—

'Sergeant it's time to go, we've finished ... Sergeant, you OK?'

Sergeant Jugg turned his head to look into the black eyes and pale face of the young Asian forensic.

'OK son ... just thinking of another time.' He turned and waited until the body was stretchered away before wiping his eyes. He had a final glance round the room, spotted the roll of scotch-tape. He picked it up, lobbed it over his head, spun round and caught the roll with his hand before it touched the floor. He grinned and shouted at poster Jesus, 'I'm still the best.'

As he started to close the door he looked again at the poster. He whispered, 'but you're never there when you're most needed.'

He locked the door and walked away, at first as if stepping over the ghost of the woman he had earlier killed.

During the ride back to the Precinct, Hooker's mind concentrated on the rail ticket to Syracuse and the arrival stub from Philadelphia with that day's date: *the Ferret was too clever to leave a trace back to its lair; if things go wrong the two tickets would send the cops in opposite directions. Doubtful if we will ever find out where she came from. If ever she was caught she would sit tight lipped, get sentenced and sit in death row until one day a female social visitor would arrive for a private chat requested by the prisoner; but the visitor would never leave, her place taken by the Ferret; the visitor's body discovered too late. Then those coded adverts would start reappearing again. But all clever people have their Achilles heel – and hers was Toby Jugg.*

He cast his thoughts back to his comment about the death of the youth being military: *There are no females in the marines, so where would she have learnt that killing technique?* He was aware the method was taught in the training of agents dropped into France prior to D Day, and many of them were women. These agents had their own chosen nicknames amongst themselves to keep their identities secret, even from each other. There had been a number of these loose cannons around in society since the war. Teach them to kill and then expected to return as normal civilians. *Bit of a long shot, but think I'll make a call to that British army Captain I had to liaise with when stationed in the UK near a place called Southampton.* That's where he would lay in bed and listen to the sound of light planes taking off from a nearby field, returning in the middle of the night. The Captain insisting he was just a logistic office boy. Office boys don't disappear for days on end, reappearing and carrying on as if they hadn't been away with everyone tight lipped; such strange times. When they parted after D Day, he gave Hooker a telephone number, saying, that if ever, in the UK after the war, then to give him a buzz.

He may not have survived the war of course. Worth a try if I can find that phone number after eleven years.

Thor

Thor

17

Sam's Grapes: At first he became aware of a rustling noise, then a breath drawn in quickly; a trace of light barely detectable through half closed eyes; a distant humming, the dull griping pain in his shoulder; suddenly the nightmare image of watery eyes; the obscene smile with the thin face jerking back with such violence. He heard himself groaning and felt his hand being squeezed. His eyes gradually focussed into a dazzling white light, two blurry eyes, the moving lips, but he couldn't hear any words. He opened his mouth to speak but found his lips dry. Then the voice he would know anywhere.

'Freddie. Freddie.'

He gradually focussed on her face and indicated his dry mouth. Stella put a straw from a glass to his lips. He sipped the water and gasped, 'God that tastes good ... what happened?'

'You're OK and safe in hospital. Oh Freddie why did you open that door? If it wasn't for the Sergeant—'

As he became aware of his surroundings, the nightmare memory started coming back through the throbbing headache. He croaked, 'those staring eyes and the sergeant suddenly shouting ... there were two deafening bangs ... I can't remember any more ... yeah, of course there was the car with its noisy siren and somebody shouting.' He looked slowly around the room to get his bearing, and then at his bandaged shoulder and the sling. 'Hell that hurts Stella—'

Stella interrupted him, 'listen to me Freddie, the Sergeant shoved you and you hit your head against the door. You've got a slight concussion, but there's nothing to worry about. The doctor said you'd be fine. You've just been given a jab to make your shoulder more comfortable, so you'll rest better.'

He lifted his good hand to feel the dressing on his forehead. Gradually the fog in his mind started to clear as further memories returned. He licked his lips and coughed to clear his throat. 'I remember the electrician shouting so I opened the door. I just didn't think.'

'They found the electrician in the basement. He was out cold.

'How could he get past the uniform at the front?'

'Last night when I left, I checked the rear entrance and all the windows ... they were secure. The guess is the Super must have lowered your landing fire-ladder to the sidewalk. He's now in custody and tight lipped ... won't say much ... too scared I guess. Oh Freddie I've been through all this before ... I bring bad luck on those I get close to. I didn't think it would happen again.'

'What do you mean ... again?'

She shook her head and remained quiet.

He put his hand to ease his shoulder. 'How bad is it?'

'The surgeon said the bullet clipped your collar bone so they've had to pin it back into position. He said it could have smashed into fragments so you've had a lucky escape. But you'll have to have that sling for about three months.'

'Oh hell, I just wouldn't take the threat seriously.'

He suddenly put his good arm up and pulled her face down and kissed her.

The startled Stella whispered, 'my my, Freddie Vermeer, that's the first time you've ever kissed me.'

'I've been waiting for the right time, and reckon this is it!'

At that moment came the pungent whiff of Cuba. They turned their heads to find a chubby figure, dressed elegantly in a dark-blue Astrakhan coat with a white silk scarf tossed casually around his neck. He was drawing on the largest cigar Stella had ever seen. His black hair, oiled and smoothed flat behind large ears, emphasised his prominent nose; dark brown eyes twinkling with mischief as he observed the couple; his dimpled smile, warm and boyish. He hovered in his own cigar smoke and in one hand he clutched a paper bag, his other arm supported an enormous bouquet of flowers. An unsure nurse paused behind this larger-than-life man. He turned to thrust the flowers at her. 'Here honey,' he growled, 'you deal vith zeese.'

Freddie shook his head and stared. 'Sam!'

'Who else bring you zer flowers?' he barked; his rich mid-European accentuation bounced around the room. Dropping the paper bag on the bed he pulled out a bunch of grapes.

'Zee Freddie, I have zeese flown up over night from zer California for zer patient, straight from my vineyard.' He popped one juicy grape into his mouth, and with his dark brown eyes full of mischief, smiled suggestively across at Stella. 'Taste just like you honey ... fresh and sweet.' He leaned across the bed and gripped Freddie's cheek to give it a friendly pinch. 'Gotta look after my buddies ... ain't zat vite Freddie?'

Freddie felt the injection starting to work and could have done without Sam's overbearing arrival, but managed to say, 'I didn't know you had a vineyard Sam?'

The man removed his cigar and shrugged his shoulders. 'Vell not mine, but good buddy down zerre owe me big favor.'

'You did that for me Sam?'

He shrugged. 'Sure.' He waved his cigar indicating the room. 'Zis is down to me Freddie, my boy. To put your life on zer line for your art bring tears to my eyes. Such dedication to our new movie ... I ask too much vom you ... it make me zo emotional.' He pretended to wipe his eyes and prodded the cigar in Freddie's direction. 'Zat's vhy you ask vatever you vant and you vant for nothing. Hey I like zat line Freddie, quick somevone, vite it down.' Turning to the nurse, now concerned with the ash scattering across the bed, he growled, 'zat means everything.' He prodded the cigar in her direction. '... zer best steak ... caviar ... champagne.' Glancing at the tube in Freddie's arm. 'Fresh blood ... zer vorks, honey.'

The bemused nurse nodded and grinned at Stella. 'Yes sir ... the works.'

'Who's zer gal Freddie? I catch you two kissing.' He looked closely at Stella. 'Zay. Maybe you're Blondie in the script. Talking about zat draft you zend me, I luff it; it's exactly vat I vant. Vants zome more vork of course, Sam's touch? But vhere's zer ending?'

'It's nearly there Sam, a few more days and you'll have it.'

The larger-than-life man exhaled a further cloud. 'Zink in black and vite, Freddie. Black and vite! It vorked vor Vaterfront. More atmosvere vot ve need! Zee if yah can get it on my desk middle next veek.' He nodded at Stella. 'Yah gal can zype it. Bet you zype, Blondie. Zer following veekend I'm off to Jordan and I vanna read it on zer plane. Having a meeting vith zer King Hussein.'

'King Hussein?' exclaimed Freddie.

'Sure, his Majesty himself. Trying to negotiate viz the damn phone don't vork. He keeps zaying the phone line iz bad az he can't understand my accent! I need his army riding zer camels. I'm trying to zell him big film,' he rubbed his fingers together, 'I tell him, bring lots ov bucks to his country. Do vonders for his tourist trade.' His eyes widened. 'My adviser he zay, ve have to zit on zer sand in zer tent and eat zer sheep's eyes before negotiations begin.'

Stella studied her fingers, biting her lip, trying not to giggle.

He growled, 'I take my own food, *and* my own chef.'

'What film is this then Sam?'

Thor

'Lawrence ... managed to get zer rights. The Brits have been trying to film vor years; zank goodness zey didn't, it needs a Zam 'piegel touch. I promise you, it's going to be big Freddie ... I can smell zer Oscar.'

'How's the *Bridge* going?'

'Crazy. Von minute zay cry, "blow it up". Then zay no, "ve von't blow it up". After zer sheep eyes I'm going on to Bangkok and I kick zer arses.'

He puffed on the cigar. 'I have to go, big schedule today, car engine zill running.' He moved to the door, suddenly turning. 'Luff your title, "Body on zer Roof*."*. I luff it.' He waved the cigar round scattering more ash, ignoring the nurse's disapproving stare and pointed his cigar at the wall as if indicating a poster. 'Zay ... how's about ... *"Blondie with zer Body on zer roof".*' 'I zee it now.' He turned back to stare again at Stella. 'Zat's you Blondie. Have you tried zer acting? You're a pussycat and you have zer nice foreign accent like me ... zink about it. Look after my boy here; at least until he vinish my movie.'

He turned to make his exit but suddenly pulled a manila envelope from his pocket and threw it on the bed. 'I managed to zort it Freddie, zo you now owe me vone.' He jabbed the cigar towards Freddie again.

'Next time you have zer gun pointing at you, do az I alvays do.'

Freddie sighed and asked, 'Oh? And what's that then Sam?'

'*Duck* .. Freddie ... *You Duck!*' He chuckled to himself before making his smoky exit, exclaiming to the nurse, 'he do it vor art, zuch dedication.'

Stella burst out laughing and rolled her eyes. 'Pussycat ... never been called that before! So that's the great Sam Spiegel. I think he's sweet ... he's a real darling.'

Freddie grimaced. 'Why do all the women say that?'

She tapped him on his nose. 'Listen to me Freddie Vermeer, if you knew his secret, you vould be az rich az zer Mr. Spiegel. And vat does he mean? I have zer accent? Cheek! He's the vone vith zer accent.'

They both laughed and Freddie picked up the envelope to push it into the side drawer, wanting her to open it when he wasn't so drowsy.

She sat down on the bed and gripped his hand. 'Freddie, I tell you now, you owe your life to Sergeant Jugg. He must have reacted so fast. Don't be fooled by the Sergeant ... that's why the Lieutenant likes to have him around.

Just then the door opened and the two men in question entered. The Sergeant clutched a bunch of grapes and Hooker sniffed the air. ‘Guess that’ll be Spiegel, we spotted a cloud of smoke and an Astrakhan coat heading for the elevator.’ He leaned over the bed to peer into Spiegel’s paper bag. He pulled out a bunch of grapes. ‘Assume Spiegel brought these in?’

Freddie made a facial gesture. ‘Sure Lieutenant, all zer vay from zer California.’

Stella stifled a guffaw.

Hooker glowered at first but twigged and tried not to smile. He glanced at the Sergeant. ‘Makes your grapes look pathetic, Toby.’

Stella snapped at his remark. ‘That’s unkind Lieutenant.’ She looked at the sergeant who screwed his nose and winked back.

Freddie asked. ‘Did you bring those for me, Sergeant? It seems that I owe *you*. I was such an idiot opening that door ... I just didn’t think ... it all happened so quickly. Thank God you reacted so fast.’ He offered his good hand to the Sergeant who took it, but embarrassed.

Hooker grinned. ‘Why do you think I put up with Toby? He’s got me out of some dodgy moments over the years. Ain’t that right Toby?’

The Sergeant nodded and sat down

eating his own grapes. 'Yeah man, right between the eyes.' He raised one hand like a gun and went 'bang' at Hooker, 'right between the eyes.'

Hooker continued. 'But the Ferret we've been chasing all these years is not quite what we expected. *He* ... turns out to be ... a *She*!' He waited for their reaction with a sense of profound amusement.

The two stared at the man, trying to take in his news. Freddie broke in. 'A *Woman*! You're kidding!'

Hooker slowly shook his head. 'Nope! *He's* definitely a *She,* and all this time we'd been looking for a *He*! If you can follow? No wonder we've always drawn a blank.' He then went on to describe the clever disguise.

Freddie suddenly perked up from his drowsiness. 'Say, this is great. Sam will love it. He loves a twist ... the unexpected!' He looked at Stella. 'Hey, vite zis down somevone.'

She turned her face and stared at the wall with Sam's imaginary poster, biting her lips, trying not to laugh.

Hooker ignored him. 'Sure, but we're keeping quiet. All that's got out is somebody's been shot. But we've got to act fast, what with the press sniffing around. For the moment let them think it's just another gang dispute. When it gets out the cops have been fooled all these years by a *woman* ... we'll never live it down. We know she always made contact by putting coded messages in the personal column of the Washington Post. We've never been quick enough to know in advance as the wording always changes with each new contract. We can't spend our lives studying the paper each day—'

The Sergeant muttered quietly from the corner, 'Yeah, apart from the crossword.'

Hooker glared, ignoring the smirking Sergeant. He added, 'I doubt if we will ever know her true identity. We found a used ticket from Philadelphia and an unused rail ticket to Syracuse for that same day, but I reckon that was to point us in different directions should things go wrong for her. The Grand Central killing,' he looked at Stella, 'you can explain that to Freddie here. He was too busy getting shot and wouldn't know. Well the killing was just after the Philadelphia train came in, so I've been in touch with them just in case they get reports of a missing woman with her description, but wouldn't be surprised if coming from Philadelphia and Syracuse was another decoy. Good riddance to her. Never thought I would refer to a dame as such, but there it is. She was after you Freddie, but thanks to the Sergeant here, you're still alive and he's rid the world of a psychopath, for that's what she was. We're keeping this close to our chest and released a press statement calling it an on-going gang revenge killing. That means the Mafioso will think it's you that bought it. We're keeping that Speedy-Super out of the way until this is wrapped up. I have a way of outsmarting the press.' He looked at the Sergeant. 'Ain't that right Toby?'

The Sergeant stared back. 'What?'

'Outsmarting the press! I can small talk them.'

'Sure boss, if you say so.' He glanced at Stella and smiled.

Stella was beginning to like the Sergeant.

Hooker pinched a grape and popped it in his mouth. 'We're expecting action at the bank any day ... probably this weekend. I was right about the bank security. This morning, before I got the call about you Freddie, I had the news I'd been waiting for. We knew the delivery was to be this morning and about midday one of the securities came out from the bank to make his call.' He shook his head side to side and laughed. 'A simple message for simple minds, "the pizza you ordered has arrived and needs collecting". Can you believe it? Such imagination! We traced the number and guess what, surprise,

surprise, our friends at Edwards and Rivera, the friendly Estate Agents.'

Freddie commented, 'I wonder where Mister Edwards is?

Hooker tipped a pile of prints onto the bed. 'He's probably feeding the fishes off Cape Cod if Rivera has anything to do with it. I want you to look at these photos. See if you recognise anybody.' He glanced at his watch. 'Hey we must go, but have a look at those pictures ... after all ... you've nothing else to do.'

He left with the Sergeant in tow and Freddie shuffled through the photos. 'Stella, what's this about Grand Central?'

'They think that woman Ferret was responsible for the death of a young kid there when she probably picked up the gun.'

'Oh hell! What a mess. Why couldn't I have left that blasted attaché case alone.'

'That had nothing to do with it. You witnessed the killing on the roof. That's why.'

He nodded and looked at the prints. 'Yes I recognise these three. They're the ones I saw on the roof, especially the dwarf in his black and white gear. I don't know which one actually had the gun.'

Stella pulled out a photo. 'Recognise her?'

He stared at the woman standing in the

agency doorway. 'Should I know her?' He blinked his tired eyes and peered closer. 'Say that's not you, surely?'

She grinned and nodded. 'How do you think that film got into the camera? Don't I look alluring? What do you think of my glasses, aren't they great?'

'But where's Madame Butterfly?'

'You're supposed to be admiring me. Apparently your girl friend didn't need much persuading to telephone in sick, so I was sent as replacement to get the film in.'

He chuckled and yawned. 'You look outrageous. Great legs though. Remind me, are you Stella or Thor in that outfit?'

'I'm glad we met at the concert otherwise you'd think I only dress the way you saw me in the precinct.'

He suddenly went quiet; his breathing heavy; the injection kicking in. She turned as the door opened and the nurse came in carrying a medical tray.

The nurse paused. 'I was going to see to his dressing, but we'll leave him to rest.'

Stella leaned back over the bed and kissed his forehead. 'I'm just going out for a while. Yes Freddie Vermeer you definitely need me to look after you.' She then whispered, 'I know Charlie would give me his blessing.'

She put the photos in the drawer before

picking up her things and leaving with the nurse.

Freddie suddenly came to from his drowsiness and opened his eyes. He grinned at the ceiling, 'if you say so miss bossy boots.' He closed his eyes and murmured, 'Charlie?' and promptly slept a disturbed sleep.

Later Sergeant Jugg entered, tiptoed over to slip a "Macy-Manhattan" carrier bag and a large envelope into the bedside cabinet. He grabbed a few grapes before leaving the room.

***

During the next few hours the reluctant patient drifted through a dream sulcus: .... *sensing the sweet and sharp smell from the Balsam fir his father had just taken his axe to; the rich fragrance of leaves, pine needles, fallen branches rotting into humus, together with the sweet smell of Hemlock. A faint mist hung in the still air, slowly drifting out beyond his father's hunting cabin called ChompChomp, obscuring the shadowy woodlands before crossing the nearby Penobscot River. He ignited the dry cedar; it crackled and spat as he poked the fire, smoke heading up in a spiral towards the crisp night sky. He crouched on his heels and spiked the brook-trout he had caught earlier and held it over the hot embers. The stars hung sharp against the majestic mauve color stretching over the forests of Maine. Suddenly the sound of an animal heading back home, the branches snapping back as it hurried by, nervously keeping its distance from man and fire. His father Joey sat facing him, squatting on a log and speaking of the night his son was born. He raised both arms embracing the night sky:*

'Frederic, that night you were born, the Aurora Borealis, what we call the dancing spirits of the north, were filling the whole sky, horizon to horizon; it was glorious and had great significance for you.' He lifted one hand to point in the direction of the Big Dipper and then up to Polaris. 'They told us that your destiny will come from the north. A pale Psuhun will appear and when she does you will know; but she will be dancing like a leaf blown in the wind so you will have to be quick and snatch her before she passes you by.' He leaned across and took his son's hand. 'It is very important. You must catch her in the palm of your hand. You will know ... she is your destiny ... you must wait my son for your pale spirit ... only her.' Just then the full moon moved into view to cast its icy light across his strong Indian

features and the son vowed a promise to his destiny ... he turned his head as a stick snapped nearby—

The door clicked open and his *Psuhun of the North* entered the room and kissed the palm of his hand. He opened his eyes realising what she had just done. He patted the bed. 'Please sit here Stella. I've been reminded of my father's prediction—'

A cleaner, who had followed Stella into the room, could see he wasn't wanted, so he made his exit, quietly closing the door.

The wager: Two blocks away, Hooker sat at his desk, absently drawing on his cigarette, blowing silky circles at Carver's back who was looking out the window.

Carver turned round from the view to murmur, 'what are you going to do when this is over Sherman?'

'Do ... what do you mean ... do?'

'Well, I'm having a break; it's been a long year chasing and tying up all the loose ends. Still it's coming to a close any day now. Trying to keep all this under wraps ... who do you trust? We have bad apples of course. I always think of my grandad talking about having trust in people. He once said to me: "r*emember lad, not all doughnuts have holes*". I didn't really know what he meant then, but I guess he was right—'

Hooker laughed and clasped his hands round the back of his head as he leaned further into his chair.

Carver continued, '...never forgot him saying that. Don't think I've ever been happier for any job to come to an end. Edith and I were discussing this couple of days ago. I guess I must be getting too old for such capers. We've decided to head north for a couple of weeks, do a spot of fishing. Edith can do her painting; put our feet up so to speak.

'Why don't you ask the Commissioner if you can borrow his "SummerWind" for a couple of weeks?'

Carver puffed his cheeks. 'Doubt if he would want it to leave his mooring in case some rival pinched it; to convenient for the bar. How about you, any plans?'

Hooker growled, 'my nearest and dearest is tearing around at this very moment trying to find a hat for her nephew's wedding. You'd think she's planning an expedition to the other side of the world, not our local church.'

Carver pulled a face and grinned. 'When was the last time you saw the inside of a church Sherman?'

'Don't get me wrong, but all that religion ain't for me. City Hall is where we got hitched.'

'I never thought of you as an atheist.'

'There times when I think surely there must be a God!' He shrugged, surrendering. 'But then I always end up arguing with myself. So I and myself decided to make a pact and go our separate ways. Maybe we'll meet up again someday and see who's right.'

Carver turned back to stare out the window. 'If only religion was that simple.'

Hooker scribbled a note. 'That reminds me I've got to get to the barber's for a haircut and collect my shoes, they're being refurbished especially for the wedding would you believe.'

'Buy yourself a new pair.'

Hooker shook his head. 'No, they're my favorite. They'll be as good as new. There's a many sidewalk mile still left in them.' He chuckled. 'Toby thought he was getting his feet into them.' He glanced down. 'I don't normally wear brogues.' He slipped the note into his pocket. 'After this job finishes, I can't see you fishing and relaxing, you'll be fretting around, ringing the office every day; seeing what your people are up to.'

'No, I don't think so; it's a young man's job. It's not the world that I'm used to.' He sighed. 'I've been unhappy with this operation from the start as there seems to be political pressure putting obstacles in the way. I think there are people higher up who'd rather I went away. Sometimes I wonder if this particular operation is just some public exercise by Hoover, showing he's still the real boss.' He continued to stare out the window before turning and grinning at Hooker, waving a rolled copy of the New York Times. 'Mind you, give me a chance to get some crosswords completed for the paper. I seem to have got behind, had the editor chasing only yesterday.'

'Well there you are. Go and enjoy yourself man, you deserve it. Give you and Edith a chance to spend some time together, just the two of you, no kids.'

'Probably spend a time with our daughter and her family.' He paused. 'You haven't any kids Sherman have you?'

'I left the honor of breeding the next generation to Toby and my sister. Actually I've never understood what kids are for.'

'Oh I can see you bouncing a little diaper bottom on your knee.'

'It's not the baby... it's what in the diaper that frightens me.'

Carver laughed. 'It's interesting Sherman, but your villains think of you as cold and unfeeling; no humor. I'd love to be a fly on the wall with you in a session with a Psychologist.'

'The villains I deal with think humor is a weakness; a chink in the armor. The only time they'd laugh is at my funeral.'

'What made you become a cop with your academic background?'

Hooker doodled on the pad for a moment. 'Uum ... never been asked that before. My dad was a beat man all his life and rose to Sergeant. He knew his area like the back of his hand. He was trusted; even the villains respected him. When I said I wanted to become a copper like him, he told me to get qualifications. He said, "After this war's over, it's going to be qualifications that'll get you to the top." So when I returned from Europe I had the chance to go to university on a GI army grant and got a law degree. Being a lieutenant gives me authority on the street and the opportunity to keep clear of political nonsense higher up. Stuck behind a desk, you haven't a clue what's happening on the pavement. That's why I turned down promotion last year. At this level, I get my hand on the villain's collar, and that's a good feeling.'

'Yes and you turned down my offer to join my team last year.'

'But you work in the shadows and too many villains know me. I like to look into the bastards' eyes and watch them squirm. I relish being disliked by these villains because that means they're always looking over their shoulders in case that bastard Hooker's around.' He angrily scribbled out his doodles and dropped the pencil. '*And* ... at this level I make my own rules. Just a few more years then I'll aim for promotion to increase my pension. I had it all planned out when I joined the force.'

Carver shook his head, feeling in his jacket to pull out a slip of paper. He read it before tossing across to Hooker. 'Try that.'

Hooker read out loud: '"*was that really milk she was pouring or a distortion through the 'obscura' lens? Ask her arty Netherland employer ... seven letters."'* He read it again and stared at the enquiring face of the man by the window. 'I'll have to give this one some thought Sebastian. I'm not going to be beaten.'

Carver said. 'No, I doubt if you ever will. Just think about it Sherman, It came to me when a certain person dropped into our lives recently. Hell, I've given the game away.'

'Damn you Carver, you've got me on edge now.' He snapped his fingers. 'Of course, you made it too easy.' He counted his fingers: 'Yes, seven letters ... Vermeer

... the girl with the milk Jug. He was supposed to have used that "*camera obscura*". I think artists started using it about that time.'

Carver nodded and picked up the slip of paper. 'Yes you're right. Johannes Vermeer, well done. Talking of Vermeer how's our movie writing patient?'

'Oh he's OK. He'll live. His prides been dented that's all. Talking of such things, what's happening to this young lady when this is over?'

'Oh you mean our Thor. She'll go back to her own unit, but I have to say she'll be missed. Sadly I can't keep her here indefinitely as they want her back home. I only managed to get her because the Commissioner demanded help from Mayor Wagner, who then had to fight a reluctant Hoover. Makes you wonder if we're all sailing the same boat!'

'Got a feeling she'll be getting out soon anyway.'

'Out?' queried Carver.

'Sure. I get the feeling she wants to move on to other things. The point I'm making, she's probably fussing around him at the hospital right now.'

'I doubt it, she was working all night. Tucked up in bed getting some shut-eye I guess.'

'If that's the case, I can't see him being

happy with her out on night jobs.'

Carver nodded. 'It's her choice. That comes with the work. I wouldn't have thought she would have wanted to get close to anybody again after what happened couple of years back.'

'Oh?'

Carver shook his head. 'Naturally I had her background file before she arrived. She's a woman of our time.'

'And what does that statement mean?'

'Well Sherman, this is the fifties and the world is changing fast. The war pushed it on of course.' He shrugged. 'But the Thor's of today want a slice of the action.' He wagged his finger. 'You'll see, our so called gentle sex will be out there demanding and getting their slice of the cake. The Thor's of the next decade won't be at home ironing their husband's vests, they'll be here,' he looked around the room, 'running your department.'

Hooker exclaimed, 'never!'

'We could do with a few more like her Sherman. You'll see, one day. Don't misjudge them, or *her*. Get used to it.'

Hooker grinned and took a twenty dollar bill from his wallet and dropped it on the desk. 'Not in our life time Sebastian. Twenty bucks says so.'

After Carver had gone, Hooker took out an empty army-issue cigarette pack and looked at the scrawled name: "Andrew Travers-Jones (Capt)," with a London telephone number. The night before, he had rummaged through his army trunk and found the pack tucked into his uniform. Andy had been a flamboyant Englishman he worked alongside in the UK before the Normandy landings. He liked his warm beer and his pride and joy was his Morgan open-tourer. Andy would introduce him to his English friends as: 'the Yank they named the Sherman tank after.' That always seemed to get a drunken laugh; the Brits had such a strange sense of humor.

He looked at his watch, trying to work out what the UK time would be and picked up the phone. 'Leo I want a call booked to the UK with this number ... Yes London! ... England! ... Europe ... remember?'

17

The nylons: Before entering the hospital, Thor removed the bandana to let her hair down; she wanted Freddie to see Stella, not Thor. She found the reluctant patient on his feet, dressed and clean shaven; jittery, pacing round, frustration on his face, trying to tie his hair back with his good hand. She did it for him.

'I've got to get out of here Stella, hate being cooped up. I'm trying to get the doctor to let me go.'

'But what's the hurry?'

He was agitated. 'I've got to get this script finished. You heard what Sam demanded. That nurse won't even allow me to have a smoke so I have to sneak outside. She's even demanding I give it up.'

She opened his side cabinet and a Winston pack fell to the floor. She held up a half empty Jack Daniels bottle. 'Oh Freddie, how did you get all this?'

He looked sheepish.

She grimaced. 'Yeah, I know. Bet it's that Sergeant Jugg. He knows the rules.'

'I feel I should be buying for him, I owe him.'

She put her arms around him. 'Look, he

was doing his job. That's what he was there for, to protect you. If he hadn't, he'd be the one with the conscience.' She laughed. 'Getting cheeky is the Sergeant. Would you believe it but the other day he was staring at my legs?' She giggled. 'Then he blushed.'

'No harm in looking.' He ran his fingers under her eyes. 'Hey you look tired. I guess you've been up all night?'

She nodded. 'Yes, as usual, down at the docks, that's where I seem to have been since I came here. I'm supposed to be working part time in a snack bar just inside the dock gates. But now Carver and Hooker want me to get involved with the planning as we're raiding several addresses at the same time.'

'Being that involved must be a sort of promotion!'

'Guess so. I get the impression that Carver is trying to persuade me to apply for a permanent replacement here.'

'Hey, that sounds good. That means you won't be leaving then?'

'Not so fast Freddie. I need time to think. I'm getting pulled in all directions. Please don't confuse me.'

'OK. But what's so important about that snack bar?'

'You'd be surprised at the street intelligence we can trawl: casual talk with names that keep cropping up again and again. I report to Carver and he treats it just like a jigsaw and gradually an overall picture emerges. He's a clever man and I have such admiration for him. Now I've met Hooker I can see why those two get on together. I might have to put up with the odd pinch, but on the whole they're a good bunch of hardworking guys; besides they tip well.' She peered closely at him and grinned. 'You're jealous?'

'I think I am.'

'Look I'm whacked. I'll go home and grab a couple hours sleep. I'll come in later, I promise.'

'Well I'm not going anywhere. And in answer to your first question the other day, sure, the idea of you looking after me is very appealing, and secondly ... tell me, who's Charlie?'

'You rat Freddie, you were awake all the time.'

He shook his head. 'No, but I caught what you said and want you to tell me.'

'I'll tell you tonight when I come back, I'm so tired and there are things I have to explain, but somehow the time never seems right ...' she tapped him on the nose ... 'and I need to know more about you, Freddie Vermeer.'

'I thought you and your friends had done a check on me?'

'No,' she frowned, 'I mean the real you.' She pointed at the cabinet trying to sound firm. 'Mr. Vermeer, I'm with the nurse, I don't want to see any more booze or cigarettes in there. Please Freddie, I want you well and back home; your real home, not at Mulberry.'

'You didn't look in the cupboard properly ... fine agent you are.'

He took out two envelopes and the Macy bag. 'They won't bite ... open the envelope first.'

She took out two theatre tickets and her eyes lit up. 'Guys and Dolls ... but they were sold out. How did you get them?'

'Well you don't work for Sam Spiegel for nothing ... well sometimes it happens. Now the box, that's from me.'

He watched her face as she opened the wrapping and asked, 'is that right ... Cabochard?'

She stared at the bottle of perfume and quickly kissed him. 'Yes of course. Yes of course Freddie. Of course it's right. Infact it's perfect. Oh Freddie ... thank you—'

'Hey it's only a bottle of perfume.'

She shook her head. 'No it's not *just* a bottle of perfume. It's more than that.'

From the second envelope she pulled out the Carnegie program.

'Don't you remember, you dropped it when we had that encounter with that young lad? Well I'm returning it ... notice the hand writing?'

She studied with disbelief the handwriting: "For Stella of the skies – Athur Rubinstein".

He grinned at her stunned face. 'Oh it's just another perk working for Sam Spiegel. Apparently he contacted Rubinstein's agent and luckily he was still in town. That's why I must get this script finished for him. As he said, "I owe him". Now look again in the bag.'

She started to giggle as she pulled out a pair of nylons. 'Oh Freddie, I was only teasing that night. But how did you know my size?'

'Well I've got a great imagination. I'd already sized you up when I first saw you talking to Carver at the concert. I said to myself, I reckon, she's a size—'

She put a hand over his mouth. 'That's classified info Freddie Vermeer.'

'Hey look you're tired sweetheart, go and get some sleep and I'll see you later.' He kissed her head and gave her a playful slap. 'You must listen to me Miss Thor, if those rough, hairy seamen can do it ... so can I.'

She nodded, wiping her eyes as she hurried from the room clutching her prized program and the Macy carrier bag.

He picked up the tickets she had left on

the bed; *actually it was the Sergeant who came up with her stocking size.*

***

Detective Nathan Clarke, sat in the council rubbish truck parked in Pine Street. The past hour he had photographed the odd-looking workmen who had entered the empty wing of the bank.

Moments later Hooker received the call he had been waiting for.

'Lieutenant we're now picking up what could be called drilling sounds.'

Hooker replaced his receiver. He lit another cigarette before re-dialling with a sense of mounting excitement. 'Hey Sebastian, I think this is it. Nothing we can do at this moment but I'll keep you posted as to when we need to go down to Pines.'

In his office, Carver made his call and tried to keep his voice sounding casual; in a basement on the other side of Manhattan, behind a door labelled: "Technical Research Unit", Chief Engineer Mike Grosse pulled out a single jack-plug; the last thing he wanted was to black-out the whole PBX system straight away. He adjusted his head-cams, picked up his coffee to resume his drinking and sat waiting for the inevitable irate call from the Manhattan & Western bank to report they appear to be having telephone problems.

Hooker stubbed out his cigarette and moved over to the open window, thinking of all the things that could go wrong. He had pulled in the usual suspects, releasing them, bringing them in again. It was obvious something was going on but they were too frightened to talk. He wanted these hoods to think it was just the usual cop investigation over a gangland homicide and nothing more. Snuffy Ginger and his side-kick Broccento were expendable and knew too much. Broccento's killing was no more than a mistake by a gun-twitchy ginzo. One simple fact had emerged: one gang was going to steal from another. If that happened, there'll be the usual outbreak of gang revenge. If Hooker had his way he would sit back and let them wipe each other out; didn't these goons learn anything from the past war? Carver's investigation and his had merged into one operation: "Smoke-Screen". He suddenly thought of Freddie and picked up the receiver. *I must speak to his doctor to see if he can come out. I did promise his movie ending; let's hope it's a happy one?*

'Leo, would you get me the hospital.'

Thor

Leo replied, 'OK but remember your call to the UK is coming in any time now so can you leave it till after?'

Five minutes later Leo rang again. 'Lieutenant, you have some irate female with a *peculiar* accent demanding to know who the hell are you to ring as the gong has just struck for dinner.'

It appeared the UK number belonged to Andy's mother. Hooker held the receiver away from his ear until she had quietened down. She continued, '.... *he's Major actually. Retired and runs some smelly pig farm down in Devon.*' Her voice became suspicious. '*And who might you be then*?'

He explained he was from the New York police Department and worked with her son during the war.

Her voice rose and shouted down the phone, '*What's he done? I knew they'd catch up with him sometime.*' She huffed. '*Well you better have his number.*'

Hooker wrote it down and tried to thank her—.

'... *and if you arrest him who's going to feed his smelly pigs, 'cause I'm not*!' The phone clicked dead.

He glared at the phone and noticed his hand was sweating. He quickly lit a cigarette and drew on it; w*ith a mother like that, no wonder Andy was crazy.*

He picked up the phone again. 'Sorry

Leo, but would you book another call to the UK.' He snapped back at Leo's response, '*NO!* They're not all like that, and then get me the hospital. Please.' As he waited, he crossed fingers for the coming days; not always with one of those cliché movie endings. He felt a twinge of nerves.

Imagine trying to interrogate her!

Jessica's Dikt: After a disturbed sleep, Stella turned over to stare at the clock-radio, trying to focus on the time before reluctantly sitting up. Her mind was confused by recent events and now her growing feelings for Freddie; an unexpected intrusion into her life she was finding difficult. She was intrigued with the idea of his ancestry and curious to know more ... strange with that message on the poster being identical to her family bible. She yawned and stretched and moved to the window to pull back the curtain. The evening dusk was now beginning to settle over East Village.

Thanks to Carver she was lucky to have found an apartment overlooking Tompkins Square. The ornate park-lights were already switched on, their yellowish glow flickered as if carnival time with tree branches moving from a slight breeze starting to drift from the East river. Within the park she watched an assortment of people hurrying home from work while a few kids roller-skated amongst strangers sleeping rough on benches with nowhere to go. Just inside the park entrance, two elderly men sat at a wooden table playing chess. They suddenly started to pack up, shook hands and walked away in opposite directions. Outside the railings, a couple slowly strolled along the sidewalk hand in hand; she felt for them lost in their own secret world. *I must write that letter home to Mom and Pop.* Suddenly, she spotted a cat being chased through the bushes by a fox. Perhaps the cat was teasing the fox? — She was back in Dalsland, in her nursery with Pop reading her favorite poem:

"It's time to go out; I peer through the gaps.
Cats starting to hunt; cats looking for scraps.
I'm watching one cat; it searches the gloom,
Cat waiting for mice; for mice to consume.
With non blinking eyes, it searches through rocks,
But suddenly finds ... the eye of a fox.
The fox makes a pounce; the cat makes a run,

Thor

*The mouse starts to laugh... another night won."**

The cat scrambled up a large elm. It turned and glared, with its back arched, hissing. The bewildered fox turned its head to look at the watcher in the window as if for help. It raised one leg in anticipation, but suddenly gave up and slunk into the shadows; cheated once again.

She felt an urge to be down there strolling hand in hand with Freddie. She picked up the perfume he had given to her; her mind thinking of another time when she first had that perfume in Paris on her honeymoon, trying to stop Charlie buying as it seemed so expensive for such a small bottle. Paris was worlds away from where they first met. He was her first instructor when she entered the FBI training academy; her memory sketchy over the visit from the Agency that Black Saturday: Charlie's best friend Nick, standing on the doorstop, trying to look anywhere but into her eyes. She remembered staring at white knuckles showing through his tanned hands; such strong hands and then that numbness in her stomach as he whispered that Charlie tried to stop a hold-up and had been shot; he wasn't even on duty. He'd only popped out for groceries. Her friends and family had expected her to leave the Agency, but it made her even more determined to carry on ... for Charlie.

The sound of a distant police siren brought her thoughts back and she kissed the bottle of Cabochard before placing it next to Charlie's. She wiped her cheeks. She rarely used it, but when she knew she was going to meet Hooker's witness at the concert, she surprised herself when she hadn't hesitated to reach out for the tiny bottle. She pictured Freddie walking down the precinct corridor and that strange feeling in her chest as he turned to look back at her. Her visit to the library; *must mention the Rose room in the letter*.

Checking the time, she switched on the radio and tuned in to RKL for their regular early-evening programme of piano music. She then turned on the coffee machine. A refreshing shower woke her up. Wrapping herself in a warm towel she poured a mug of coffee before returning back to the window. Her finger touched the scar, still sensing his touch, reflecting on Freddie's remark after the concert that it would tingle occasionally ... a good sign? What could he mean by that? She was lucky to get out of that situation with just a gash from the broken bottle; one undercover job which went dreadfully wrong.

The Carnegie concert seemed such a long way off now. She didn't think she could possibly have any feelings for anybody after Charlie's death and would withdraw when acquaintances started getting too close. She had an unfair reputation of coldness, especially from those who didn't know her story. Had she thrown herself at Freddie? Was she becoming too involved? She'd made it quite obvious and knew there could be problems with the Agency. One of the first things drummed into you, she recalled it was Charlie saying on one of his first lectures: '*never get too close*;' easy said ... she suddenly spotted two cops chasing a youth in the park ... they cuffed and led him away. Maybe just another desperate Alix in another park; wonder what happened to him? Did Deno get him that job? Charlie had this dream of helping kids; the ones he came in contact with were always from broken homes. She could still hear his voice: '*hitting kids over the head and throwing them into jail wasn't the answer. Maybe one day we can do something positive for them'.* Charlie always used the word *we*, including her in his plans. She had thought of him when she decided to give that young lad Alix the ten dollars. *Why did I play Charlie's music for Freddie at the restaurant*? She hadn't wanted to play it since he died. Tomorrow was her weekly piano lesson at the Juilliard School of Music; luckily Claremont Avenue was only a short walk from her apartment ... *damn - I won't be able to go this week.* She was lucky to get the special weekly lessons, but only because her father was a friend of the school president William Schuman who sanctioned her audition as he already knew her high standard. That had been one of her dreams and this transfer to Manhattan gave her an opportunity she couldn't resist. She shouldn't have gone into Chinatown with Freddie, especially playing the piano; drawing attention after she had strict instructions not to leave the apartment; she would have to talk to Carver and get it off her chest before he hears from others ... *probably get a reprimand ... what the hell.* What would her family think of Freddie and his culture? Her parents didn't have an ounce of prejudice, and after Charlie all they could wish for was her happiness. A few days ago if someone had told her about pale spirits from the north, Mars and Venus aligning, she would have laughed and said it was just Indian superstitious myth ... but now... maybe she just wanted to believe?

Thor

She sat down at the kitchen table to write her monthly letter home. She hadn't been in touch, apart from that brief call she made to them on her return to Manhattan when she knew they would be anxious for her safe arrival. She pulled the towel tighter and chewed the pen ... pondering:

"... My weekly piano lessons have helped me so much. Can't believe I'm having lessons at Julliard. Thanks pop for arranging it with Mister Schuman, oh yes I bumped into him the other day and he asked to say hello to you and mom. I didn't mention anything on the phone, as the line was so bad, but I had this revolting salesman sit opposite me on the journey. He'd been drinking and kept staring at me and making me feel uncomfortable; old enough to know better of course. I could have called the inspector I suppose but suddenly remembered that game I used to play on our visitors as a girl; remember pop? Remember that line Dick Tracy would use in your favorite comic strip? Well I went over and flashed my badge. You should have seen his face; you would have loved it pop. I whispered in his ear, just like Dick Tracy would, that several of my fellow agents were with me on a stake out

as there was a desperate escaped prisoner sitting in the carriage. He was dangerous and not to be approached. His face went purple. (I was worried in case he had heart problems) I said that if he foils the coming arrest then I would personally charge him under section 4 (Dick T's favorite line, remember?) with assisting the man's escape. This is the best bit: I said that he could get 30 years inside if he doesn't leave that minute. Well he was up and out like a shot rabbit. I still laugh thinking about it. Wonder if there was really a section 4, or do you think that was made up for the strip? I must look that one up".

She screwed her face, thinking about that repulsive man. *I bet he won't ogle any women again for some time;* she shuddered at the image and then swallowed, *I think this would be a good time to vaguely mention Freddie:*

"... I met an interesting man who works for Sam Spiegel, you know the famous movie producer. Well he is working on a new film for Mister Spiegel; he's writing the script for it would you believe. He is half American Indian and half European and so interesting. His name is Frederic Vermeer Maliseet, love his name although

I call him Freddie, he's about my age and so nice and we met at a concert at Carnegie Hall by Artur Rubinstein no less, you know, my hero; he plays so wonderful; can't believe I was actually seeing him. Freddie loves classical music, especially Chopin, and last evening I had the chance to play for him in a restaurant he took me to. Only friends of course, but it would be nice to keep in touch when I finish here. You never know I might get invited to a premier. Oh yes I even met Mister Spiegel the other day. Wow, a real movie mogul. I suppose this is normal for the big city." She hesitated, *mustn't mention why I met him or where, they worry enough as it is—"*

She jumped at the phone's shrill ring. 'Hello Sir ... they've actually started at the bank ... briefing first thing in the morning ... Good night, Lieutenant.'

Again that sinking feeling in her stomach.

Putting the receiver back she clasped her hands tight together; *thank goodness I'm not on duty tonight. I must talk to Freddie before the morning; there are things I have to tell him. Perhaps he'll pull away from me? Oh hell, I should never have come to New York.* She suddenly felt choked and started to chew her bottom lip and dashed into the bathroom to splash her face. She stared in the mirror at the dark rings under her eyes ... then quickly turned away as if Charlie was watching in the reflection. The tears started to trickle down her cheeks. That phone call meant her time would be coming to an end in Manhattan and she'll soon be returning back to Minnesota ... away from Freddie ... but really she knew she was becoming unsure of her ability and what was expected of her. She couldn't hide behind Thor forever. She threw herself on the bed and wept.

***

Freddie studied the girl sitting on his bed as she explained about Charlie; her eyes still hinting those dark lines. He sensed her vulnerability as she fingered her ring finger. She had been staring down at the faint mark but suddenly looked up.

'I've been trying to pluck up my courage Freddie.'

'Why has it been so difficult?'

'In case you wouldn't want to get involved with my problems. I was frightened you would pull away.'

'No,' he said, 'just the opposite.' He ran his fingers gently down her hair and murmured, *'Woliqe.'*

Thor

She could only guess at his meaning, *so much to understand.* He squeezed her hand as the door opened and the doctor entered, followed by his duty nurse who seemed to guess his every gesture. He stared at the patient. 'Can I have a word?'

He picked up the chart from the end of the bed. 'Do you fancy going home tomorrow, Mr Vermeer? You're making great progress and I guess home will be better than any medicine we can give you.' He glanced and smiled at Stella. 'I'm sure Mrs. Vermeer would agree.'

Stella smiled back. 'Mrs. Vermeer definitely agrees Doctor.'

The doctor frowned at the patient. 'You're going to have that sling for some time yet and Mrs. Vermeer will have to be your nurse. Don't forget she's in charge ... no arguing ... do as she says.' He replaced the chart. 'Oh by the way, Lieutenant Hooker tells me he'll be picking you up tomorrow morning as he's particularly anxious you should come out. He didn't explain why.'

'Thank you Doctor, I think I know why.'

The doctor swept out with his nurse shadowing close behind. As the door clicked shut, the patient and the grinning Stella glanced at each other. Her eyes now shone, the tiredness had gone. 'You heard doctor's orders ... *Mrs.* Vermeer is in charge ... *Mr.* Vermeer.'

Hooker stared at the pile of memos sitting on his desk. He picked up the unopened pile and dropped it into the trash can. His forgotten call to the UK came through just as he decided to leave the office. He lit a cigarette and settled down into his chair wondering if this ringing the UK was such a good idea. He immediately recognised the English voice with its cultured tone. They spent the first few minutes exchanging pleasantries.

'... *how the hell did you get this number from that bat I call mother? I had a call from her shouting something about New York police coming to arrest me ... serves me right and don't expect her to come and feed my disgusting pigs. Mind you, she does a super pork casserole when she's not drunk. How can I help old chap*?'

Hooker gave him the background story of the elusive Ferret, and the method used to kill the youth, and as a long shot wondered if it was possible to trace any female using the name Ferret in the SOE records.

At first he was hesitant at the mention of the SOE. '*Well officially I haven't a clue what you're on about. And naturally any records would be locked away because there are people still around who would like to catch up with any ex agents who let them down, shall we say; scores to settle if you get my drift. Sorry can't help you old chap, thirty year ban, and more on some info of course. As we've caught up again I might feel like writing to you, very soon, so give me your home address. Talking of old times, I think I'll make a telephone call to London and chat with an old war chum of mine. He still owes me a drink by the way. Sorry about my mater Sherman, no wonder people support euthanasia. Now you can see why my old man fled to Africa and went native. Just bear this in mind Sherman: at least she was on our side in the war!'*

He slowly replaced the receiver as the door opened. Detective Harry Henshaw poked his head round the door. 'What we doing about Miss McDonald's memo to you?'

Hooker growled at him. 'How about some respect for your superiors, detective ... Try knocking first.'

'So, I wiped my feet. Say Lieutenant what we doing about her memo?'

'What memo?'

'The memo with all the others I placed very respectfully on your desk this morning.'

Hooker picked up the trash can and rummaged inside. He pulled out a crumpled envelope and recognised the hand writing. He sniffed it. 'Yeah this must be it, "Heather Mist". OK before I open this sealed envelope, tell me what it says.'

'Are you suggesting I opened a private and sealed envelope behind your back Lieutenant?'

'Of course not. So what's in it?'

'Apparently Captain Mulligan was rushed to hospital with a suspected perforated ulcer. Apparently he's going to live but the boys are taking bets, and the odds, so far, look good for him. She suggests that Floor-3 should have a whip round and send a card.'

'What type of card does she have in mind then?'

'Well the boys had a show of hands and we assume she means a "Get Well" card, but we also thought we would send him some girly flowers.'

Hooker nodded. 'OK. here's a buck then.'

'A buck! Say Lieutenant you're surely pushing the boat out. But then you always had a soft spot for the Captain.'

Hooker smiled. 'Tell you what, also get him a box of candy and write that it's from me.'

Thor

‘What candy shall I get?’

‘Something soothing for an ulcer...like acid drops!’

‘OK. Will do Lieutenant. Oh when I leave your office, do I show respect by also wiping my feet on the way out?’

The trash-can hit the door as it shut.

Sergeant Jugg turned the unmarked police car to drive slowly into the service alley running behind the bank parallel to Pine Street. Halfway along they passed two men dressed in Western Electric coveralls and hard-hats; they appeared to be doing maintenance in a small telephone unit. One familiar looking engineer was working at the top of a ladder propped against a telegraph pole which was directly opposite the side passageway linking the service alley into Pine Street. As they passed, one of the engineers looked up to acknowledge Hooker. The Lieutenant glanced in the car mirror. ‘That security door over there is the entrance to the bank’s rear yard, Freddie. Not much going to happen today, but thought you’d like to see where the fun should be tomorrow.’

He raised his eyebrows. ‘So that *was* that you up the ladder? ‘Are you Thor or

Stella today?'

'When I'm with you, I'm Stella of course.

Sergeant Jugg put his foot down on the throttle and headed for Brooklyn. Freddie took her hand. 'Looks like you're coming with us?'

'Of course ... I'm taking you home Freddie. Remember I'm in charge. Doctor's orders'

He leaned his head back. His shoulder was aching and he felt a wave of tiredness, but he also sensed his father's protection and his "*Psuhun from the North*" expressing a promise to his future; he felt content.

Freddie led Stella from the apartment elevator as Hooker and the Sergeant followed carrying bags.

Hooker called out, 'let me have your key Freddie, I'll open the door.'

'Thanks, but I would like Stella to do it,' he insisted.

He handed her the key as she tried to hide the pleasure crossing her face. She turned the key and pushed open the door. As he followed her in, he paused to hold his good hand up with the palm facing the room.

She hurried around the room, quickly taking in the paintings and his record collection. She looked out the French window, then paused to study the costume in the glass case.

'My Grandfather's,' he explained before she suddenly darted into the kitchen.

Hooker put down his boxes and moved over to stare at the paintings. He nodded his approval, quietly asking, 'who's the artist?'

'My Grandfather.'

The Sergeant stared over Hooker's shoulder at the pictures, gum clicking. 'Yup, lots of color,' he offered.

Hooker growled, 'if you took your shades off Toby they'd be even more colorful.'

Stella suddenly appeared at the kitchen doorway. 'You've got a lovely cooker Freddie ... at least you won't need another electrician.' She picked up her bag and disappeared, calling out, 'I can't wait to use it.'

The Sergeant winked. 'Have to watch her Freddie; she'll be moving in next.'

'That's very astute Toby,' agreed Hooker studying his wristwatch. 'We must be off. Freddie I need your phone number so to keep in touch. The Sergeant here will pick you up first thing in the morning, and then, hopefully, you should be able to finish your movie.'

'Can I get you a drink Lieutenant ... coffee ... beer?'

The Sergeant's eyes lit up. 'Ah beer!'

Hooker pushed him to the door. 'Come on Toby, we've got shoes to collect, and get my hair cut. You didn't remind me.' He tugged the Sergeant's untidy hair. 'And you could do with a cut Toby, my sister's starting to moan about both of us now.'

Stella hurried back into the room and handed over a note. 'Here's Freddie's telephone number, Lieutenant ... just in case!'

Hooker stared at her. 'Don't forget, no wandering around Brooklyn tonight playing pianos. Let's get those goons inside first.'

Her eyes widened as she blushed. 'How'd you—

Hooker muttered. 'Hooker knows all, young lady.' He opened the apartment door and pushed the sergeant out, paused and looked thoughtful at Freddie. 'When this is over, don't let this dame return to where ever she comes from, chain her up ... otherwise you'll regret it. Get my drift?'

He adjusted his hat and clicked the door shut behind him, Freddie suddenly felt drained. 'Home sweet home. Thank God!'

18

The Sting: Early next morning, at the hint of first light, Mercury appeared briefly in the east before sinking back. At the same time, Venus and Mars start to move away from their current alignment to which they wouldn't return for many years. With the dawn's promise of yet another warm day, the sun started to lift the blanket of mist slowly drifting across Manhattan. The inhabitants were already prepared for the last holiday of summer with the next day being Labor Day. It would be a quiet weekend in the city; highways without the usual heavy rush-hour traffic, making that morning's ride from Brooklyn so easy. As they drove over Brooklyn Bridge, Stella watched the private yachts and the small pleasure boats passing Governors Island as they headed for the distant Verrazano-Narrows Bridge; ferries already snaking back and forth taking day trippers to the funfairs on Coney Island. Liberty's torch suddenly appeared through the lifting mist to glitter in the morning sun; she loved it all.

Before leaving Manhattan at the end of her tour of duty, Stella had promised herself to walk over the Bridge. She felt an excitement that maybe now Freddie could walk with her, and then of course, she'll be going with him to see Guys and Dolls. Her day dreaming ended as Sergeant Jugg pulled into the service alley running behind the bank with the pretend Western Electric engineers still restoring a faulty line. The bank's rear security access was open and Hooker came out to greet them. Stella had sat in the front next to the Sergeant. She was dressed again in her coverall and as she opened her door to get out he noticed how her posture changed into Thor. She hurried over to an engineer who directed her further down the alley. Freddie becoming aware that not only was the alley sealed either end, but also the narrow walkway leading into Pines that hugged the bank's wing from where the suspect tunnelling was now taking place.

Hooker turned to Freddie and nodded towards the two parked trucks. 'Go and get yourself into the smaller truck.' The Sergeant drove the car further down to where Thor now waited by the telegraph pole. He turned his car sideways to block the side alley leading into Pines. Hooker returned back into the bank yard as Freddie entered the truck through its side sliding-door to find Lieutenant Carver perched on a stool next to a radio consul.

In the corner sat an engineer with head-cams intently tuning a radio dial. He glanced at the stranger but quickly turned to whack an angry insect that had taken a dislike to him. Carver pulled a stool over for the newcomer.

'How's the shoulder young man?'

'It's OK, Lieutenant ... I think I'll live.'

Carver nodded. 'Good. You have to understand that you ignore what's in this wagon. I understand Lieutenant Hooker said you were cleared for today's fun.'

Freddie didn't think he sounded convinced by Hooker's clearance assurance. 'Don't worry Lieutenant, I suspect you'll see my version of today's events before Spiegel does, and that'll be a first.'

Carver nodded. 'I understand Hooker involved you in his investigation right from the beginning. I could do with someone having your imagination in my department, would you consider it?'

Freddie shook his head. 'Thanks for the offer but I like what I do,' rubbing his shoulder, 'and even prepared to get shot for my art.' Carver chuckled as Freddie continued, 'tell me Lieutenant, what's happening?'

'Apart from the men here, we also have two of our men as engineers working on the exchange box outside the bank in

Pines sealing the front entrance. There's no way out for those inside. Western Electric has a special department that we liaise with, shall we say, for unusual jobs. The bank think they have a line problem and demanded it fixed before the end of the holiday period.' He growled to himself, 'they do have a problem but we created it. So the engineers were expected to be here. From the top of that pole we have a good view of the surrounding area ... the alleyway and the back-yard. The other truck is a rest room but to the casual onlooker, there appears to be only five engineers on site at one time, not the ten we do have.

Freddie nodded. 'I noticed the Lieutenant is in the bank yard.'

'It's important we're in there of course, but the bank doesn't know; can't trust their employees. The only security officer patrolling the bank this weekend happens to be one of Hooker's men.' He looked at his watch. 'We have several teams around the city awaiting my signal and then they'll move in fast.' He crossed his fingers. 'Months of hard work will be wrapped up. Lieutenant Hooker will have his local villains and I'll stop this loot run.'

He looked knowingly at Freddie. 'I had intended Thor to be at the docks, but the

Lieutenant requested that I use her here.'

The hours dragged as he waited in that truck with Hooker popping in occasionally for coffee from Carver's seemingly endless thermos. Freddie found himself reading the newspaper adverts over and over. The expectation was great but the waiting frustrating. Hooker was right: "Not like one of your movies Freddie, just a five minute reel of film".

His shoulder started to play up so he took extra tablets. Carver suggested he went for a stroll around the block which he gladly accepted if only to take his mind away from hum of the equipment; the irritating engineer still whacking the canny insect; surveillance wasn't for him, easier to pretend in a movie. As he walked he thought of Stella and the job she was doing as Thor. He had this omen she was in impending danger and it was going to go all wrong; how he wished the anxiety he felt would go away. He felt for a cigarette, the pack wasn't there. Damn. He had cut back on his smoking. He wanted to please her but he could do with one at that moment. He came to the corner of Pines and stood next to an employment agency window. He waited in the doorway to watch two engineer-agents supposedly working on the telephone cabinet built into the bank wall.

One looked across at him before glancing at his watch, making Freddie check his own. He decided to return as he didn't want to miss the show but suddenly heard a squeaky voice behind him singing...

'Ma n'atu sole, cchiù bello, oje ne'

O sole mio sta 'nfronte a te!'

Suddenly a meticulously dressed dwarf came skipping round the corner and bumped him; it was Dandy-Dandy Angelica carrying a large paper bag. The bag went flying but Freddie grabbed it with his good hand.

'Oh, mi dispiace signore,' squeaked the walking mannequin

For a moment Freddie panicked and tried to compose himself.

Dandy-Dandy stared at him, but suddenly broke into a laugh. 'No, No, Signore. I was happy and singing.' He swept off his hat, bowed and sang, 'O sole mio'. He replaced the hat, studied his reflection in the agency window and tweaked his tie-knot. He then smiled at Freddie who handed back the bag.

'Molte grazie signore.'

The dwarf held the bag high and skipped across the street in little jumps.

Freddie quickly turned as if to study the vacancies displayed outside the agency. If Dandy-Dandy had recognised him, it could have blown the whole operation. He watched the midget's window reflection as he walked up the steps. At the top he suddenly turned as if to stare across at Freddie. But he laughed and walked back down to the two engineers to gesture with the bag. Freddie couldn't believe what was happening as the two engineers pulled out a doughnut each. Then they all laughed as the dwarf skipped back up the steps. At the top step he turned and sang, 'O sole mio,' before entering the building. One engineer spoke into his mike before biting into the doughnut. Freddie suddenly felt hungry.

He crossed to the alley entrance where Thor's pigman from the docks was taking a break, drawing on a cigarette, rocking on his heels. He glared as Freddie approached, as if weighing him up through biased eyes.

Freddie nodded at the cigarette. 'Any chance, I've left mine behind?'

Pigman reluctantly pulled out his pack. Freddie gratefully took the offered cigarette and the man lit it with his own burning tip, he stared openly g through his strange droopy eyelids at the American Indian. The two men stood in silence for a while looking along the alley.

Pigman gestured with his cigarette at Freddie's sling. 'You were lucky the Sergeant was with you that morning, otherwise you wouldn't be enjoying one of my smokes.'

Freddie nodded, unsure of the man's tone. The man motioned along the alley with his burning cigarette. 'Why we have to have bloody broads in the team, God knows? This ain't dame's work,' his voice now more aggressive. 'I can't imagine why Carver has her here today, things could get hairy. When it gets tough, they get girlie and wanna to go home.' He laughed. 'Have you heard the story about—?'

Freddie felt his blood surging as he studied the man with his deep jawed face: features of an old hardened red-neck; a chauvinistic pigman. He thought the war had brought an end to that type of prejudice, but it was alive and well in Manhattan that weekend.

'OK,' he asked, 'how would you do undercover work in a woman's environment?'

The man shrugged. 'Sure they're useful for that or working in the office at base.' He scowled. 'Like doing the dishes—'

Freddie ground the half smoked cigarette into the gravel and walked away; the man's cigarette didn't taste so good. As he approached the truck, Hooker peered from the yard doorway and quickly beckoned him over. Freddie noticed Thor coming out from the second truck making for the Sergeant's car. What the man had just said seemed to make her vulnerable. Maybe he's right? Maybe she shouldn't be here? His stomach tightened.

Hooker put his finger to his lips and indicated, whispering, 'Come in and be quiet.'

Freddie quickly told him about Dandy-Dandy and the doughnuts. Hooker nodded and growled, 'yeah I heard, he must be acting as lookout. He wouldn't get his hands dirty in case he has to straighten his tie. This time I'll have him, he won't be skipping when I've dealt with him. Listen! If I shout *drop* ... then *drop ... no heroics!* This ain't some movie.'

Freddie quickly took his position in the corner, sensing the mounting tension. Hooker joined three blue-clad officers standing by the bank's rear wall. They continued to stare at the gravel. One man with head-cams knelt down with a listening pad, suddenly smiled and nodded. Hooker looked over to Freddie to give the thumbs up; his face animated

Freddie acknowledged the Lieutenant's excitement. He also noticed Carver was standing at the open gate. The engineer at the top of the ladder stared across as they watched the gravel. Freddie found the silence unnerving, the anxiety he had felt earlier intensifying; he tried to comfort his aching shoulder.

Suddenly they heard scraping, then occasional tapping ... muffled shouts. Hooker now had his gun out. The group of four men stared down at the gravel which began to sag and crack. They slowly backed off. Suddenly it collapsed with dust gushing from the sudden air pressure, followed by curses and coughing. A pair of grubby, blood stained hands shot out to grab the sides. Muffled shouts became louder. A dirt-covered head poked out coughing from the dust; the face bewildered, sweat poured into eyes trying to take in the unexpected daylight. He tried to pull his unwilling body through the hole. Hooker's men leapt forward, grabbed his arms and dragged him out. They pushed his face into the gravel. He shrieked with fear and tried to struggle, but Hooker pinned him down across the neck with his recently refurbished Allen Edmonds shoe; being careful of course not to scuff the highly polished leather. The click as cuffs snapped on unwilling wrists yanked behind a sweat-soaked vest. Hooker turned back to the hole and waited with his legs firmly apart. He stared into the hole with his .38 gripped tight in both hands. A second head appeared running with sweat. It jerked round at the sudden commotion, eyes red and bulging.

Hooker shouted, 'just try it José ... just give me an excuse, that's all I need.'

The head squealed with disbelief, 'HOOKER! ... WHAT THE HELL!'

He tried to turn back as Hooker screamed, 'OUT! ... NOW!' Rivera tried to pull away from grabbing hands but was roughly dragged out and flung unceremoniously to the ground; Hooker again enjoyed the careful pinning down with his shoe across the thick neck. They heard more shouting and scrambling with someone retreating back along the tunnel, followed by a sudden gun shot. Hooker looked across at Freddie. 'That'll be the other team going in from the front.' He leaned down to growl with bared teeth into the crumpled face of José Rivera pressed into the gravel. 'You're trapped like rats on a sinking ship, Rivera.'

The two protesting men were hauled roughly to their feet. Rivera snarled,' I'll make you for this Hooker.' His expression looked as though he had just spilt his cream; Hooker looked as though he'd just discovered his.

Hooker took out a cigarette. 'Guess you could do with one of these Rivera.'

Rivera nodded. 'Yeah.' he gasped.

Hooker put one between his own lips and lit up, staring at Rivera. He blew a smoke curl into the man's dripping face. 'Well you'll have to have a word with the governor of the penitentiary. I hear he's quite obliging to long term guests.'

Rivera spat at Hooker who flicked his head away. 'I'll get you Hooker, you bastard, see if I don't.'

Hooker smiled. 'Well before you get *put away*, you and me, or should that be, you and I? are going to have a little chat about your partner Joey-Joey Edwards, I haven't seen him around lately. I quite liked him: quiet and clever type, didn't like leaving his dabs messing up my evidence.' He nodded at his men. 'Take him away boys. Not too rough. He's like me, very sensitive at being touched.'

Rivera glared. 'Typical of you Hooker,' he snarled, 'if you knew we were digging this tunnel, why couldn't you have got us before we started? My back's hurting—'

'What took you so long Rivera? I'm starving, and look ... I've broken a finger nail.'

The two wretched men were dragged from the yard, shouting and blaming each other.

Hooker winked at Freddie and turned to one officer. 'Stay here and make sure no more try to come out this way.' He put his hand on Freddie's shoulder as they moved to the gate. 'That worked a treat

Freddie, they had no idea Lieutenant Carver altered the basement plans. Hey, I didn't realise Rivera had back problems. I'll send in some liniment for him.' He chuckled, his eyes glinting. 'Now that's what I would call a great movie ending ... Your mister Spiegel will love—'

The sudden shattering of glass and shouts made them run to the gate. A shot rang out, the man on the top ladder yelled, 'LOOK OUT!' Hooker charged out the yard followed by Freddie who immediately thought of Thor with that gun-fire. A heavy egg-head pounded from the passageway. Sergeant Jugg darted to head him off but caught his foot on the ladder which threw him against the wall. The man spun round and rammed his gun against the Sergeant's head ... w*ith one movement of the wrist, Thor sent her hard hat spinning across the alley to smash into the man's wrist. The gun jerked with the slug ricocheting down the alleyway. She lurched forward and brought him to the ground. Before the others could react, he jumped to his feet, grabbed the gun and swung it sideways at her head. She ducked and threw him across the car. The impact smashed the windshield. As he slid to the ground she screamed and jumped on his back, grabbing his arms ... the cuffs snapped with the man screaming in pain* *from his dislocated shoulder and the shattered wrist.*

Freddie started to run towards her, but Carver restrained him, shouting 'don't interfere!'

Thor was on one knee, her heart pounding from the effort. The Sergeant pulled her up. Freddie watched the smiling pigman walk over and try to pat her on the back; she shrugged him away; *a powerful victory for her!*

The Sergeant picked up his hat and shades, stood awhile, scratching his head, staring at the gap where his windshield should have been. Hooker ignored all this and hurried down the walkway to the shouting coming from Pines, wanting to be the first to grab Dandy-Dandy's collar and dangle him kicking and squealing.

Carver indicated with a nod of his head for her to go into the truck as the technician came out holding a squashed insect between his index finger and thumb. He grinned with delight. 'Got it,' he growled and dropped it on the ground. Having missed all the drama, he went to look at the Sergeants car.

Freddie followed her in. 'If he had caught you with that blow to the head he could have killed you.'

'Freddie I'm OK!'

'For one moment I thought I'd lost you.

I've had this bad feeling all day that you were in danger. Jesus Stella, I can't believe what you did. You even frightened *me* when you screamed.'

She slowly shook her head, anger in her eyes. 'At that moment I wanted him dead.' She then laughed as if from relief. 'But listen to me Freddie. I'm still good at Hella. I haven't lost my skill. If my hat had been a real disc it would have taken his hand off. I wanted that thug dead.'

He tried to cheer her up. 'There's a lesson for me, never get into an argument with you, I wouldn't stand a chance.'

She tried to smile. 'I was so angry. I suddenly saw what happened to Charlie. I wanted to kill him. I wanted revenge.' Her body shook and she rubbed her arm. 'The director was right! I should have listened to him. I shouldn't have come.'

'What do you mean, you shouldn't have come? Who's the Director?'

'Oh it's a long story.' She sat down. 'I don't think I can do this job any more. What happened out there frightened me. A while back I would have loved it.' She grabbed his hand. 'Since I met you my values have changed. Listen to me, I want other things now ....'

One mile away in Brooklyn, Sonny Pretsy, Chief Security Officer for the

Manhattan & Western Bank, returned home with his family after a trip to Coney Island to be met at his front door by two plain-clothed officers; by the look on their faces he quickly realised the planned family trip for the Labor Day Monday wasn't going to happen.

And about the same time, down in a basement, behind the half glazed door: "Technical Research Unit", the phone rang. Mike Grosse lifted the receiver and nodded as he recognised the voice at the other end. He re-arranged the jack-plugs: the PBX in the bank started flashing; phones started ringing throughout the deserted bank. He grinned as he picked up his paper and flask; he was going home to spend Labor Day with his family after all.

Hooker entered the truck without a word and picked up his newspaper. He suddenly said. 'Well done young lady that was text book. You've got a lifelong friend in the Sergeant, and you Freddie have a great ending for your movie, but the problem is your Mister Spiegel will argue the public won't buy it, "that don't happen in the real world." Oh yes, I've had a word with the singing dwarf: I've booked him for the Precinct Christmas concert, special rates.'

As he turned to go, he looked back at

her, his expression darkened. 'Hey, you realise you'll be in trouble with Western Electric and the police department.'

Her face dropped ... 'Why? ... WHAT NOW?'

'The hat has a dent, and what's the Captain going to say about Toby's windshield?' With that he roared with laughter and stepped out the door.

Just then Carver entered muttering to himself, smirking and kissing a twenty dollar bill just handed to him by an amenable Hooker.

'You'll be pleased to know we've picked them all up in one go. Oh I know they'll re-group, but it'll take time, and next time we'll be waiting.'

She asked, 'how about Europe?'

'We haven't heard back yet. At least our end is busted.' He smiled at her and rubbed his hands. 'Your help in all this has been appreciated—'

Freddie interrupted. 'She frightened me to death; I don't want to see that again. But tell me Lieutenant, what was that breaking glass and how did that thug get into the passageway if the front was blocked?'

'Just above the passageway, there's a special fire escape window from the bank. Hit it with a sledgehammer outside and it won't break, but hit it with your fist from the inside and it shatters outwards just like the Sergeant's windshield. That's how he got out.

Carver picked up his belongings. 'I suggest you go home now and we'll debrief first thing in the morning. I think you've done enough today. We've got a replacement car coming through and the Sergeant will run you both home. That business outside was pure text book. Good day.' With that passing remark, he hurried out.

Freddie was amused. 'Do they always say ... '*text book?'*

She kissed him. 'That's their only way of giving praise.'

Just then a car pulled up outside and the Sergeant blasted its horn.

She took his arm. 'You heard the Lieutenant, we're going home.'

As they got into the car she asked, 'Toby I need to pop back to Tompkins square to get some things from my apartment; I'm moving in!'

He slipped a wad of fresh Wrigley into his mouth, grinned and winked at her in his mirror before pushing his foot hard down on the gas.

After Tompkins they drove over Brooklyn Bridge. Freddie had his head back against the seat, his eyes closed. She had her arm through his, studying his face, reflecting on past events: that night at the concert ... She shook her head, crazy thoughts. She moved closer to rest her head against his shoulder. That moment of satisfaction she had felt with her uncontrolled violence against that thug; frightening: "*one day in your career you may lose it and step over that threshold, that's the time you should pack up and move on ... you'll recognise that moment*"; she knew that moment had arrived.

Thor

19

A letter from the UK: Hooker slowly read Captain Andrew Travers-Jones untidy scrawl:

"Dear Sherman,
Super to chat again old friend. Gosh I miss those exciting days and sorry I was a bit vague, but you know how it is, walls have ears and all that nonsense. Remember, you got this from an anonymous source. Yes your hunch was right: there was a female with the code name 'Ferret'. Her real name was Marie-Élise Lefèvre, born in France, educated in the UK early 30's and as a Jew fled back here when France was invaded. Spoke fluent English and French of course. Lost her family as they couldn't get away in time. Like many of them, she wanted revenge so joined up. Found herself recruited in the SOE. Did two drops, distinguished herself, awarded the Croix de Lorraine. Sounds quite a girl. Several did go off the rails post war, only natural I suppose. You'll be interested in this: she converted to the Catholic faith in '46 when she became a GI bride marrying a Sergeant Joseph Walker, Army Corps of

Engineers and moved to Chicago when he was demobbed later that year. Before the war he worked for the Tucker motor manufacturer as a vehicle designer. So it's possible he returned there. That's it!

Hope this helps and of course this means she settled in the good old USA for her sins. Sorry the photo enclosed is a bit fuzzy; I managed to get a copy from her war time ident-card. Is she like your Ferret? Must say it's all exciting and in a way I envy you.

Had a call from mater and it appears she's coming down this weekend. I think she's feeling guilty she's never been introduced to my pigs. She reckons she's bringing her wartime gas mask! Damn cheek! Keep in touch Old Boy.

ANDY.

PS: Remember your promise, not a word. Not me so much but could finish my friend's career in Whitehall!! Once read, prefer you burn! Like old times, eh!

Despite the poor quality of the photograph, the young face was definitely that of the dead woman. It was a good feeling as his hunch had paid off. He wanted to pick up the phone and tell Carver, but hesitated; he couldn't tell anyone. How frustrating! But there was one thing he could do to close the case.

He asked Leo to put in a call to his cousin Henry, a desk sergeant in the Chicago police. He couldn't reveal the full details to his cousin, only a basic background check, saying, 'it was unofficial!'

A few hours later Hooker was sitting down to a meal at home when the phone rang ... it was his cousin.

'... Joseph Walker was easy to trace as he's a descendant of James Walker, one of the pioneers who built Chicago in the last century. When he was demobbed in '46, he returned from Europe with a French bride called Marie –Elise; that was the name you gave me I think? Yes? Well they moved into an expensive area called Walker's Grove at a huge family house he inherited just before the war. Rather sad for her, because a few months later he had an accident falling down the stairs and broke his neck. It appears there was some question mark on how he tripped, but that was not resolved so the coroner left it open. Terrible for her of course, only just married, in a strange country.'

Hooker's pulse surged. 'Does she still live there?'

'No. Sold up and moved away, probably returned back to France. I guess she would have been a wealthy young widow from the sale of that house.'

That call became the closure of the

Ferret story: she would be buried and recorded with just a number in a file to gather dust in an official basement. Despite what she became, he still felt a sense of sadness for her; but he could never break his promise to Andy!

Later that evening he went into the back-yard for a smoke. As he lit his cigarette, he put the match to Andy's letter which symbolised yet another legacy from the war. A few days later he attended her funeral: just him, the minister and an official together with the gravedigger. To their surprise he laid one lily on her coffin: at least she deserved the flower of France for her bravery in the war. He refused a lift from the official as he needed to be on his own.

The next two weeks passed by quickly with many arrangements to be made. Stella proving her worth as Freddie's secretary, the draft script delivered to Sam Spiegel's office the day before his return. Then, with much soul searching, and a few private tears for the lost past, she handed in her badge and her .38.

20

Brooklyn Bridge: Mr and Mrs. Vermeer-Maliseet emerged from City Hall with the promised rain starting its gentle fall. Freddie opened his umbrella before they crossed to the road that sloped up and onto the gantry crossing the Bridge.

On the roadway below them, traffic swished through the gathering puddles. The newlyweds deliberately took their time, the umbrella held tight, the light rain making Stella feel special and the walk romantic. She knew she would never forget her first ever walk over the bridge with Freddie now her husband. Even Governor's island seemed to convey its blessing through the rain. As they reached halfway, Stella suddenly paused to watch the transatlantic liner Queen Mary as it passed under Verrazano-Narrows Bridge on its homeward run back across the Atlantic to Southampton.

Freddie felt her body tense as she gripped his arm tighter. 'What's the matter?' he whispered.

She stared at the distant liner as memories flooded back. 'Freddie, how strange, but Charlie and I went to Europe for our honeymoon on the Queen Mary. And there she is.'

Thor

He held her tighter.

She wiped her eyes and looked at him. ‘It’s OK sweetheart. I know it’s telling me to go for it, start a new journey. He’s telling me that you will look after me.’ She anxiously studied his face. ‘You will look after me won’t you Freddie?’

His reply was droned by a distant farewell blast from the liner. Just then the rain suddenly stopped and the sun peeped through the breaking clouds.

He nodded. ‘Look even the sun is telling you that you’re going to be OK. And yes of course, I’ll look after you.’ As they watched the liner disappear, he asked, ‘I suppose today is where you also say goodbye to Thor?’

She remained silent for a moment before turning her head to look at him with a mysterious grin. ‘You must listen to me when I say, I have another use for Thor, but you’ll have to wait and see.’

On the roadway below, a car suddenly pulled up and two men got out. They climbed the iron maintenance steps leading up onto the overhead walkway to greet the surprised newlyweds, waving a bottle of champagne and four glasses.

Stella cried, ‘Lieutenant, Toby. What are you doing here?

Hooker chuckled. ‘We’re toasting the happy couple of course.’

Freddie shook his head. 'But we kept it secret. We didn't want any fuss. How did you know we were here?'

'Well you can't keep secrets from Carver.'

Sergeant 'Toby' Jugg broke in, 'Sherman for Christ's sake, pop the cork, I'm thirsty!'

As they raised glasses, Hooker pulled out his newspaper and asked Freddie, 'today's movie question Freddie. "B.D. asks romantic astronomical question to end the '42 movie before captions roll."?'

'Heaven's above Lieutenant, give it a rest, I'm on my honeymoon. Like all good movies, you'll have to wait until the end of the story.'*

Stella suddenly turned to look back at the Verrazano-Narrows Bridge: just drifting mist, no Queen Mary, and no ghost from the past.

She felt a sense of release!

Thor

Part Two

THOR and "Project Charlie"

Thor

Thor

19

Thor's Odyssey to ChompChomp: Stella nervously telephoned to tell her parents about their marriage. Her mother cried of course and asked to speak with Freddie. He then spoke to her father and the conversation turned to fishing so she knew Pop was happy: she guessed her letters home had paved the way.

Freddie then made his call home and spoke to his father Joey and his mother Sibylla. His father asked to speak to Stella.

'One evening I dreamt my son had caught the spirit of Psuhun in his hand. She came to me with dark green eyes and hair to match the sunrise. I feel there's been a long sadness for her but now happiness. One day came tingling on the right side of my face, and I sensed my son had placed his fingers on your injury.' Stella touched her right cheek. He then surprised her with, 'I know my son's body is now healing because of your presence.' Freddie had kept quiet about the shooting!

Her next call would be very difficult as she spoke to Charlie's parents.

A cool Sam Spiegel rang Freddie trying not to sound too pleased with the finished script; to Freddie this meant that Sam was pleased. He commissioned Freddie to draft a more detailed version with various changes he wanted; Sam of course, had to have the final word. Freddie knew that, *if* the film came to realisation, there would be many more Spiegel changes. Spiegel was riding a success wave after Waterfront; he needed to catch that enthusiasm with backers waving their dollars and the punters filling seats.

Stella was amazed at the speed with which Freddie's shoulder was healing and he was given the OK to remove the sling long before the doctor had indicated at the hospital. She was also aware how her own scar was fading; she so wanted to absorb his beliefs; she so wanted to be his *Psuhun* from the North.

They managed to get time away and caught the overnight train to Minnesota to visit her parents. It was an emotional visit over two days, but a great success and then straight up to Maine to visit his folk. Before they left, Freddie mysteriously asked her father to give his daughter one brand new dollar which he then insisted she put safely away. Her father also handed Stella a parcel that she had requested from her uncle Vida; this time it was her turn to be mysterious.

On the long journey north Stella was restless, unsure. However when the two tired travellers got off at the Loaders-

Crossing Halt, she was welcomed with open arms by his parents, Joey and Sibylla

Stella felt immediate warmth for his father: tall, upright and with a firm handshake; his deeply lined face and umber-brown eyes conveyed tenderness. She loved it when he smiled and placed his hand to her face, which he described as, 'pleasing.' She felt a strange spiritual generosity from him, making her relaxed and comfortable; this is what she had experienced from his son; she knew she would get on well with Joey.

They drove through the small county town of Loader-Crossing where there appeared to be some sort of police activity. The hour-long journey home first took them across continuous Downs, and then through miles of forest she had read about on her visit that day to the Rose Room, described in the old manuscripts as: "*The Uninterrupted Forests of Maine*". Twice they were flagged down by a parked patrol car but recognising Joey, the cops nodded and waved him on.

Joey growled, 'nothing better to do, ah guess.'

Eventually they turned away from the tarmac road onto a gravel track. Nailed on the first tree was a mail-box: "Wikuwam" with its red flag up. Freddy collected the mail and they continued for half a mile before pulling into their homestead yard.

Wikuwam was a shingle-roof, white-painted clapperboard frame-house which Joey had cleverly built on two levels. It sat back into an embankment that followed the curve of the passing track. This embankment helped to protect against the winter's north-easterly blow. Its deep, colonial porch created a welcome shade from the summer heat, and essential net-screens that covered all the windows. The second-level extension continued further back beyond the ground floor onto the shoulder of the embankment. The house was surrounded by pitch pine, hornbeam, maple and unusual white birch trees known locally as "Lady of the Woods". A snow-plough blade stood ready at the side of the yard for a quick attachment to a truck, and snow-guard strips ran across the roof as a reminder of changeable weather in the coming months. A narrow, covered walkway projected from the house and led to an open wood-shed protected from inclement weather by a deep overhanging shingle-roof, supported by pine stanchions at each corner. Inside this shed, a small, wiry man of about Joey's age was busy splitting stove-length logs and stacking them into neat cords; Stella loved the smell of freshly-split logs. The man wore a chequered lumberjack shirt with the sleeves rolled up his dark muscular arms. He wore weathered jeans, and the traditional Bean-leather boots. The bowery cap was turned backwards to shade his neck when working outside from the sun that could be fierce that time of year. An old mackinaw coat hung on a metal spike hammered into one of the corner stanchions; this spike also held a double-bit axe, and to the visitor its blade looked very sharp and lethal.

His name was Smokey, and he rushed forward with a wide, shy grin to give Freddie an excited bear hug, quietly murmuring, 'welcome home lad.' He turned and offered Stella a respectable handshake, adding a slight bow; seemingly a man with old world manners and few words. His round leathery face was covered in sweat and wood dust.

Attached to the other side of the house was the essential barn. Later a proud Joey would take her down under the barn to see his bark-lined root-cellar, now being stocked with the new season's crop. The whole ambience of the barn came with the sweet smells of horse leather, greased iron tools, creosote and raw vegetables. This took her back into her childhood just outside Malmo in Sweden. It was this moment she felt a sense of destiny as she and Freddie had shared a similar upbringing, although thousands of miles apart: their meeting was surely written.

The interior of the house had a defined European touch that reflected Sibylla's background, obviously influencing Freddie's perception and taste and Stella found it very homely. That evening there was an air of mysterious anticipation from Freddie and his parents over the next morning's visit to ChompChomp. This was Joey's log cabin hidden deep in the forest beyond. She knew this was where Joey had predicted her coming to his son, but wondered what they had in store for her? She was getting excited.

After the evening meal, the two sat alone on the porch and Stella started to write a letter home to her parents:

"Dear Mom and Pop,

It has been such a long day but we arrived here safe and in good spirits. We were met at the station by Freddie's mother Sibylla and his Father Joey. They have made me so welcome; you remember how nervous I was? And their home is just lovely, reminding me of Uncle Vidal's house. Isn't it amazing that Joey also has a log cabin just like uncle. They call it "ChompChomp" and even a root store under the barn here! It's almost as if I've been here before - very strange feeling. This evening we've been getting folks from around, popping in to give the new Bride a once over. I feel just like a princess!!!

Tomorrow we're all going up to ChompChomp, but they seem to be planning something up there – oh dear?

Joey has a life time friend here called Smokey who works for him. He seems part of their family and he's also Maliseet. He is very shy but so courteous to me. Oh dear someone else is popping in, I'll continue later..."

They stood as a black Chevrolet pulled up in front of the veranda with the sign of "County Sheriff" on its door.

Freddie commented, 'I knew he wouldn't take long.'

The Sheriff had to pull himself from the car. He waved and pushed his khaki-colored Stetson to the back of his head and boomed, 'Freddie, good to see yah. Come to look the bride over.'

He heaved himself onto the veranda and shook hands before turning to study the new bride. The Sheriff was a bearded giant of a man, standing head and shoulders above the many; his holster-belt showing considerable strain round his rotund stomach. With his other hand he clutched a bundle of handbills which he dumped on a chair.

Freddie put his arm around Stella. 'Stella this is Sammy. Sammy Polanski, County sheriff for our sins.'

The man gripped her hand and continued to hold it. 'Folks round here been saying yah quite a looker, prettiest gal in Maine they reckon. An' they're sure am right Marm. Ah' just had to come an' take a look myself. Yar's a lucky man young Freddie.'

Stella was glad the light was fading as she was starting to blush.

'Where's Joey, ah' want a word with him,' he growled.

'Right behind you Sheriff, got you covered, so don't move.'

They shook hands. 'As ah' was a-passing, ah' thought ah'd drop in to see catch up with Freddie here an' see if ya'll goin' up to ChompChomp?'

Joey nodded. 'Sure, tomorrow, come first light. Thinking of joining us for a spot of hunting?'

The Sheriff shook his head. 'Ah'd like that ... but heck no!' He glanced towards Stella but looked back at Joey and lowered his voice. 'We gotta couple of armed nasties ... tried a bank raid down south in Loaders-Crossing this morning an' failed, but they got away. They winged a passerby who'll live, but they don't know that. Probably thinks he's dead, and so that makes them kinda dangerous, ah' guess. Abandoned their car when they ran outta' gas. According to the car's direction they must have been headin' east, away from here. Pinched another wagon an' so they're probably miles from our area by now ... nothin' to concern yah folks about.'

Freddie glanced at Stella, even in the half light he could see Thor in her eyes and was amused by the Sheriff talking low as not to alarm her.

'Just keep yah eyes peeled Joey. If yah see anythin', yah can always get us by using the fire-tower radio near ChompChomp.'

He went to leave but not before reassuring the visitors. 'All was OK! 'It's nothin' to fret yahselves with! They're outta our neck o' woods; someone else's problem!' He turned to go but remembered the fliers. 'Here Joey, take these an' hand them round to the folks 'bout here. Only few days now to the darn election, last minute fling with these fliers. Otherwise ah'd be outta job an' lost.'

They waved goodbye and Stella held one of the fliers up to the porch light. She giggled. 'Hey! Listen Freddie...'she read the flier out loud, as if making a proclamation: *"County Sheriff Election! Re-elect SAM POLANSKI! Sleep secure in yah beds folks! Remember - SAM's yah MAN!"'* She shouted to his car as it disappeared back along the track, 'Oh Sam Polanski, I'd vote you in as President with that slogan!' She laughed excitedly and flung her arms round Freddie to kiss him.

Later in bed, Freddie commented on her obvious excitement with the Sheriff's visit. 'Do you miss your days as Thor? Do you wish you were back with the FBI?'

'No,' was her firm reply as she snuggled closer, 'and Freddie listen to me, Thor still has a lot of schemes up her sleeve.' She went quiet and did some thinking. 'Freddie, what on earth made you take that attaché case and not report it? You must have been crazy. You could have gotton into a hell of a lot of trouble. You saw a homicide and you messed around with evidence.'

'Yeah, I've often think about that. I guess Sam was putting me under pressure and I could see a great story there. But you're right, I was mad. But hey, it worked out in the end. After all Rivera's doing twenty years in the pen, and if Hooker had taken him when he started tunnelling then he would have only got ten years for attempted burglary, but letting him be arrested on the Bank's property, then it became an actual entry making it federal, so he got his just deserts.'

'You were lucky it was Hooker who took the call. Anybody else would have nailed you. Imagine if it had been someone like that nasty pig agent. Hooker has a reputation of sailing close to the wind.'

'He told me he never breaks the rules or even bends them. He might make them curve occasionally.'

'Oh yeah! And your statement?'

'He dictated and I typed. It read well, even I believed it. Hooker told me that as one of the Angelica brothers confessed to accidently killing Broccento, then my part wouldn't even come into it. I think the Lieutenant fancied himself as a writer.'

'Oh Freddie. From now on I'm keeping an eye on you. But I'll tell you one thing—'

'Oh?'

'If it was Thor she would have nailed you.'

'Never!'

'Oh No?' came her tetchy reply.

'At least Rivera got his just deserts ... years to think about it. Hooker was aggrieved he couldn't pin Edwards's disappearance on him. Bet he won't let that drop, and I bet he's frustrated about the identity of the Ferret.'

'Why frustrated.'

'We'll never know who she was. Surprised he didn't follow that up, you know what he's like, won't let anything go.'

She went quiet for a moment. 'You're right, he'd never let that go and that's why I reckon he does know. Just a feeling I have.'

'What makes you say that?'

'The ambiguous way he tied up all the loose ends at the coroner's court. I can read the Lieutenant like a book and I think he was doing the right thing; whatever that could mean. Only a feeling and I could be wrong of course.'

'Changing the subject, don't forget to take your father's one dollar bill up to ChompChomp tomorrow ... very important.'

'You're being most mysterious, husband Vermeer.'

'And you are with that parcel you want to give Joey.'

'ChompChomp is the perfect place to give it. Oh Freddie I'm so excited, because tomorrow we're going to be where your father told you to wait for me. And you did wait for me, didn't you?'

After a pause she added, 'I really like Smokey. He seems, well, he seems a true friend to your family ... and he has manners ... he's a real gent!'

'Yes. He's been around all my life of course. Lives up the road from here, got no family that I know of. They were at school together and Joey said that Smokey hardly ever turned up for class. He only appeared at the start of each term to sign on as required by the State. When I was into scrapes as a lad, he would sit me on his knee, always having the answers to my problems. OK, not much education maybe, but he seemed so wise. That's when I first learnt that wisdom doesn't necessary come from books. I've met the most educated at times and usually they turn out to be the most ignorant and foolish.' He chuckled. 'He reckons any fool can run a country, but it takes fast thinking and rapid feet to catch and pluck a chicken. He still wears that old cap of his. Don't think I've ever seen him without it. He's always claimed that's where he kept his savings. Safer than a bank he reckoned. When I left to go to New York he gave me some advice: "If you end up in the so called big time, be wary of the banks lad, they like to gamble, not with their own money ... it'll be yours until it runs out!'

She suddenly said, 'I've been thinking ... well, Thor's been thinking.'

'Oh dear, and what has Thor been thinking?'

'If she was being pursued and run out of gas, and had to abandon the car, she would turn the car round to point in the opposite way to where she was really heading, to confuse her pursuers into the wrong direction. If Thor's right, then that means they're heading back in this direction ... not away ... back here.'

'No sweetheart, the Sheriff knows what he's talking about. Tell Thor to go to sleep, she has a big day tomorrow.'

'What should I wear tomorrow?'

'Go as Thor. We're going-a-hunting.'

'Then I shall wear my bandana?'

Freddie laughed, leaned over and switched off the light.

**

The next morning they were on the road by 6am. Joey and Sibylla had already left taking groceries and camping gear. Stella and Freddie followed with Smokey driving his one-tonne flat-bed across the barrens, now changing into mauve from the ripening blueberries. Micmac Indian pickers were already out stacking wooden boxes along the roadside, preparing for the seasonal blueberry harvest. Mexican casuals started to unroll white marker tapes to indicate the area for that coming day's harvest. The early sun was already casting her orange fingers across the rolling landscape. Stella couldn't help but be spellbound by its raw, fragile beauty. She rolled her window down, refreshing her senses from the smell of the earthy humus, still damp from the overnight drizzle and now beginning to warm; scent from tall clumps of pinkish-white, meadowsweet and orange tiger-lilies growing in clumps along the roadside. They suddenly turned and drove through a dense forest of birch with its scent of crushed apples from the abundance of the wild, pink rosa-rogosa roses. They followed the trail Joey had cleared earlier of fallen branches brought down by a recent storm. Smokey unexpectedly swung away from the track to splash through spring-water bubbling up through the ground. He finally stopped by a fast flowing tributary of the Penobscot River. The intrigued Stella watched as the two men pulled out a birchbark canoe hidden behind some bushes, letting it slide into the river before hitching to a branch.

***

Thor

She later continued her letter: *"...it was all so mysterious because Freddie made me get into the canoe with Smokey. I was in the front and Smokey sat in the rear. Freddie just smiled and pushed us off. He called out something about seeing me later, blew a kiss and got back into Smokey's wagon and drove off. I asked Smokey but he had his permanent grin under his bowery cap and told me to start paddling. It was all so mysterious and lovely, just like being back with Uncle Vidal. I felt safe with Smokey and boy was he good with that canoe, especially with the speed of that strong current"*.

Before they started paddling, Smokey leaned forward to quietly whisper, 'Miss Stella, the hour is early and the forest giant is still asleep, which we must respect. As we paddle, you have to concentrate and listen to him: it is the poetry of nature that I want you to hear, and be aware of as he starts to awaken. I would often take Freddie as a boy along this same water to listen and to learn. This morning I promised him I would take you on that same journey. I will guide the canoe and as you paddle you must concentrate and let your heart be your ears.'

She whispered back her promise, and as

she concentrated, she could sense the silence of a sleeping forest cathedral. In the distance came the subtle sounds of trees beginning to stir, the occasional snap of a twig, a sudden rustling in the canopy hanging above them from the gentle movement of air, as if the giant was breathing. A distant branch would rub against another, its groaning sound as if the giant had just yawned and stretched. The lapping of water against the canoe as if he was now licking his dry lips. The unexpected snap and crash of a falling branch made the giant jump; a sudden gust, making the overhead trees sway and stretch out their branches as if embracing the early intruders. Then the sun broke through the mist as if he had suddenly opened his eyes to see them in his cathedral. Nearby came the sudden sharp whistling from a black-cap chickadee warning of strangers. A sudden snapping of twigs and the distant rumble from a moose calling as if to make the canoe gently pitch.

"...I thought I was in heaven. It was so magical paddling through the forest with the sun breaking through the mist; the air so fresh and clean; and that early morning smell of wild sage; sweet oily odor from spice bushes; the birch trees

starting to wake and stretch. Wow!! But where was my Freddie, what was he up to? After a time we suddenly came round a bend as the river widened into a small lake called ChompChomp. There was Freddie standing on a wooden jetty with Joey and Sibylla. Behind them stood the log cabin set back into a clearing. It was so picturesque with smoke from the chimney and the nearby camp fire. Joey helped me from the canoe, quietly greeting me with words I didn't understand. But because of that special journey with Smokey, I felt so peaceful, wanting to hold Freddie but they kept us separate and we walked into the clearing where two small stone circles had been set. In the centre of each circle was a pile of split wood where Freddie and I had to stand side by side. It was then I realised it was to be a simple, symbolic wedding ceremony as a gesture to me; what a lovely idea and that explained the mystery. Later I understood why Smokey took me up the river as the bride must arrive by canoe to be greeted by the groom's father; the groom waiting.

There was me dressed in my old Tee shirt as Thor, but somehow it didn't matter. Sibylla draped me with a beautiful wrap covered in small colorful beads that was very old and passed down over the years, bride to bride. She asked me to remove my yellow bandana so she could place a beaded band around my head and push a symbolic eagle feather into it. Around my neck Freddie hung a necklace they call wampum, made of copper and brass rings with hanging stones, shells and carved bone beads. Sibylla handed one for me to hang around Freddie. I tried not to laugh as he looked so cute. Whilst this was going on, Smokey played a beautiful lament on a flute; he plays so well. Next, Joey filled a jug with water from the river and poured it over our hands to wash away our past single lives. The water was then poured over our joined hands for our shared life ahead. Freddie took a burning stick from the camp fire and lit the wood in his stone circle, and then I did the same with mine. When the two fires were burning well, Sibylla sprinkled sage and sweet grass into the flames, and then Joey pushed the two fires together to bring our future lives as one. He read from an ancient parchment which sounded so beautiful even though of course, I didn't understand. Next they named me "Possesom" which means little star; I was so moved. I then realised what the dollar bill you gave me was for; it was my symbolic dowry from you, pop, to Freddie's father. You will love this pop,

traditionally your new son-in-law now has to spend the first year hunting for you. Ha Ha!
Then Freddie handed me a posy of wild flowers before we kissed. It was over and we were man and wife in their tradition.
Oh how I wish you both could have been there. Mind you I cried on your behalf mom. I was so happy and felt so honored to be accepted into their heritage with my own name too. It seemed the right time to offer my parcel to Joey. He was amazed and mystified as he had never seen or heard of a Hella disc. I promised to teach him later after the feast Sibylla had prepared; no wonder they had left so early that morning. I will probably finish this letter when back home ..."

***

She would never forget Smokey's love of the forest and the privilege of sharing it with her; understanding what Freddie meant when he said, "Smokey was special".

What Stella decided not to write, were the events that happened later at their wedding feast?

Freddie sat fishing and watching Stella teach Joey and Smokey the techniques of throwing the Hella. Joey had felt the smoothness of the disc by running his fingers across the surface, holding it up sideways to examine closely the slight concave curve. He let it rest in his palm absorbing its weight. He heard Stella explaining about the round edge that could be ground down to slice through an object; or left round it would even break a bone.

He watched his mother Sibylla as she busied herself preparing the evening supper over the camp fire and at that moment the outside world didn't exist. He felt relaxed away from the pressures of Sam, enjoying the way Stella and his father were bonding; he loved the way she had one arm around his father's shoulders and the other arm gripping his hand as she demonstrated the flowing movement of spinning the disc. Occasionally they would laugh as the disc flew off course: was it that long ago when he first clapped eyes that morning on the street-girl called Thor in Hooker's precinct? Now here she was as his wife, laughing and having fun with his father at ChompChomp where Joey had predicted her arrival all those years before; who would have believed it? He watched as Smokey strode out sixty paces to place a beer can on a rock. Stella ran her hand around the disc feeling the edge, judging the weight. She quickly glanced over to Freddie before leaning backwards, rapidly swinging her arm forward. The disc spun from her hand, seeming to streak in a downward curve, lifting upward by force of the air pressure under its concave shape to strike the can which burst with a hiss.

The cheer from the watchers echoed through the trees. Sibylla clapped her hands and called, 'supper's ready!' As they walked over to the fire Smokey suddenly turned his head sharply and looked at Joey with questioning eyes. He whispered, 'did you hear that Joey? That was no animal.'

Joey nodded. 'Have a look Smokey.'

Stella later commented to Freddie, 'Smokey just disappeared. I couldn't believe it. One minute he was standing next to me, and then he'd gone. Not a sound.'

Freddie looked at his father. 'What's the problem Joey? Where's Smokey gone?'

'There's a-nothing to worry about my son. Come let's eat, I'm hungry. My new daughter has built up an appetite in me.' He turned to look sadly at Stella. 'I don't want you to return to New York, I want you to stay forever and throw your Hella discs with me.'

She smiled at him. 'And I have something I want to do back in New York.

I'm keeping a promise for someone.'

He understood not to ask.

Sibylla waved a spoon at him. 'You've got all those logs to cut for the coming winter, no time for spinning discs.'

They all laughed but a sudden angry shout made them jerk round. The voice came from a heavy-built man who stumbled into the clearing with a shot-gun. Sibylla shrieked and Freddie grabbed Stella. Another man followed gripping a belly-gun. He suddenly dropped onto one knee as if exhausted. Their faces were drawn, unshaven and their clothes torn and covered with mud ... there was no mistaking who they were.

Freddie felt Stella stiffen. 'Don't do anything stupid,' he whispered in her ear.

She whispered back, 'Thor was right.'

The big man spun round to her, his eyes flashed. 'Shut yah mouth ... both of yah. Yah won't be the first who got hurt today.'

Joey started to move forward. 'Tell us what you want. We mean you no harm, there's no need to threaten us.'

The man jerked his gun round. 'Stay where yah are. Don't move any of yah.' He pointed his gun at Joey's wagon. 'Yah got plen'y gas in that there wagon? I wan' its key.'

Joey chucked it over and the squatting

man leaned forward and picked it up. The big man snarled, '...an' food. We want food. That's how we found yah. We smelt cooking.'

Joey replied, 'we've plenty of food and drink. You are welcome to sit with us and eat your fill. Then you can take the wagon and go on your way. As I said, we mean you no harm. This is a wedding day for my son and our new daughter-in-law.'

The man continued to threaten and wave his gun to cover the group. 'Shut yah mouth and move back so 'ah can see yah all.'

They started to move back but he jerked his shotgun at Stella. 'No, yah stay, yah's coming with us. First get the food.' He screamed at her, 'MOVE!'

She stared back, assessing the wretchedness in those wild eyes: *she had been cornered before - her scar started to tingle – that jagged bottle ... she should have reacted sooner!* She had sworn never again – never again! She glanced at the crouching man whose head kept tilting forward, desperately trying to keep awake. He had one hand on the ground supporting his body and his gun started to droop. Pulling away from Freddie and still holding the disc in her hand, she moved to the fire, her eyes fixed on the big man's eyes pulling his concentration away from the others. She tapped the disc. 'I'll put food on this plate for you.'

He raised his gun and she noticed his finger whitening as it squeezed the trigger. He screamed again, 'get 'arn with it woman!'

She turned her back to him, leaning forward as if reaching for the food, but she suddenly spun round, the disc streaked towards him on its upward curve to smash violently into his thigh! As his femur cracked he jerked the exploding gun skyward; birds scattered wildly from tree canopies; a frightened moose bellowed and crashed through distant undergrowth. The man gave a high pitched scream as he collapsed to the ground, desperately gripping his smashed thigh. Thor launched towards the other man as he tried to stand and swing his gun at her. His head suddenly jerked forward, his eyes rolled upwards as if into his skull as he fell flat on his face.

Smokey stood behind the fallen man, casually tapping his open palm with a cudgel made from a broken branch. His face grinned with satisfaction from under his bowery cap. A man of few words!

They secured the two men and Smokey took the wagon to radio from the nearby fire-tower. He repeated Joey's message to a dumbfounded Sheriff Sam Polanski:

'"an' donna' forget to send an ambulance Sheriff."'

***

"... *after the wedding we had a beautiful feast Sibylla had prepared. Unfortunately, some people we weren't very keen on arrived uninvited at supper time, and I had to use the Hella by taking down a moving beast that could have been dangerous; they would have shot it but I think my way was best as it was only stunned; caused a bit of excitement though. Apart from that it was very peaceful.That night we slept under the stars. It was so quiet apart from the beavers chomping at their wood and then realised that's why they called the camp ChompChomp. I thought it was an Indian word. Freddie found that funny. Then another relaxed day with Freddie fishing and watching Joey and Smokey mastering the Hella. I also think they were impressed (amazed actually) with my shooting skill using Joey's hunting rifle!*

We're now back to the hustle and bustle of the big city and Freddie's writing. I enjoyed the break so much, but maybe a little too quiet for me. Not a lot of excitement seems to happen around Maine.

Thor

Write soon, lots of love from your honouree Indian daughter "Possesom" and of course, my beloved Freddie.

Stella Elisabet XX

Hey! Just had telephone call from Joey that his friend Sam Polanski has been re-elected Sheriff again with an increased majority. As they say in Maine... "Darn it ... Now ain't that great!"

20

Project Charlie: Freddie got the call from Spiegel that the finances were in place and the filming would start in two months time. The same morning he had watched with pride at a ceremony when Stella and Sergeant Jugg received their commendations from Commissioner Washington. They were both rather bemused by the attention: the flashing bulbs, the Sergeant awkward and fidgeting in his smart uniform; looking strange without shades and gum. Later Stella found herself next to the Commissioner's wife Ella Washington. They instantly hit it off and Freddie overheard Stella talking with passion of her dream to start a martial-arts class for the kids from the deprived part of New York, to turn their anger into self discipline.

'The first time in their lives, their aggression becomes controlled and they'll form a comradeship with a fellow human being ...' Stella would occasionally glance at Freddie for his support and his encouragement. She took a slip of paper from her handbag for Mrs. Washington to read who instantly nodded her approval.

Thor

On their journey home in the taxi, he asked about the paper.

She handed her handbag over to him. 'It's just inside, have a look, I've been unsure of showing it to you ... not sure of your reaction—'

'No young lady, you must open your bag. It would be as if I was entering your soul, every woman should have a secret.'

She laughed. 'My darling Freddie, forever the writer.' She leaned across to kiss him, nervously taking out the paper.

He unfolded the paper.

She explained: 'It was written by Charlie. It was his dream, and now I want it to become mine. That feeling I experienced in the alley is what those kids go through every day of their lives. They don't have families to help them. No wonder they're in such a mess. Charlie believed their aggression could be channelled and that's what his dream was all about.'

He read: "*C-Courage, H-Hope, A-Ambition, R-Respect, L-Love, I-Integrity, E-Excellence = CHARLIE*".

She anxiously studied his face for some reaction.

He carefully folded the paper and slipped it back into her bag. He appeared to be thinking, and suddenly said, 'why don't you call it: "*Project Charli*e".'

Thor

'You approve?'

He nodded. 'How could I not. I think it's great ... go for it Stella. I'll back you all the way.' He nodded positively. 'Yes, call it "*Project Charlie*". I glad Mrs Washington is interested. That could be important.'

An excited Stella gushed, 'Oh she was, she promised to get back as soon as possible. "*Project Charlie*", I love it.'

He so loved her enthusiasm and he wondered if the Commissioner's wife knew what she had let herself in for. His one piece of advice: to keep the project away from the local council's involvement as she would get bogged down with bureaucrats trying to take over and get the credit for any success. When they reached home Mrs Washington was already on the phone and she also agreed with Freddie's awareness of bureaucracy. She talked of her own "hands on" involvement, unaware that this was where the person called Thor would have other ideas.

Stella's first task was to find a venue to hold her "*Project Charlie*" classes. Here she met opposition when the owners were told what she intended to do. Typical reaction: '"We've enough problems with these kids and now you wanna teach them how to kill each other ... *get wise lady*!"'

Thor

Eventually she was put on to a Father O'Connell who ran the annex behind his church; he seemed to be her last hope. She caught up with him as he was about to enter his church. He was a tall, broad shouldered giant of a man, with a deep voice to match; but he had twinkling eyes. He turned out to be ex-marine who entered the church after his war in the Far East. His broken nose was testament to his army boxing and he possessed the biggest hands she had ever seen; he looked promising.

He stared at her and patiently listened to her story, before commenting in his deep voice, 'you realise what you're taking on don't you? These kids are broken and abandoned. I've had lots of do-gooders here before, thinking they can change the world.' He looked her up and down, and took in her smart clothes. 'But the reality is, your kind is the very last thing these kids need. At first you give them hope and then you get bored, so off you go on some other whim!' He turned to walk away declaring, 'when you commit to these kids, it's for life ... not a short tram ride ... it's a long train journey with no halts to get off!'

Stella felt her anger rising as she pulled out her "Project Charlie" paper and shoved it at him. 'Please Father, just read this. This is what it's about.'

He looked her up and down yet again before glancing at the paper, grimacing. 'I'm sorry, I sense your desire to help, but all you do is to raise their hopes and dash them once again. I'd rather you went home. I'm sorry.' He turned and opened the church door—

She shouted at his broad back, '... and you call yourself a man of God,' immediately regretting her words.

He hesitated before entering the church and quietly closed the door behind him.

Stella wiped her eyes, trying to control her frustration, taking a deep breath before crossing over to the nearby East River. She watched the fast moving dark waters as if carrying her dreams out to sea. She focussed on Brooklyn Bridge where she fulfilled her walk with Freddie on their wedding day. Turning to go home, she suddenly caught her image reflected in a shop window; *she had dressed to impress*.

She decided to continue walking along the river to the bridge. Crossing over to the middle, she leaned against the cold iron structure where she had stood that day with Freddie. At that moment she wanted him there with her. Looking across to Ellis Island brought back memories as a young girl: her arrival from Europe and that first glimpse of liberty with its hand holding the torch high as a promise to an exciting future, set against the stirring backdrop of New York. She recalled standing hand in hand with her parents at the ship's bow, with the screams of excitement, the shouts from other passengers; such expectations to take in all at once. Then they had to wait for the "steerage" passengers to be off-loaded into small boats and taken across to Ellis Island for their documentation and medical procedure; the fear of failing and being returned back to Europe. She watched them go, clutching their few belongings, not understanding why she was being separated from the young friends made on the voyage over: too young to understand that she was an "upper-deck" passenger and her family had been cleared of these formalities before departing Europe.

Brooklyn Bridge with its solid steel girders had seemed so overwhelming; her first awareness of the vast America where everything had to be so God-given big. The Bridge far bigger than her memory from that black-and-white American movie she had seen back in Malmo as a very young girl: the beautiful blonde actress in the film had hurried across the bridge to meet her handsome lover in the middle. They had clung to each other, kissed and turned to gaze across to Liberty embracing their new life together as the "End" appeared. It had seemed so dreamy to the youngster, and her parents later telling her about the look of amazement with her first glimpse of the bridge. After they had disembarked, she tried to get her parents to walk across, but her father had to get down to Minnesota as they were late arriving due to bad weather on the crossing. There was of course that special occasion with Charlie, but yet again there wasn't time even then. The bridge had become symbolic to her; she looked upon it as 'her Bridge'.

She then thought of Father O'Connell looking at her clothes and his words: 'Your kind is the very last thing these kids want.' Her reflection in that shop window reminding her: she was "upper-deck" and those kids he referred to were "steerage".

He was right of course and suddenly realised her mistake. She recalled what she had said to Freddie on the bridge about Thor's future. Suddenly her spirits started to rise as she knew what she had to do to persuade Father O'Connell that her dream wasn't just a tram ride ... and to apologise for what she said to him: she felt ashamed with her words!

The next morning, Thor sat on 'Harvey' waiting for the priest. The young lad

Andy in the coffee shop had told her that he always came in about ten every morning without fail to have his coffee and read the local paper before entering his church next door. She looked at her watch, a few minutes to go. Suddenly there he was, no mistaking the big man striding along the road with his newspaper held under his arm. She kick-started the engine and roared up alongside him. He turned to admire the motorcycle. Thor turned off the engine and dismounted.

He frowned surprise at the young woman handling such a heavy machine and gave her a smile as he started to open the coffee shop door.

Thor called after him, 'Father O'Connell, remember me?'

He turned to stare at the young woman with the yellow bandana, the torn jeans and the bomber jacket. 'I don't think so, but your face is familiar.'

Thor handed him her "Project Charlie" paper. He frowned again, taking in her appearance before glancing at the paper. He stared back at her and raised his eyebrows before exclaiming, 'but you're the young lady who came here yesterday.'

Thor nodded. 'Before I explain to you, I wish to apologise for what I said yesterday. I was out of order. No excuses ... I'm sorry.'

He smiled and murmured, 'accepted, and I apologise for being so abrupt. I was very rude to you. I must have gotton out the wrong side of bed.'

Thor went to speak but he held up his hand, his eyes twinkling with humor. 'Do you know what young lady; I think we could start again over a cup of coffee. Come, they make the best coffee in New York right here, and today it's on me,' he laughed, 'but next time it'll be your turn ... agreed?'

They shook hands; Thor's hand looked like a child's.

As they entered the coffee shop, Father O'Connell raised two fingers at young Andy, but noticing his guest's face, he bellowed with laughter. 'No I wasn't being crude young lady ... I was simply ordering two coffees.'

She felt happy as it was Thor who found him.

The next few weeks were tied up with distributing fliers to all the local bars and shops. Freddie and Father O'Connell joined Stella, now dressed as Thor, tramping around the area explaining the purpose of the Judo club. Mostly they took the fliers but shook their heads: 'it won't work lady, they'll only be there for the "free coffee and doughnuts".'

Freddie persuaded Sam to lean on his

contacts into supplying the mats needed. These duly arrived with the promise of clothing kit to come later - should the club survive?

The evening before the opening, there was a gathering of interested people. Mrs Washington turned up, Father O'Connell of course and several local council members all wanting to give their support and to attend when Stella opened up for business the following evening. The group sat in a circle, each offering advice and enjoying the coffee organised by the young lad Andy from the nearby coffee shop. Freddie remained standing and leaned against the wall. He smiled as he noticed the slight flush appearing on Stella's cheeks; he knew what was coming.

Stella clapped her hands for full attention, expressing her thanks for all the help and the encouragement they had given to her. She took a deep breath and started. 'I know how much you want to be here, but I don't want you to think I'm being ungrateful when I ask you not to come tomorrow.' She let it sink in before continuing, 'you all represent the establishment. Problem is these kids are suspicious of the establishment.' She noticed Father O'Connell nodding in agreement. 'I couldn't have got this far without your help, but I think the next few weeks we have to tread careful.'

Mrs Washington raised her hand and spoke up. 'But surely Stella, you are as much *establishment* as all of us here?'

Stella nodded. 'Yes I am, but I won't be coming.'

They stared at her as she continued, 'a friend of mine is coming called Thor. She is qualified to teach and she dresses just like them; she's definitely not establishment. I am sure she will be accepted.' She looked across to Father O'Connell. 'Would you not agree Father? You have met her.'

They all turned puzzled to look at the giant man who wore a cheeky grin on his face. He nodded. 'Yes I have met her and I think Stella is right. I agree we should leave her friend Thor to get the thing off the ground.'

Stella looked over to Andy. 'Andy has agreed to deal with the coffee and doughnuts and they know him anyway as he's one of them.'

Freddie spoke up, 'even I won't be here. Stella is right and I'm as anxious as the rest of you for it to succeed.'

Mrs Washington didn't seem convinced, and as they started to leave, Father O'Connell took her by the arm and asked, 'could you pop in to the church next door with me as I need your thoughts on a matter.'

The priest led Mrs Washington into his church and they sat down in a pew. He told her of his first meeting with Stella and the reason he turned her down; of Thor's arrival on her Harvey the following morning. He chuckled. 'Don't underestimate that young lady; she knows exactly what she's doing.'

Mrs Washington eyes lit up. 'Good for her. I promise to keep out of the way ... well some of the time,' she added.

Now all the others had gone from the meeting, Freddie and Stella were finally on their own in the empty hall and ready to go home. She had one last look around and turned out the lights. Freddie suddenly put his arms around her and they kissed.

The Suspicious Kids: The next evening Thor purposely parked Harvey near the entrance to the hall; she wanted the kids to see it as hers. The maverick bike certainly attracted the curiosity of the kids as they drifted into the hall, assuming the young woman, sitting on the refreshment table swinging her legs, dressed in torn jeans, a faded T-shirt, trainers and wearing a yellow bandana, was one of them.

They were surprised when she then

introduced herself as Thor who was going to be their instructor. At first they were more interested in her Harvey, amazed that a woman would ride one, never mind owning it. Thor was relieved when three girls strutted in, making ten in all. It was obvious that they were there just for a giggle and at first unsure of this Thor person. They all seemed to know each other and reassured to find Andy serving coffee.

As they scoffed the free doughnuts, Thor told them how she first learned Judo to stand up to school bullies and how it changed her life. They were impressed, and what with answering questions about her Harvey, she began to feel they were coming on board. She explained "Project Charlie" and her late husband's dream and how he died. They remained silent for a while until one lad piped up, '*OK Thor, what's the catch?'*

She wasn't quite ready for that question, so she explained that they didn't have to come, won't have to sign anything and could leave as soon as they had their coffee and doughnuts. They can make their own rules and even elect a leader to help run the club that would belong to them.

She handed out a card to each person with "Project Charlie" printed across the front, and pointed out what was printed on the back.

"*C-Courage, H-Hope, A-Ambition, R-Respect, L-Love, I-Integrity, E-Excellence = CHARLIE.*"

'That's it, no catches, just my belief in you kids.'

"*Project Charlie*" had difficult beginnings as distrustful kids would come but pull back as they tasted discipline and order for the first time; they didn't like or understand boundaries. On these low times Freddie would walk a despondent Stella across her bridge to the half way point, reminding her of the promise she made to the kids.

A few of them who left, kept returning to stand in the hall entrance, sensing something unknown was happening to them; comradeship, family, belonging? The low point came one evening when she arrived to find the mats had been vandalised; she was devastated and so angry. She couldn't believe they would do this to her. She exploded with rage and screamed at the kids who were dumbfounded at her reaction. She slumped into a chair and held her head in her hands, trying desperately not to burst into tears. A tiny Chinese girl called Mei tried to pull her up, but she shook the hand off, stormed from the hall and ran into the street. A cab drew up and Freddie got out. He held her tight as she wept into his shoulder.

'Freddie what are you doing here?' she sobbed.

'After you left home, I somehow just sensed you might have trouble tonight as it had run too smoothly up to now, so I grabbed a taxi just in case.'

He held her hands as she told him what happened. He looked into her eyes. 'Now Stella, or Thor, it's important that you return and confront the problem straight away. You knew this had to happen at some time. You have to give yourself one more chance. Go straight back and tell them that this is their last chance, otherwise you won't be back. It's the only way. Do that and from now on, I bet your journey will be smooth? I can't believe Thor would give up so easy.'

She wiped her eyes. 'No, Thor wouldn't give up?' She took a deep breath and they walked hand in hand back into the building.

The kids had started to tidy up, trying to make repairs to the slashed mats. When the two entered, the kids crowded together and stood in a silent group with their heads bowed. One boy nervously stepped forward. He towered above Thor, staring at the ground as if to avoid her eyes. She put her arms around him and the boy started to sob. He admitted to causing the damage and kept saying sorry. He didn't understand why he wanted to hurt her, but was frightened she would let him down like all the others: he wanted attention of course. She took his arm and stared at the worried kids. Her voice trembled as she tried to control her anger, her eyes showing the hurt.

'You must listen to me. For the first time in your lives there is someone who cares for you ... *me*!' She looked over at Freddy. 'My husband Freddie ... *he* cares for you. This is probably the only chance you'll ever have to make something of your lives ... otherwise you'll end up in the gutter, *all* your lives. I'm offering you a chance!' She held out both hands. 'You've got to learn to come towards me. I can't do it on my own. I'm prepared to work with you ... *together*. I want *you* to answer this question ... are you *with* me ... *yes* or *no*? It's a simple question! *YES or NO*? Make a decision now!' she pointed at the door. 'Otherwise I'm walking out that door ... going home and you'll never see me again! And then you can all go to hell ...!'

Freddie knew this was the make or break moment that would decide the future of her dream. Thor felt her heart pounding as she began to think she had lost them. She glanced at Freddie, her eyes showing her feelings; where had he seen that look before? ... Central Park of course.

Suddenly the tall lad pleaded, ‘I’m with you Thor. Don’t go,’ he shouted. The next minute they were all urging her to stay. Some tried to hide their tears. She knew this was probably the first time they had ever experienced the emotion of crying for another person, or even themselves.

Freddie was right, it had to happen and he watched the scene with such pride; she was a remarkable person. That did prove to be the turning point in the success of the club. They had hurt the very first person who had ever reached out to them, and that had a sting; it was a lesson they would never forget. The damaged equipment was miraculously replaced; Freddie suggested that Stella shouldn’t ask how or where it came from. She later confessed to Freddie that the tall boy, Danny, was the one who she didn’t expect to stay before he caused the damage. He later proved to be the most rewarding of all.

One evening two Harley-Davidson motorcycles waited in the shadows outside the hall. The two men were dressed as Hells Angels and watched as Thor arrived and hauled her machine up onto its stand. Sitting on the back of the front bike was a young pale-faced girl. She had her arms around the man, who was built like a mountain. He spoke to her over his shoulder but she didn't reply. The three watched Thor open the front door and hook it back against the wall before disappearing into the hall.

Then gradually the kids started to arrive. At first a couple, then a single figure, then a small crowd all laughing and jostling as they entered the hall.

The big man pulled himself from the bike and lifted the reluctant girl, as if she was a doll. They walked hand in hand over to the entrance and stared at the activity inside. He tried to reason with her but she shook her hand loose and returned to the bike. He called after her but was ignored. He turned to look back into the hall before gripping his hands with frustration. The girl waited, staring at the ground, ignoring his pleas, so he came back and lifted her back onto the pillion. The second man shrugged his shoulders, kick-started his bike and drove off into the night. The big man slowly drove past the entrance and they both stared into the hall before he too accelerated into the

Brooklyn night; the girl buried her face into his back and clung tightly to him.

The tall lad Danny hurried from the hall to stare after them, his hands on his hips.

***

Alix Palos, cub reporter, sat next to the New York Times copy editor who was teaching young "cubby", as he was known, the process of final proofing before the paper was put to bed for the night; only then could they go home – job done.

The editor turned the pages of the final draft-copy and suddenly stabbed his finger on an article, exclaiming, 'bet someone will be out celebrating tonight!'

They both leaned over to read the headline: "Rare Chinese vase discovered by auctioneers in Manhattan. Surprised owner wishes to remain anonymous!"

Alix felt tired, it had been a busy day but he still felt the excitement of working for such a prestigious paper. He suddenly frowned and took a second glance at the: "Special People in Town Today" column. He stared at the photo of a woman with two youngsters dressed in judo gear. Her face abruptly brought back that night in Central Park; no mistaking his angel!

Thor

There she was! The times he would think of her and the kindness in those eyes: a kindness he didn't think he would ever see again after the death of his mother and father during the Greek civil war in '46.

The article covered the story of: "Stella Vermeer, known to the kids as, local Angel called Thor, who started the Project-Charlie judo club for street kids, and how youth crime level had gone down in that area; an idea now being taken seriously across several cities". He scribbled down the name of the church hall.

He thought back to that morning when Deno listened to his story with much nodding, and who had piled him with ham, eggs, beans and mugs of the best coffee he had tasted since leaving his home in Thessalonica. Deno had admitted to him, that when he first arrived in America, he'd got into trouble with the law and nearly kicked out but for the kindness of an official. This meant having a criminal record but he was determined to pull himself together; he had looked with pride around his bar.

'Don't make the same mistake young man. Keep your nose clean. What do you want to do with your life?'

'I want to be a journalist,' Alix had replied with determination.

'A Journalist, Uh huh, you're aiming high.' He stared at him pensively for a moment before picking up the telephone directory. 'Right son, first you earn your breakfast by washing those dishes ... I've a phone call to make.'

That call took him to the desk of Times crime-reporter Tommy Stanley. Tommy was a frequent visitor to Deno's bar; a useful source of information – both ways. Tommy's first action was to ring a friendly lawyer who explained the procedure for illegal hopefuls: *"If you can act as guarantor and he can prove he's had a steady job for one year, then there's no reason he can't be made legal. It's down to you ... your risk."*

Deno received a call back from Tommy and so he went to find Alix. He put a friendly hand on the boy's shoulder. 'Go and see my friend who's going to wait in the bar directly below the large Pepsi sign in Times Square. You can't mistake him ... he's bald as a coot. He wants to look you over and see whether you're worth giving a chance. He's tough, so you won't fool him, and Alix, smarten yourself up and comb your hair.' He grinned. 'He's very sensitive about hair ... and just be honest ... promise?'

The youth nodded. 'I give you my word Deno. I won't let you down.'

Thor

He spent his first year as a junior boy-Friday: sweeping the floor, making coffee in the manic atmosphere of a newspaper giant – loving it – and then one day he had been called into the sub-editor's office. Told he was giving him a break by working with Tommy as a cub reporter. 'If you turn out half as good as Tommy, I'll eat my hat.'

Tommy had grinned at the editor. 'I think you'll learn to regret that remark, boss.'

That night a smiling Alix Palos had walked tall back to his digs. He stopped to buy the late edition of the Evening News, nonchalantly telling the newsboy to keep the change; he had arrived! He studied the front page of the competitor's newspaper feeling like an old pro, but resolving that one day his name would appear on a front page – as a reporter.

***

Thor's esteem in the community grew and she could leave Harvey outside the hall knowing it was sacrosanct; a promise given by the kids. However, one evening Danny frog marched a young lad into the hall over to Thor. He had caught him rifling through the pannier bag on her bike.

Thor

Thor asked the lad, 'why steal from me, what harm have I ever done to you?'

He looked down and mumbled, but she pulled his chin up and demanded he look in her eyes; eyes having the usual sad, hopeless look. He shrugged his shoulders; he had no answer.

'What is your name?'

Danny tightened his grip

He mumbled and Danny snapped, 'speak when Miss Thor talks to you.'

'Tony.'

'Right Tony, look at this.' She handed him the *Project Charlie* membership card and pointed at the word "*respect*".

'Do you understand why that's there and what it means?' He pulled a face and shrugged. 'You will go round to the church library at the back of the hall and ask to speak to Father O'Connell. You take this card and ask him to look that word up in a dictionary and he'll read it to you. Do you understand?'

He shrugged his shoulders again. 'Maybe?'

Danny growled. 'There's no such word as maybe in my dictionary. He will Miss Thor, I promise, he will!'

Thor looked at her watch. 'I think its break time. First of all Danny, get Tony a coffee and a donut, then go and see the Father. '

She watched Tony at the table eating his donut, his eyes taking in the hall and her family ... hopefully he sensed the comradeship; she crossed her fingers behind her back.

One evening as she was locking up the Hall, Father O'Connell came to tell her that an upright piano had been given to the church and the only place it could be stored was in the hall. Would she give an assurance that it wouldn't be touched by her kids?

'Yes of course,' she replied firmly, but added, 'why do you have to ask?'

He grinned. 'Old habits Thor, old habits.'

Thor arrived early one day to find the piano tucked into the far corner of the empty hall. She pulled back the cover to reveal an early Bechstein "Model-8". Her heart leapt; she couldn't contain her excitement. Hurriedly raising the lid she ran her hands across the keys; it had even been tuned to suit the hall. She glanced at her watch ... yes there's plenty of time before the kids arrive. She pulled the stool out, sat down and rubbed her hands, stretched her fingers, and played; the music swept her into that other world she loved. The piano was an absolute joy and she didn't notice the time passing. As she finished she was startled by the sudden clapping behind her. She swung round to find the kids sitting on the floor.

'Did you like that?' the surprised Thor asked.

In unison they shouted, some nodding. 'Yes!'

The little Chinese girl Mei asked, 'what was that last music you play Miss Thor?'

'Did you like that Mei?'

'Yes it was so gentle. I think it make me cry.' One boy laughed. She glowered back at him.

'It is called Gymnopédie and written by a French man called Erik Satie a long time ago. I'm glad you like it as it's one of my favorites.'

Danny put his hand up. 'Play some more Miss Thor.'

She looked at her watch. *Maybe these kids had never...* She nodded. 'OK. One more piece, then we must get on.' *Maybe the Shaker Hymn "Simple Gifts" ... why not?*

She had just started when she heard a voice quietly singing; it was the young lad Tony that Danny caught stealing from her pannier bag ... his confidence increasing as he sang:'

'Tis the gift to be simple, 'tis the gift to be free
'Tis the gift to come down where we

ought to be,
And when we find ourselves in the place just right,
'Twill be in the valley of love and delight.
When true simplicity is gain'd,
To bow and to bend we shan't be asham'd,
To turn, turn will be our delight,
Till by turning, turning we come 'round right.'[12]

As Thor finished, there came sudden clapping from the hall doorway. Father O'Connell walked over and continued to clap with his big hands. 'Young man you have a beautiful voice, please explain, how do you know that Hymn?'

The young lad Tony started to blush, realising what he had done, aware of the staring faces. He shrugged his shoulders. 'My mother used to sing it and get me to join in. I've always known it. I'm sorry Thor, I'm sorry to spoil your playing.'

She looked hard at him, her eyes shining with emotion. 'Oh Tony, you gave us such pleasure. You must listen to me ... don't ever apologise for giving enjoyment by singing.'

The priest raised his eyebrows and looked at her. 'And I was concerned about the piano! I think we've all learnt something today.' He rubbed his hand around his chin. 'I know it's an old cliché, but God certainly moves in strange ways.' He turned his dark eyes on the lad. 'I know we had that chat and agreed to differ on God and religion, baseball and the "Red Sox" young man, but there's nothing to say you can't sing in our choir is there? After all, the choir is not just for Sundays,' he grinned at Thor, 'or even a short tram ride, come to that.'

Tony looked at Thor as if seeking approval. She smiled back and nodded a firm 'yes' to reassure him.

They raised money and awareness by holding piano recitals. Ella Washington proved to be a staunch supporter and would rally her friends and contacts to attend the concerts. This later proved unnecessary as her concerts were always well attended. Their friend Ling willingly supported the project and also would play for her.

At the recitals she became aware of the little Chinese girl Mei, who would stand in the corner of the stage as if mesmerised by the piano, so she began to take a special interest in the girl. Her background and parents were unknown as she had been abandoned as a baby; she didn't even know her surname of course and Stella felt she had become a mother figure to the young girl. When Mei said she wished she could play like Stella, it was the look in the girl's eyes that persuaded Stella to start giving her lessons. She proved to have a natural talent and with encouragement she was making astounding progress. Stella and Freddie joined up with Ling to set up a Trust, and with an arm twisting contribution from Sam they were able to send her to Music College. Her progress was such that years later she eventually ended up teaching at the Juilliard School of Music. She took the name of Vermeer as her surname.

There were failures of course, kids fell through the net and Stella would take their failure personal. The hard lesson was that some of them had been too numbed as kids and would never make it. Her spirits were raised one day when Lieutenant Hooker and Sergeant Jugg called in to confirm the reports that the youth crime-statistics indicated a remarkable drop in their area since *Project Charlie* had started.

One day there came an opportunity for Thor to show herself as Stella to the kids. Her concern was that now she had gained their trust, 'Stella' would be part of the establishment they hated. The chance came when Freddie and Stella received an invitation to a formal social evening dinner that clashed with a club night. She gave it great thought and just prior to the event she asked Freddie to show her how to tie his bow tie. She kept practising to tie the bow around a flower vase much to his amusement.

It also was an opportunity to give Danny the responsibility of opening and running the club on his own that evening as he had been voted in as leader. That afternoon she packed a case with two dresses, one blue and one deep green, some jewellery together with various shades of makeup and two pairs of high heeled shoes. She finally put in her *Cabochard* perfume. She arranged with Freddie that she would go down to the club in a taxi dressed as Thor and later he would arrive with his bow tie undone, his cuff links in his pocket and carrying his tuxedo jacket; all very mysterious.

The kids were naturally surprised to see Thor carrying a case and she explained that she was going to an event to meet influential people that could help the club. As she couldn't make up her mind what to wear, she decided to ask the girls if they would help her to dress. They were excited to be asked and the giggling females disappeared into the small committee room followed by whistles and cat calls from the boys.

They loved the two dresses and the decision made with the deep green color to match her eyes. Mei asked if she could comb and set Thor's hair pulled back into a coil; what she called an 'upstyle' a hairdressing friend had taught her: one loose strand hanging down the side of her face as a teaser. The other girls tried out various shades of lipstick on her, choosing a soft red to match their chosen necklace with color matching pearl studs in her ears; she wouldn't have thought of that color, but it was their choice ... yes they were right. She then finally explained the subtle technique with perfume; less is more.

Now she was ready, but before they went out to show the boys, she gave the girls little packets of chocolates she had tied with ribbons earlier as a thank you. She felt her heart racing; how would the boys react? She took a deep breath and waited for Mei to open the door and lead her out. At first the lads were quiet, staring, not believing the transformation from Thor into this sophisticated woman wearing high heeled shoes. Then of course came the whistles and shouts; she had won them round. Just then Freddie arrived in a taxi to collect her, his timing perfect. The girls proudly pushed her to stand in front of him so he could admire her; his face said it all.

He asked Stella if she could see to his bow tie as he was all fingers and thumbs. As she tied the bow she asked them to watch as one day they would be doing the same when they were invited to special occasions. Freddie asked one of the boys to fit his cufflinks. Then Tony helped him on with his jacket.

Stella took Freddie's arm and they faced the kids as if asking for their approval. They responded by clapping, murmuring definite approval. Stella asked Danni to escort her to the waiting taxi whilst Mei and another girl grabbed Freddie as his escort.

As the cab pulled away, Stella punched the air. 'YES!'

Freddie laughed, 'now don't get emotional and spoil your make up.'

'What makes you think I'd get emotional?' she replied, dabbing her eyes with a tissue.

One Sunday the group were busy decorating the tired gray walls. Thor stopped to watch her group of volunteers. They were so keen to please her – they were her family and she had grown to love them. Danny suddenly whispered to her. 'I think you have a visitor Miss Thor.'

Thor

She turned to see a young man standing in the doorway clutching a bunch of flowers. He was smartly dressed in a pressed suit and tie and she couldn't help noticing his highly polished leather shoes. The scrubbed face seemed nervous under his curly black hair. She went over and smiled to ease the young man who looked familiar?

She asked, 'are those for your young lady?'

He grinned and pushed the flowers towards her. 'No, these are for my angel.'

Thor took the flowers and frowned, puzzled. She stared at him. 'For me? Thank you. We've met before haven't we? Now where would that have been?'

His look became more anxious. 'Central Park, one dark evening, you practised your judo on me ... remember?'

Her mouth dropped and she looked startled. She put one hand to her mouth and gasped. 'The young boy. I can't believe it ... is it really you?'

He laughed excitedly. 'Yes it is really me. Alix.' He held out his hand. 'Pinch me. I'm real.'

She took his hand and then flung her arms around him. 'I can't believe it. Tell me. Tell me all. I've often wondered what became of you.'

The rest of the group had stopped

decorating to watch the couple. Danny became unsure and started to move across but Mei put a restraining hand on him. ‘No. Leave her. She’s OK. I think this is special.’

Thor sat Alix down and he told his story. As she listened, she tried not to show her feelings. He pulled out his wallet and from its back took a folded ten dollar bill. He handed it to her. ‘This is the *very* bill you gave me that night. I did go to buy food but my restaurant friend wouldn’t take it. He said, as it’s from an angel I should keep it to bring me good luck. Deno wouldn’t let me pay for the breakfast.’ He grinned. ‘But I had to wash dishes for him that day. Tommy the reporter gave me an advance on my wages so I didn’t need to use your money after all. I’ve kept it as a reminder of your trust and with the hope that should we ever meet again, I could return it to you.’

Thor felt the tears trickling down her cheeks. She was choked and lost for words. She studied his young handsome features and handed back the money. ‘Please Alex; I want you to keep it. Then one day you can hand it on to some other person that needs help. Then you can tell him, or her, our story.’

He leaned forward to gently wipe her cheeks with his fingers. ‘I didn’t know that angels could cry.'

That evening Stella retired early to bed; trying to read, impatiently waiting for Freddie to return from his evening meeting. She found herself reading the same page over and over again. When he came in, he poked his head round the bedroom door and raised his eyebrows. 'I see one of your boy friend's been spoiling you with flowers.' He came over to kiss her and tried not to grin at some paint on her nose, recalling a smudge that evening when he took her into Chinatown. 'How's your day been with the decorating?'

She patted the bed. 'Darling Freddie, please sit down. I've a fairy story to tell you.' He sat down and she took his hand. 'Once upon a time, two people went for a walk in a very dark forest called Central Park. Suddenly a monster leapt out to rob them ... but he wasn't really a monster Freddie, he was just a frightened kid called Alix ...'

21

Karma's story: Thor checked all was well in the hall before turning off the lights; it had been a good evening but she was looking forward to getting home and to the meal Freddie would have prepared: a special treat he promised. As she was locking the door, she hesitated on seeing two Hell-Angel riders closely inspecting Harvey. One middle aged man was tall and muscular, dressed in a dragon Tee-shirt and marine cap, a gray bushy beard, pigtail and ear rings. He towered above the other man of a similar age: small, wiry, covered in tattoos with a red bandanna pulled tight round his head. They looked up as she approached and stared at her with faces showing no emotion; she felt uncomfortable.

The big man spoke, 'you Thor?'

She nodded and stared back. 'And who's asking?'

'It's OK! We're just admiring yer bike. We think that model number comes from down South. We don't get many of those up this way. We heard there was one in the city.'

'So I believe.'

He moved closer. 'I'm Mussey and this here is Ratty. I wan' you to come with me. I wan' you to meet someone.'

She glanced at her watch. 'Sorry, but I don't go anywhere with strangers.' She deliberately paused, ... 'especially someone called Ratty.'

The man called Ratty glared and mounted his bike.

'Look, I'm expected home, I'm tired and hungry.'

The big man fixed his steel-gray eyes on her. 'It won't take long. You'll be OK. You're quite safe. Hooker suggested you.'

'Lieutenant Hooker? The cop?'

'There's only one Hooker, Ah hope.'

'What's it about?'

He nodded at the hall. 'Ah want you to help ma niece.'

'Well she can come here anytime. Tell her she'll be welcome.'

'Ain't that simple, miss. You need to come and meet her at home. Follow me, and Ratty will cover your back.'

The man called Ratty waited, revving as if impatient. She locked her pannier and sat astride Harvey. Mussey kicked started his bike and waited for her reaction. She bit her bottom lip, taking a deep breath before following the big man as they tore off into East Brooklyn; not an area to feel comfortable in. She knew Freddie would be worried and probably angry that she went off with these strangers. They suddenly turned down a narrow cobbled alleyway, coming to a halt outside an old, three-story terrace. Mussey switched off his engine, dismounted and waited for her.

'Don't worry about yer bike. Ratty will stay here.'

Thor stood fast. 'Before I go in, tell me what this is about? Otherwise I'm off home.'

His face suddenly dropped as if he was thinking what to say. He shuffled his feet. 'Look, ma niece is fourteen, and two years ago she was ... well ... she was—'

She prejudged him. 'You mean raped!'

He nodded; relieved she had broken the ice. 'Yeah. Difficult talking about it. But she needs help. Ah tried to get her to yer club, but when we got there she chickened out. Problem is, she sits at home and hardly speaks. Ah don't know what to do.'

'Have you tried counselling?'

He turned his head and pretended to spit. 'Been down that road. Ma dog could do a better job than those shrinks.'

'How about the police?'

He gave a bitter laugh, pretending to spit again. 'They didn't believe her.' He growled, 'the cop said it was ma fault for letting her hang around the likes of me!'

'Who? Hooker?'

'No. Wish it had been. Ah didn't know him then.'

'What happened to the man?'

'He was one of us. Yeah, one of us, the bastard. Don't worry he was dealt with.'

Thor was aware of the Angel's code and the likely outcome for that man.

'How can I help?'

'Look, Hooker said yer a musician as well as all this ...' He waved his hands at her clothes as if unable to explain himself. 'He reckons yer might help her through music. She seemed to have a flair playing the violin, but hasn't touched it since ... Ah try to encourage her, but he thought someone like you with yer club, and yer music knowledge might be able ... well yer know what I mean, surely!'

She nodded. 'Ok Mussey, as I'm here, let me meet her, but how about her parents?'

'Her mother ran off after she was born, and ma brother brought her up on his own. Before he died, ma misses and I promised we would look after her as if she was ours.' His shoulders seemed to sag. 'Honestly Thor, she's a-breaking our heart. We hate to see her like this.' Strange words coming from this big man dressed as a rebel.

He opened the house door and she heard the sound of a violin.

Thor

He shook his head. 'That ain't her ... Ah wish. That's a record.'

She followed him to the end of a narrow passage where he opened a door into a small sitting room. Although sparsely furnished, the room was neat and tidy with the warmth of a coal fire burning in the grate. One wall was covered with shelves of books, LPs; on the floor was a pile of sheet music; in the centre of the room stood a music-stand with an open manuscript; a wind-up gramophone played on a side table. She noticed a dusty violin case on the floor as though abandoned. On one wall hung a picture of a middle aged man sitting on an early Harvey-Davidson.

A young, dark haired girl sat dealing cards at a damask-covered table. She looked up as they came in and stared at her uncle before her amber eyes settled on Thor. Her eyes expressed no communication at Thor's presence. Her dark hair emphasised the pale skin, and despite her dull expression, she was very pretty. Thor was immediately drawn to her long delicate fingers: musician's hands.

Mussey bent over and gently stroked her head. He whispered, 'Karma, Ah brought a friend to meet you. She's called Thor and she plays the violin like you. She would like to have a look at yer music.'

The girl didn't say anything but continued to deal her cards.

Thor picked up the violin case. 'Hello Karma. My playing isn't that good, but would you mind if I have a look at your violin?'

The girl screwed up her nose. Thor looked at Mussey and he opened the door.

'Ah just going to make ma self a coffee.'

Thor opened the case and took the violin out. 'Your uncle told me how well you're doing with your playing.'

The girl shrugged her shoulders.

'That record you're playing is one of my favorites: Bach's *Partite*, I love a Sarabande.' She held the violin under her chin and pulled the bow across the strings. 'Oh dear it needs tuning. Would you mind if I do it for you?

Karma screwed her nose again and tried to study the cards as if not interested.

Just then the record finished and Thor went to lift the arm. Karma quickly stood. 'Don't touch, it's mine!' She hurried over and turned the machine off. She took the record, slid it back into its cover and placed it carefully in its empty slot on the shelf before hurrying back to the table and her cards. Thor could see her likeness to the man in the hanging picture.

Thor

Thor began tuning the violin with the girl now closely watching. Then she turned to the open manuscript on the stand. 'Oh Karma, I love *Meditation de Thais*. I haven't played this for years, but here goes.'

As she played she was aware that the girl sat transfixed, her eyes not leaving Thor's face until the music came to an end. Mussey appeared in the doorway with his mug of coffee. He came over and put his arm around the girl. She clung to him with tears running down her cheeks. He whispered across to Thor,' hey this is the first time she's—'

Thor went to put the violin back in its case, but decided to leave it on the table in front of the girl.

Mussey said, 'thanks for coming, sorry to have kept you ... Ah be in touch. Ratty will see yer home ... and Thor, Hooker was right.'

'Oh?'

'He said you're a *bridge builder* ... thanks.'

As she left the room she noticed the girl's hand was now feeling the violin. Thor went out to where Ratty was smoking and chatting to a woman dressed in leathers. He ground his cigarette with his foot and started the bike. The woman climbed up behind him and they watched

Thor. She sat on her bike and looked at the house for a while. The experience with the young girl was moving, and she wondered if that short time could possibly help; would she see Karma or the big man called Mussey again? It was lovely playing the violin after all this time, but my goodness she was rusty; she was glad her teacher hadn't heard as it would have made her cry! She started Harvey and headed home with Ratty and his woman following close behind.

Fancy Hooker saying, bridge builder! ... She had an idea, but best to leave it for a while!

***

The following couple of weeks, Thor made several calls just to show her face to Karma and gradually the barrier thawed. One night as she was closing the club, Mussey and Ratty were waiting. The big man was grinning.

'Thor, Ah just want to say yer visits seem to have done some good. Karma has started playing the violin again. Mind you, it's not when we're around. Our neighbor hears her when we go out, and stops when we return. The violin is always back in its case; it's as if she can't admit it. And this morning, she suddenly asked about you.

She asked if you were coming again as she enjoyed yer company.' He shook his head. 'Ah tell you Miss Thor, Ah longing to get her into yer club.'

Thor noticed even Ratty looked more amenable. She said, 'I'm so pleased Mussey. Yes it's a start. Look I've been thinking, can you bring her to the promenade end of Brooklyn Bridge tomorrow morning, about ten?'

He frowned. 'Ah guess so.'

'You don't have to tell her I'll be there. Just make some excuse to go. I'll wait on one of the seats and keep an eye out for you. OK?'

He nodded.

'And if it's raining, bring an umbrella because you might have to wait ... Karma and I will be having a stroll over the bridge.'

The sky was indeed clouding over but Thor wasn't bothered, if it rains, it rains. She carried a large umbrella. She felt nervous as Karma would either turn and run, or not even appear. Why would a young girl want to walk over the bridge like Stella wanted as a young girl? What could it possibly achieve? Karma certainly wasn't stupid and probably would guess it had been arranged.

Her thoughts were interrupted when a voice said, 'hey look, it's Miss Thor.'

Thor

She looked up to see Mussey and Karma walking towards her. She must have looked surprised as her thoughts had been far away. She greeted them. ‘Hello Mussey ... and Karma!’

The girl smiled shyly but clung to her uncle’s arm.

‘Ah persuaded Karma that we could do some shopping this morning. She hasn’t been out for some time, so here we are.’

‘I was just thinking about having a stroll over the bridge, well only to the middle. Hey Karma, how about coming with me whilst your uncle does his shopping? Girl talk, just you and me?’

Karma looked at her uncle and screwed her nose.

He nodded. ‘Ah think she would rather do that than shop with an old fogey like me. That’s fine by me. Hey, how about it Karma?’

Karma nodded, and for a moment her face lit up.

Thor pretended not to notice the clumsy way he wiped his eyes.

He cleared his throat. ‘Ah expect Ah’ll be about an hour so no hurry, take yer time.’

He hugged Karma, turned and walked away. The two watched the big man’s back for a moment before Thor picked up her pack and started walking over the bridge with her new friend Karma. After a few steps, Thor suddenly felt the girl slip an arm through hers to grip it very tight. She pulled the girl close and those nerves she had felt earlier, vanished; she felt good.

As they walked, Thor spoke about her feelings for the bridge. The time when she first set eyes on it, and the times when she felt that the world was against her, so she would walk to the middle on her own. She spoke about Charlie and the way he died. Her first walk over with Freddie on her wedding day and the opposition to her starting the club to help the kids. It all poured out and she began to sense the closeness of the girl. She hadn't meant it to be like this, she was the one trying help but Karma was comforting her. In the middle they leaned against the cold ironwork and stared out to the Verrazano-Narrows Bridge. Suddenly Karma started telling Thor about the man who assaulted her, the mother she didn't know, and yes that was her father in the picture. She was calm as she told her story; there were no tears, just dark eyes filled with intense anger; her pale face was now beginning to express her emotions. She admitted she had started playing the violin again, but didn't want her uncle or auntie to know until she played better. She suddenly asked, 'Thor would you mind if I do the same as you, come and talk to your bridge when I hate the world, and kick it?

Thor laughed. 'I think it is strong enough for both of us to kick. From now on it is our bridge. Agreed? Shake?'

Karma nodded, and so the two confidants shook hands in the middle of Brooklyn Bridge. They hugged and as they walked back arm in arm, the young girl couldn't stop talking and laughing, almost hysterical; she had held it in for such a long time.

***

The Premier: Freddie and Stella alighted from the taxi and paused amongst the gathering fans and the passing curious outside the cinema, taking in the large colorful neon sign glowing above the foyer entrance: "Manhattan Alignment". He turned his head to look at her excited face. His thoughts returning to those early days in his rented Mulberry apartment when all this started: did he really witness the Macbeth-style death of a Chaplin look-a-like; their meeting in Carnegie Hall with lucky-seat number 32; that magical walk through Chinatown when Thor played just for him the night when Mars and Venus finally made an alignment over Manhattan.

Thor

The gathering crowd had suddenly started to get noisy so he squeezed her arm and they walked into the foyer to await the arrival of Sam Spiegel and his entourage. Freddie chatted to Lieutenant and Mrs Hooker, whilst Sergeant Jugg and his wife were exclaiming with Stella and Ella Washington about the success of the club. They all stopped talking to watch as Alexander Swindon, manager of the Manhattan & Western bank, walked self consciously along the red carpet. He approached them with his arm around a most attractive woman and shyly introduced her as Mrs Swindon. Hooker recalled their first meeting in his office and how he had imagined his wife. She was charming and clearly adored the man. He nervously, but excitedly, tried to be modest over his appointment as a vice executive of the bank.

Stella noticed that Freddie kept looking at his watch and eventually his face lit up as Butterfly came hopping into the foyer with a broken shoe heel. She took off her shoes and tossed them into a trash-can before slinking, cat-like across the deep red carpet with stylish elegance; her long legs dressed in Christian Dior sheer-silk stockings; her designer sack-dress was a cool, cosmopolitan red-sheen. Pinned at a saucy angle in her long dark iridescent hair, she wore a large red dupoini-silk butterfly. From her ears, dangled two red gem-stone droplets, and from her slim neck hung a silver chain with a large matching red gem-stone butterfly. In her hand she held a black Tiffany clutch-bag with a red gemstone clasp: she looked a million bucks! She did a twirl for Freddie, breaking into a nervous giggle before giving him a big hug; her large dark oriental eyes excited and shining.

She exclaimed, 'how do I look? My Chinese-thingy-pottee paid for all this. You didn't come back for your free lunch, so I think what the hell. OK. I'll blow it on a new wardrobe to impress Mister Hollywood tonight.' She giggled and hugged Freddie again.

Stella immediately warmed to her as a girl definitely after her own heart, and at least they both had something in common: they both wanted to bash Rivera. She breathed a sigh of relief as the giant figure of a grinning Father O'Connell headed towards them head and shoulders above the crowd followed by her club family. She had been nervous and worried they might chicken out at the last moment, but no, they had dressed in white trainer slacks and black T-shirts bearing their logo: "*Project Charlie*" across the front. But what made Stella and Freddie laugh;

they all wore red bow-ties, even the girls. For a moment they grouped together, unsure, and then the priest pushed a shy Karma forward to give Stella a box of chocolates.

Sam Spiegel finally arrived with his entourage. He swept in like an unstoppable battleship, waving his huge cigar, savoring the attention. Freddie took Butterfly's arm and manoeuvred her through the admirers to meet the film mogul.

She immediately flashed her antennas and gushed, 'Oh mister Spiegel, I 'ave followed your career and 'ave seen *all* your movies.'

His face lit up as he took in her appearance. He put her arm through hers and patted her hand with his eyes twinkling with mischief. 'Vell my dear Butterfly, you must zit viz me tonight. I think ve have lots to talk about.' He glanced at her shoeless feet. 'Zay my dear, Vot's happened to your zhooes?'

Her antennas almost touched his cheeks as she used a tissue to dab her moist almond eyes. 'I broke my heel and threw them into the trash-can.'

He laughed. 'No problem my dear girl. Before ve go to my party later tonight, I have a friend who has zer zhooe store and he owe me big favor, he vill open zer store vor you. You can choose wot you vant.' He tapped her hand again. 'Don't cry my dear Butterfly, Sam vill look after you.'

Butterfly winked at the grinning Freddie as Sam led her into the cinema; butterflies reflecting dangerously as little red spots in the depth of her black eyes. Her wink saying to Freddie, '*I'm not bothered if this guy squeezes his toothpaste tube in the middle!*'

Stella and Freddie burst out laughing as they followed.

The film was received with much acclaim and Sam Spiegel bathed in the glory of the moment, not realising he had even greater rewards the following year with "Bridge on the River Kwai", and later with "Lawrence".

Freddie went on to become one of Hollywood's most respected writers, nominated many times, but he would say to Stella that the success of her *Project Charlie* was his greatest reward. *Project Charlie* became copied in many cities, but Stella would never forget the year, 1960, watching Danny receive his medal in Rome.

Thor

SUPERIMPOSE MOVIE CREDIT:

THE END

Final Thoughts:*...each new book starts with a blank page, never knowing to where the story will end. However, this is not the end of our story, just the end of the beginning... Frederic Vermeer Maliseet*
...yes, Angles do cry sometimes... *Thor - Stella Elisabet Vermeer - Possesom Maliseet.*

Hooker's crossword : "B.D. romantic astronomical line ending the '42 movie before captions roll: Movie? 7 letters: Bette Davis, "Oh Jerry, Don't let's ask for the moon ... we have the stars". Answer - Film title: "Voyager".
*"My time of day."
(Frank Loesser – Guys & Dolls)

(Jessica's Dikt – Den Musen)
It's time to go out. I peer through the gaps,
Cats starting to hunt; I'm hiding my scraps.
I'm watching one cat, it searches the gloom,
Cat waiting for mice, for mice to consume.
With non blinking eyes, it searches through rocks,

But suddenly finds ... the eye of a fox.
The fox makes a pounce; the cat makes a run,
The mouse starts to laugh... another night won.

It's time to go out. I peer through the dark.
I'm watching the shapes that live in the park.
I'm spying an owl that hoots through the night,
Who's staring with eyes, saucer-round bright.
With time on his side, the owl yawns and waits,
But suddenly hisses ... the mouse is on skates!
The owl does his swoop! The mouse does a trick;
Jumps head over heels ... A back-worthy flip.

It's time to go out. I haven't a care.
I'm sensing some fun, I'm wanting a dare.
The Owl makes his hiss, the cat cries meow.
The fox makes a call, the mouse takes his bow.
There's nothing to eat. There's nothing to bite.

Thor

There's nowhere to hide. It ain't blooming right.
So I'm going home, back through the gaps,
Into my nest to woof up my scraps.

My eyes start to droop, it's nearing the dawn.
It's been a long night, I'm starting to yawn.
The fox sits and waits, the owl gives a hoot,
The cat goes back home, the mouse gives a toot.
He's riding his bike, he hasn't a care.
I'm closing my eyes and saying a prayer.
I'm falling asleep and hiding my scraps.
And when I awake, I'll stare through the gaps ... goodnight!
(Joey Morino)

Thor

Other books by same author

morinojoey1955@gmail.com

The Greek Doctor's Visit
'Back in 5 Minutes'

Printed in Great Britain
by Amazon

84662220R00254